Helen closed her eyes and smiled as Alison's body surged and closed around her fingers. Waves of heat followed the rush of moisture that flooded over Helen's hand. She moved her thumb away from the swollen nub of flesh and slowed her pace. Alison moaned softly as her thighs trembled, and Helen slowly withdrew her hand.

Even in the dim light of the bedroom, Helen could make out the heightened color of Alison's face. "I feel kind of selfish, Helen."

"Don't be silly." Helen gave her a quick kiss on the cheek and struggled with the rumpled sheets until she was sitting up. "I wanted to make love to you. Sometimes it's more fun to be on the giving end of things."

"But if you're feeling good enough to take care of me . . ." Her hands strayed to Helen's waist and she tried to pull Helen closer. "I'd love to return the favor." Alison put on a ridiculously somber face and intoned, "I'll be gentle, my dear. And it's already morning, and I already respect you, so what the hell?"

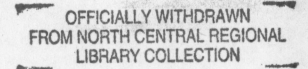

Fallen from Grace

A Helen Black Mystery by

Pat Welch

C3

THE NAIAD PRESS, INC.
1998

Printed in the United States of America on acid-free paper
First Edition

Editor: Christine Cassidy
Cover designer: Bonnie Liss (Phoenix Graphics)
Typesetter: Sandi Stancil

Library of Congress Cataloging-in-Publication Data

Welch, Pat, 1957 –
    Fallen from grace : A Helen Black mystery / by Pat Welch.
        p.   cm.
    ISBN 1-56280-209-7   (alk. paper)
    I. Title.
PS3573.E4543F35   1998
813'.54—dc21   98-11949
                                                                        CIP

For Riffraff

Acknowledgment

Many thanks to Christine Cassidy
for all her help

About the Author

Pat Welch was born in Japan in 1957. After returning to the states she grew up in an assortment of small towns in the South until her family relocated to Florida. Since attending college in southern California she has lived on the West Coast, moving to the San Francisco Bay Area in 1986. Pat now lives and works in Oakland. *Fallen from Grace* is the sixth novel in her Helen Black mystery series. Her short stories have appeared in several Naiad anthologies.

Prologue

Later that day, when she'd had a chance to think about the death that had taken place, Vicky Young decided that she should have known that something horrible was going to happen. She should have known the minute Leslie Merrick smashed the champagne bottle against the wall, letting the clear sweet liquid bubble across the polished floor of the conference room.

"I should have walked out of there right then," Vicky told Helen the following week. "Just walked right out that Wednesday morning, found another temporary assignment through the agency that very day."

Instead, Vicky remained at the office, a small and seemingly insignificant element of the events rumbling toward denouement in downtown Oakland before Wednesday became Thursday.

Vicky sat quietly, all alone, at an enormous desk in a deserted hallway of the fifth floor of the Centurion Sportswear Headquarters building in downtown Oakland and tried to gather her thoughts. Not ten minutes ago she'd been questioned by some police officer.

"No, I wasn't on the eighth floor when it happened. Yes, I'd been sitting there at that desk on the seventh floor for hours. No, I haven't seen anyone come or go while I've been sitting here. Well, except for people who wanted to use the fax machine. Yes, I just started my temporary assignment here this morning. I didn't hear a thing. How could I, with all those drills and machines going across the street, where they're working on that reconstruction? No, I never met the — the woman who died — before this morning."

The only thing about this particular man in uniform that made an impression on her was his thick mustache. Why did male firefighters and the police delight in growing hair on their upper lips? She'd seen the boredom glaze the man's eyes as he clicked his pen and slid the small notebook back in his shirt pocket. After all, she was only a temp and couldn't be expected to contribute much information toward their investigation. Vicky watched him walk back down the hallway to the group of officers gathered by the elevator, mutter a few words at them, then accompany the others into the elevator which would presumably take them up to the eighth floor. That was where the woman had fallen from the window to her death.

About an hour before it happened, Vicky had been sipping at the fruit punch offered by the well-girdled, well-heeled woman who was showing her around the premises of her new temp assignment. The punch was much

2

too sweet — a brilliant red, sticky and too warm. Like a watered-down children's drink, Vicky thought to herself as she forced a smile across her lips. Next to the punch bowl sat a white plastic basket filled with candies resting on tufts of shredded green plastic common around Easter. Vicky glanced over the assorted chocolate eggs and bunnies and jelly beans, but decided against sampling the treats. Easter had come and gone two weeks ago, and the delights offered in the basket were sure to be stale by now.

"Come on to the meeting," Miss Tight-Butt had said, "and meet everyone. It's a sort of bon voyage thing, anyway — I doubt if we'll get any work done this morning."

Vicky remembered all too well the pep talk given her by the agency matron yesterday afternoon. She recited the litany in her mind as she glanced over the cookies and croissants arranged on paper doilies on the table in the conference room. "Always start with a smile for everyone," the woman had intoned. "Be flexible. Be on time. Be cooperative."

Too bad Jim, her husband, couldn't hear that little speech. Vicky sighed, trying one more time to forget the look on Jim's face when she told him over a year ago she was going back to work.

"But, honey, I just retired! Why can't you and me plan some things to do together, instead of you rushing all off back to work again?" The wrinkles in his brow deepened as he frowned, looming over her. "I thought maybe we could both start golfing."

Vicky had shuddered and continued to turn the pages of want ads in the Sunday paper. "No, thank you. Swing a golf club around with a bunch of old men? That's not my idea of a good time."

And now, ten months later, he'd waved goodbye to her that very morning as she backed the Lincoln Town Car out of the driveway and headed for Oakland.

At least they provided snacks my very first morning, she

3

reasoned, biting into a slightly stale cookie. Vicky smiled back at Tight-Butt, perched herself on a stool near the door and looked at everyone. The corporate universe, she decided, really was like a great big dysfunctional family. This little gathering could be like the traditional holiday dinner, with all of them uncomfortable but gamely doing their duty when they'd much rather be somewhere else.

In that respect, Centurion Sportswear was no different from any other assignment the agency had sent her on. Vicky had always been pretty good at matching names to faces. She finished the cookie and started on a doughnut as she tracked a few bodies around the room, honing her skills.

At first Vicky was distracted by the room itself. She was more accustomed to the blank square rooms of suburban office complexes, lined with nondescript and inoffensive muted colors and prints, than she was to the stately old Victorians of Oakland and San Francisco. Hardwood floors, high ceilings festooned with cherubs and bas relief classical scenes, and the polished table made of some dark and expensive wood were definitely new to her. The street sounds of downtown Oakland — cars, buses, shouts, beeps and sirens — floated up to the twelfth floor of the Centurion Building, poured across the newly renovated faux-marble facade that fronted Broadway and assaulted her senses. Someone had flung open the windows to let in the uncertain murky sunlight of a spring morning.

Vicky ventured off her stool and edged back to the cookies. Leaning over in search of chocolate chips and macaroons, she caught her own reflection in the highly polished metal of the coffee urn. Did she look perky enough? Her makeup, carefully applied early this morning, still looked okay, although by the end of the day no doubt the mascara and eyeliner would have smeared in greasy streaks above her cheeks. Thinning blonde hair, artfully arranged to cover an annoying bald spot on the crown of

4

her head, topped a round, plump-cheeked face that was only just starting to show a few wrinkles. Oh well — what could one expect after twenty years of marriage and raising a daughter?

She stood up again, startled by the boom of some man's voice echoing throughout the room. "Everyone here?" He'd planted himself between two huge windows, facing the small group that hovered over the goodies. A couple of hours ago Ms. Stethins — the one Vicky labeled Tight-Butt — had whisked her through an introduction to the man. "Mr. McFarland is in charge of the administrative offices since they moved from Santa Clara to Oakland," Tight-Butt murmured conspiratorially. McFarland, Vicky remembered, had given her a brief smile and handshake, then glanced at Tight-Butt as if asking why the fuck he was being bothered with this person. "He likes to think of us as a family, or actually a team," Tight-Butt had simpered as McFarland paraded off down the hall.

Looking at him now, as he prepared to address the gathering, Vicky wondered if he and Tight-Butt were boffing, then decided against it. Stethins probably wouldn't aim that high.

"Thanks for being here, folks. Although of course, whenever there's food around. . . ." Lame laughter for an old, tired joke. While McFarland rattled off a few announcements that had nothing to do with her, Vicky glanced around. Just a few feet away from her, on the other side of the doors that had been propped open, the security guard stood in military fashion, erect and unyielding, his arms folded across a bulk that had spent a lot of time weight-lifting. Not far from the guard was the receptionist — was it Linda? Laura? L-something, Vicky knew. Very, very pretty, sort of Asian. Maybe Filipina. And no doubt — as was often the case with extremely pretty receptionists — a lot smarter and shrewder than one would imagine.

She guessed that people were grouping themselves

5

according to department, as usually happened. Those messy, frayed guys back in the corner were probably the ones who took care of the computers. The youngest ones, sprawled over by the other end of the long conference table, the ones with headsets — those kids had to be customer service, the ones you talked to when you called the 800 number to order Centurion sportswear. Three — no, make that four — women in expensive tailored suits stood near the front of the room, by the windows, close to McFarland. Executive assistants, Vicky decided. They gazed at McFarland as if he were an ayatollah, listening to his words as though they'd gain some power from the sound of his voice. Tight-Butt was right up there with them, too. She kept glancing back at the techs and the customer service kids, willing them to be quiet and listen to The Man.

One pudgy young man — he couldn't be over twenty-five — moved away from the nerd pack and stood next to the pretty receptionist. She smiled up at him, and he grinned, stuffing a Chinese cream-filled cocktail bun between his lips. At least, Vicky smiled to herself, a couple of people around here are willing to break ranks. The young man's ID badge, clipped to his shirt pocket, flipped over as he leaned heavily against the wall and Vicky made out a last name starting with the letters TYR.

The data-entry types, the ones Vicky would be working with over the next couple of months, must be the ones circling the coffee and doughnuts. Vicky could guess by their clothing and the way they ate the junk food which ones were on the fast-track to management and which ones were going to be sitting in front of computer screens, puzzling over pieces of paper and jotting senseless notes, for years to come. A few of them smiled curiously at her as they helped themselves. She grinned back as she finished a jelly doughnut and cautiously licked her fingers. This was going

6

to be like all the other jobs she'd taken from the agency in the past year. Just show up — clean and clothed and speaking a semblance of English — and you'll get paid.

Then everyone suddenly started paying attention to McFarland. Now they'd get to hear what this whole thing is about, Vicky thought as she crumpled her napkin and glanced around for a trash can. Just as she'd located one and tossed the greasy stained paper into it, Vicky noticed one other set of people she hadn't spotted before.

"For two years now," McFarland intoned, "Centurion Sportswear has shown huge profits — profits that are due to all of us working together as a team."

They can't help it, Vicky decided as his voice became a soothing drone in the background, sending her closer to a meditative state. All these men in all these conference rooms — they're frustrated high school football team captains, or something. Her attention wandered back to the two women she'd noticed just as Coach started his pep rally. Vicky puzzled a few moments over their appearance. Who the hell were they? Obviously not clerical types — those suits were the real thing, not mass-market department store run-offs. And not casual enough for techies.

They seemed hunched together, defensive, perhaps, huddled in a corner behind McFarland. One of them was pretty enough, with long blonde hair left hanging straight in a style reminiscent of Vicky's haircut in her senior class yearbook. Big blue eyes, goofy grin — but the woman's mouth was pinched, almost as if someone had pulled a drawstring tight at the corners of her lips. Vicky had seen that before with chain smokers.

The other one — well, that was a different story. Tall, heavy, but knew how to dress for it. *Impressive* was the first word that sprang to Vicky's mind. Neat dark hair capped a plain face that was distinguished only by the eyes that smoldered, black and deep-set, above thin lips. And she was amazingly pale, with skin the dead white shade of alabaster that was offset by her charcoal-gray suit.

Vicky puzzled for a moment over the tall plain woman. Finally, while McFarland buzzed on, she figured out what was so strange. Unlike all the other people in the room, who kept up a constant ballet of slouching and fidgeting and coughing and scratching and clearing throats, this woman simply stood. Didn't move a muscle, so far as Vicky could see. Those burning black eyes stared straight ahead while the woman's arms hung limp at her sides, her chest barely moving as she breathed, her feet rooted to the polished floor.

"And so," McFarland said, reaching behind him for something on the credenza below the window, "I'd like to give this to Leslie Merrick as a small gesture of our appreciation for all her hard work in getting our international division up and running this year. Leslie" he took a step closer to the two women, offering the champagne bottle with both hands extended — "please accept this with our thanks and good wishes for your future as a consultant. Oh, and Christine —" The thin blonde started and stepped away from the dark-haired woman next to her. "Yes, you too. Folks, Christine Santilli will be staying on as one of our 800-number customer service team. Come on up, Christine!"

McFarland led the room in a spate of half-hearted clapping. The blond — Christine — glanced over at Leslie, then shrugged and waved with a cupped hand in a royal gesture. Vicky heard whispers surging all around her. From the international division to answering phoned-in orders for running shoes was quite a slap in the face for this woman, yet McFarland was trying to pass it off as a triumph. Weird.

The applause quickly died away as soon as everyone got a good look at Leslie's face. The black eyes glittered as she turned, unsmiling, to take the bottle from McFarland.

8

Suddenly nervous at Leslie's stillness, Vicky watched while the woman bent her head as if to study the bottle's label. Her arm moved slowly, gracefully, swinging the bottle to her side and against the window ledge in a lovely arc. Sunlight reflected on the shards of glass that fell to the floor, spinning and tinkling amid drops of champagne that fizzed into nothingness.

The only person in the room who moved for several moments was Tight-Butt. Vicky saw her holding a croissant at her lips, nibbling like a rabbit at the edges of the pastry, her eyes narrowed while her jaws worked like pistons at the morsel.

Then without a word or a facial expression, Leslie dropped the remains of the bottle onto the floor. The glass held together, bounced once, then rolled to a stop in front of McFarland. Leslie, her black eyes fixed on McFarland, took a couple of steps in his direction. He stepped back and jammed his ass into the credenza. Leslie planted her foot into the slivers of the bottle splayed in front of McFarland and ground her heel into them. The gritty noise of glass being pulverized filled the silent room.

No one stopped Leslie as she walked slowly out of the conference room. Vicky backed away from her, then edged herself closer to the door so she could watch Leslie proceed down the hallway to the elevator.

Vicky had to give McFarland credit. At least he didn't try to put a good face on things. He leaned against the credenza, his handsome features frozen in either fear or rage — Vicky couldn't decide which — and cautiously brushed at his shirt with a hand wrapped in paper towels, protected from any fragments of glass stuck on the fabric. Tight-Butt trotted up to him, cooing in sympathy. He muttered something to her, glancing back at the door where Leslie had exited. Then the security guard appeared next to him. How had he gotten up there so fast? Vicky wondered.

"Right now," she heard McFarland growl through gritted

teeth. The guard ducked a nod at his boss and melted back out of the room as silently as he'd moved through it.

No point in looking for something to do, Vicky decided. Everyone was clearly shaken from the drama. The others clustered in whispering knots while Vicky searched out the bagel she'd spotted several minutes ago. Yes, it was still fresh. And was that some cream cheese over there?

Tight-Butt Stethins was wiping McFarland's face, and Vicky munched her bagel and listened to everyone else around her. That was another thing temping had taught her — there was a great deal to learn from careless gossip.

"They shouldn't have tried to pass this whole thing off as a bon voyage. Leslie was pushed out of here for speaking up, that's all."

"Bullshit. She's been wacko from day one, you ask me. Did you see her eyes? And how pale she is?"

"Consultant, my ass. The first place she's going to consult right now is the newspaper. Maybe TV, too. She knows where a lot of bodies are buried."

"Guess Santilli knows which asses to kiss. I thought she'd get fired with Leslie."

"Well, would you want to stay on answering the phones? I'd be humiliated."

"Do you think they got rid of her because she's gay? Can they still do that and get away with it in California?"

"She should've seen it coming. I don't know why the hell she thought she could talk back all the time to him and get away with it. He wasn't going to let it go any higher up."

Slowly people dispersed, until only Vicky, Tight-Butt and a few other women at Tight-Butt's level were left. Even McFarland was gone. He must've slithered, Vicky realized, out through the door tucked into a corner of the conference room.

Stethins remembered Vicky once the room was almost empty. Vicky, finished with her bagel, smiled her perkiest smile while Stethins walked over to her. "Sorry you've had such an awful morning," she whispered, leading Vicky back out to the hallway.

Vicky refrained from mentioning that it had been the most exciting meeting she'd ever attended. "I guess everyone is still pretty upset," she said noncommittally. Inwardly Vicky hoped Stethins would reveal a bit more information about Leslie.

Stethins had rolled her eyes and clutched a hand to her throat. "Honestly," she hissed, "I thought for a minute in there that Leslie was going to try to stab him! With the bottle, I mean. And now we won't get a bit of work out of anyone, you watch." She steered Vicky back down the hall to her own office. "Now, you just sit right there, and I'll get your temporary key-card from Lily." She whisked out of the room, leaving a trail of floral scent.

Of course. Lily, the receptionist. Vicky sank back into the chair and surveyed the office. Pretty ordinary, really — lots of little pots of ivy, some stuffed teddy bears, the usual plain file cabinets. A group of photographs hanging on the wall behind the desk caught her eye, and Vicky got up to look at them.

Wasn't that McFarland? Sure enough, and a recent picture, too. There were news clippings, as well, talking about the move from Santa Clara into downtown Oakland. That was Oakland's mayor shaking someone's hand, with McFarland beaming in the background. And no wonder the mayor was smiling, Vicky thought as she plopped back down in her chair. Oakland had been struggling for years to revitalize itself, to bring in business and new residents. The people running the city would probably do anything, short of murder, to attract a company as big and rich and powerful as Centurion Sportswear.

Something else had caught Vicky's eye. What the hell was this thing sitting on the desk? After a few moments' study of the bronze figure that rested next to Stethins' nameplate, she figured out that it was a small replica of a tennis shoe. EMPLOYEE OF THE YEAR 1995 was engraved on the side.

Vicky replaced the trophy on the desk just as Tight-Butt burst back in the room. From her hand dangled an orange badge with a magnetic strip running lengthwise down the back. "Here we are. Now, you have to keep this with you at all times, and the security guard will want to see it every time you enter or leave the building." Stethins marched her back out to the receptionist's alcove to show her how to insert the key card. "Now, you sign in here and — that's funny, where's Brian?"

Lily gazed up at them from her huge semicircular desk. "Oh, Mr. McFarland asked him to go up and help Leslie take her stuff downstairs." Lily's eyes flickered to Vicky then back to Stethins, and Vicky was certain that Lily would have said a lot more if the temp hadn't been there. Like how the guard was "helping" to make sure Leslie left the building without causing another scene, Vicky thought.

"I see. Well, we'll just have to show you how to sign in later, won't we?"

"Yes, I guess we will." Vicky heard Lily stifle a giggle, but Stethins didn't notice the sarcasm in Vicky's voice.

If this was anything like the usual first-day drill, Vicky realized, she'd be following people around for most of the day, getting in the way and keeping them from doing their work.

Their next stop was the seventh floor. "I thought you said I'd be on the top floor," Vicky said.

"Oh, well, technically. This is as high as this elevator goes — you know these old buildings, always something that doesn't quite work out."

"What do you mean?" Vicky asked, visions of crashing elevators dancing through her head.

"Whoever built this in the first place put a second, private elevator to the eighth floor. I guess it was some kind of penthouse, or something. For now, unless you get that elevator from the lobby, you have to take the stairs up from here to the eighth floor."

"I see." At least, Vicky reasoned, she wouldn't have to march up any stairs to get to her workstation. A chime softly announced their arrival, and the doors slid open into a huge beige room that opened out from the elevator.

"All these offices right now are empty," Tight-Butt said, gesturing with a sweep of her arm at the rows of cubicles ranked in dull beige squares across the expanse of the floor, "but we'll be putting our customer service people in here within six weeks. You know — the people who take phone orders. Oh, Leslie Merrick is up on the eighth floor — well, it doesn't matter. She'll be gone within the hour." Tight-Butt sniffed. "I guess we can put you here for now." She indicated a desk off to the right of the elevators. "You'll be out of the way for a while until we figure out what to do with you."

Fortunately her back was turned so that she couldn't see Vicky roll her eyes. Vicky plopped her oversize handbag down on the desk and glanced over the bank of office equipment nestled along the wall. It was an impressive array of machinery — fax, two computer terminals, complicated-looking telephone set-up, a dot-matrix printer, a laser printer, and a huge gun-metal gray box that she realized was a large paper-shredder.

"Usually people come here to use the fax or the shredder, so far," Stethins was saying. "Somebody screwed up and didn't get fax machines and shredders for each floor." She sniffed again. "You know how it is, getting new equipment into an office — they promise you the world by the next afternoon and then take six months to deliver what they've promised."

"I understand." So she'd be pretty much by herself for the day. Good, Vicky thought, she'd probably find a solitaire game on one of the terminals. Or she could finish that mystery novel that lurked somewhere in depths of her bag, under her tuna sandwich and apple.

"Well —" Stethins presented her with a thick blue booklet. "You could read this employee handbook while I get things set up for you. Oh, by the way, you know how to put calls on hold, right? In case any calls get routed up here?"

"I think if I press this button that says 'hold' it should work."

Half an hour had gone by with no interruptions. Just in case Stethins showed up again, Vicky decided to glance through the handbook. Nothing unusual there — the ordinary statement of goals and objectives and saccharine all-American wholesome ideals, with perhaps a bit more sports metaphors than the average employee handbook. Vicky threw the booklet down on the desk, where it landed with a slap against the polished wood. Aside from her own quiet rustling at the desk, the only other sounds she heard were the annoying whines and thumps of construction equipment from the building site across the alley. She was just about to switch on her computer and look for a game to play when she heard the first scream.

"Where's the guard? Oh, God, get him up here right now! I said, right now!" Suddenly people appeared out of nowhere, dashing down the hall to the elevator, bursting out of the stairwell, one or two of them looking with strange expressions into Vicky's seventh-floor enclave. The faces looked somewhat familiar, from the meeting earlier, but no one seemed to recognize her at all.

"Have you seen the security guard?" one of them asked.

"No, no one's been up on the seventh floor but me," she said, but the man was gone before she'd finished her sentence. "Hey, what's going on?" she shouted after him.

"Don't know — an accident — on the top floor —" And he was gone again.

Mystified, Vicky ventured through a heavy door marked EXIT in the wall beside the elevators and immediately

14

bumped up against a large contingent of people crammed all the way down the stairwell. "What's going on?" she asked, loudly.

"I guess she jumped," someone said in the silence that followed her question.

"Jumped? Who?"

"You didn't hear? Leslie. Leslie Merrick. Just sailed off the eighth floor out onto Broadway. Eight floors down. Jesus."

The group surged forward, downward, pushing past Vicky, who remained frozen at the seventh-floor landing. Suddenly Vicky felt a little sick. Too many people crowded into a small space, she thought, and she fought her way back out into the carpeted quiet of the empty seventh floor.

She made her way slowly back to her desk, breathing deeply to calm her nausea. With a start, she realized that the big windows behind her desk faced Broadway. Unable to stop herself, Vicky went to the window and looked down onto the busy street below.

The charcoal-gray fabric of Leslie Merrick's suit was just visible at the edge of a group of people huddled over her broken body. Despite the frenzied activity on the street, the whole scene appeared oddly quiet and remote — perhaps because no sounds of shock and hysteria rose up high enough for her to hear. She watched the others scurrying back and forth for a few minutes, her head swimming and her hands shaking as a grim realization flooded over her.

If she hadn't been so intent on that damned booklet, Vicky reasoned, she might have seen it happen. She might have looked up and caught a glimpse, no more than a gray glimmer, of Leslie Merrick plunging through the warm spring air to the sharp shock of death on the oily asphalt of Broadway.

Trembling, Vicky backed away from the window. She sat down at her desk and waited for the police.

Chapter One

Helen tried to hide her grimace from the woman sitting across the desk from her. It wasn't the woman's fault, really — not her fault that the Monday morning sun shone right through the streaky windows of Helen's office into Helen's face, its rays like a million little arrows shot by a million little demons sent to plague her. Wasn't her fault that Helen had stayed up far too late the night before, having yet another weird combination love-making and arguing session with her girlfriend, trying to persuade the girlfriend to come out to her parents already, for Christ's sake. Wasn't in the least her fault that Helen, although every instinct

16

she had as a private investigator told her to refuse to take the case, needed the money too badly to turn it down.

Deliberately facing away from the sun's glare, even though that meant that the prospective client had to contort herself in the chair, Helen wondered just how run-down her office looked to Mrs. Tina Merrick, who perched across the room from her with expectation beaming from her placid, round face. Thank God there was at least one really good chair in the place, Helen thought, ignoring the way the room always seemed to have a faint scent of broccoli seeping in from somewhere. The rugs were worn but clean, and cheap prints covered up the worst stains on the walls. Despite staying busy and having a few really lucrative cases every year, finances had never been comfortable for Helen Black Investigations, and a client like Mrs. Merrick was exactly what Helen needed. What, unfortunately, she always needed.

So who cared if Tina Merrick had been sneaking a toot from a bottle of something or other when Helen came out from her office into the cramped waiting area to usher in her prospective client? The bag she'd thrust the bottle back into was expensive, and hopefully there was a big fat expensive checkbook to match it nestled next to that little bottle.

Helen caught a glimpse of herself in the dark glass of the coffeepot sitting atop a shelf beside the desk. Did her face show the wear and tear of the previous night too badly? It was hard to tell in the carnival-mirror distortion of the curved glass, slimy with the dregs of the morning's coffee. Helen saw her face, square and plain and dour, framed by close-cropped salt-and-pepper hair. The suitcases under her eyes were a bit more pronounced than usual, and Helen ran one thick hand through her hair, wishing she looked a little more professional. Her tailored slacks and simple beige blouse, both expensive and worth it, helped to conceal the stockiness that seemed to encroach further on her every day, and they also conveyed a sense of ease and financial stability that her strained, dark face contradicted. "I'm still not completely certain just what it is you want me to do, Mrs. Merrick," Helen began, turning away from her own reflection. She leaned forward on the desk and put her face back out of the sun's reach. "I mean, I'm very, very sorry for your loss, but it seems the police in Oakland —"

Mrs. Merrick squirmed in the chair. "But that's exactly what I mean, Miss Black! They are telling me that my only daughter, my Leslie, killed herself." Her voice broke over the words. "And it's just not true. My Leslie would never, ever do anything like that. She was killed by those monsters! And I want you to prove it!"

Giving the woman time to govern her emotions, Helen looked down at the newspaper dated last Thursday that Mrs. Merrick had slapped on her desk a few minutes ago. The headline in the *Contra Costa Times*, the biggest newspaper circulating in the suburbs east of Berkeley, didn't exactly say "suicide" or "murder," although Helen had to admit that CUTBACKS AT MAJOR CORPORATION ENDS IN DEATH left the door open for either interpretation. The article was heavy on Leslie Merrick's state of mind and said very little about Centurion Sportswear itself. Whoever wrote it had quickly meandered into a commentary on economics and the realities of downsizing.

Helen looked up again at Leslie's mother and caught the woman studying her through narrowed eyes over the tissue balled up in her fist. The tasteful black suit Mrs. Merrick wore was slightly too small for her girth, and the makeup was a tad garish, but beyond that, she was the perfect mother in distress. A little too perfect? Helen wondered as she saw the hard little eyes widened with emotion once again. "I'm curious, Mrs. Merrick —"

"Oh, Tina, please. Everyone calls me Tina."

"All right, Tina. Why did you choose to come to me?"

"Well —" Tina looked down, bending her head so that

Helen could see a thinning spot on her scalp, beneath the cap of glossy blonde hair. "I thought since you were, you know, like her, like Leslie, I mean, you might be a better idea. That is, you would know how to talk to her friends and sort of, well, have some kind of insider thing. You know?"

Ah. Of course. "You mean, your daughter was a lesbian."

"We weren't sure. I mean, Bob and I — Bob died last year — we thought she'd get over it. But of course now she'll never get the chance," and the tears started again.

Whether those were crocodile tears or not, Helen was grateful for the chance the outburst gave her to control her own irritation. After all, Mrs. Merrick was, at worst, simply ignorant. How many other parents felt the same way about their own gay kids, no matter how much they might love them? Tina, coming from a lot of money and not a lot of experience, living in the wealthy suburbs far away from the harsher realities of urban life, would take her information about Oakland and Berkeley from the local television news and the area's conservative newspapers. No doubt she was being completely sincere. In spite of those hard little eyes.

Helen looked away, angry at herself. No wonder she was short on clients. She was going to have to drum up some sympathy from somewhere.

Tina was babbling again. "And so when we saw that gay newspaper in her apartment, well, I was all set to throw it away when I saw your ad in there. And I told myself that I should talk to you."

"I see."

"Look, if it's money you're worried about, you don't have to worry. Bob made sure before he died that I'd be taken care of." Her eyes went hard and small again. Helen found herself wondering what poor old Bob had had to put up with before he died.

Helen felt a sudden burst of shame for her own nasty

assumptions. For God's sake, the poor woman had already lost a husband, and now she had to face the death, possibly by suicide, of her only daughter. Just because she herself was in a bad mood was no reason for her to project it onto Tina Merrick. "Look, Mrs. — I mean, Tina — I don't really think I could do a whole lot more than the police are already doing. They have access to all the facts, and I'm afraid their conclusions do make sense. I'm very sorry to say so, believe me."

"Well, they're all wrong. Leslie just wouldn't do that," Tina sputtered as tears spilled over her round cheeks. "She was my daughter, and I should know! I mean, except for being that way —" she had the grace to stammer and blush a bit over that one — "she was completely normal! Like the way she was planning her vacation to Mexico next month. Now, would someone ready to take her own life be doing a thing like that, planning a trip?"

"Were you and your daughter close, Tina?"

"Well . . ." Back came the hankie. "She did move back into my house, just two months ago. I think things were getting better between us, and then this!" Her voice faded into a high-pitched squeal that mercifully silenced itself in the hankie.

"Why did she come back home?"

Tina shook her head. "Honestly, Helen, I don't know. She wouldn't tell me, but I think she was just about ready to talk about it. I always figured maybe she'd realized what kind of life she was leading, maybe getting ready to change back to normal. And a girl needs her mother to help her, doesn't she?"

"But something must have taken place in her life in order for her to make a decision like that."

"I'm her mother. I would have known if something was wrong."

Helen sighed and refrained from pointing out that, contrary to popular belief, depression often masked itself quite well. "Well, Tina, I still have to ask you what exactly you would like me to do that the police aren't already doing."

"The police! That's a joke!" The tissue flew apart as Mrs. Merrick snorted into it contemptuously. "They're so scared of those horrible monsters at Centurion that they won't say a thing that might make those men look bad."

"What do you mean?"

"Just something Leslie said, once, about the people she worked with. I just know they had something to do with all this. I'm positive you'll find out they've bought off the police, and the mayor of Oakland, and I just don't know who else!" She rummaged for and found a fresh tissue in the impossibly small handbag she carried, then dabbed at eyes and nose with it. "Leslie told me they were all up to something there. She had plenty of stories to tell, believe me."

Who knows, Helen wondered, how much of that was normal bitching and moaning and complaining about work, the way people did the world over? "Can you be more specific?"

"Well, not really. But once you start digging you'll turn it up, I just know you will."

Helen flipped open the daybook on her desk, pretending to study the pages as if looking for some free time for Leslie Merrick. What the hell was she supposed to do? She really did need the money. Even if she came up with the same information the police had, which would more than likely be the case, Mrs. Merrick would pay for her services. "I believe," she said slowly, "you mentioned a memorial sponsored by Centurion to be held for Leslie tomorrow? At a church on Broadway?" Helen glanced back down at the note Tina had given her — the Community Christian Center. The address showed it to be perhaps six blocks from Centurion.

Tina nodded. "Although why they couldn't have it

21

somewhere else, like a nice hotel or something, is beyond me. I guess they just wanted to save some money, the cheap monsters."

"Possibly. Maybe they wanted to keep it quiet, too. Not draw a lot of attention to themselves, the way a more public venue would. There's been a lot of interest from the media, after all." Helen tapped on the daybook with a pencil and studied the flyer. Cheap paper from an office copier, not centered on the page, a couple of simple words misspelled. Why hadn't Tina, the woman's mother as well as the executor of Leslie's will, arranged this event herself, instead of leaving it to people who knew Leslie only from the office? Maybe this was just one more indication of Tina Merrick's lack of concern about her daughter. "And you'll be going to the service, too?"

"Yes, of course. It's at ten o'clock tomorrow morning."

"How about if I come and pick you up in Orinda, then we go together? It will look better for me to appear with you, rather than just show up alone."

"You mean — you'll take the case? Oh, thank you, thank you, Helen! Oh, I knew you wouldn't let my Leslie down!"

Tina gushed and babbled until Helen gave her the standard contract to look over and sign. As Mrs. Merrick studied the single sheet of paper, Helen watched her closely. She was indeed reading it very carefully, more carefully than most clients, who were generally too grief-stricken or distressed or shocked by the circumstances to study the wording of her contract. Tina was taking her time, and Helen saw the eyes shrink and harden. Damn, what was with the woman? One moment she was exhibiting what appeared to be genuine emotion, the next it was that steely glare that missed nothing. Helen was startled when Tina suddenly looked up, turning those cold eyes toward her.

"There's nothing in here about how long it will take."

Helen stared for a moment, dumbfounded. "Well, no, not specifically. Of course, there's no way to predict a resolution to an investigation. But if you'll look at the last paragraph, the contract does say the agreement will be terminated at the client's discretion." Tina continued to stare at her. "I'm sorry, would you like something more specific added in? I could have it ready for you first thing in the morning." Helen felt uneasy at her own eagerness to get Tina to sign the contract and be done with it. What the hell was this about?

Tina sighed and looked back at the contract. "No, I guess it's all right. We'll worry about a written termination of the contract when we get to that point. Sorry, I just need it for the insurance people. You know how it is — they hate paying out any money, and in the case of a suspicious death, they're more reluctant than usual." She looked up again. "I hope you won't mind if my own attorney draws up a form stating a termination date? We'll give you a copy — it's just a formality, anyway."

Helen hoped her face didn't register the shock she felt as Tina bent back over the contract. It was downright scary — the constant switch from grieving, long-suffering bereft mother to hard-nosed, calculating vulture who profited from the death of her nearest and dearest. Probably acted the same way about her husband's insurance policy, Helen thought. Once more Helen took in the expensive black suit, the pearls strung about her neck, the French manicure, the carefully arranged hair that only just missed covering the bald spot. Tina Merrick was no fluffy suburban housewife whose only purpose in life was chauffeuring the kids around and cooking dinner for her husband. And who was Helen to judge, if that's how she learned to survive? What did that say about Helen herself, earning a living off the grief of others?

Finally, Tina scrawled her signature over the long line at the bottom of the page. Helen pulled apart the form and handed Tina the carbon. "Shall we say nine o'clock tomorrow morning, then?"

"Oh, yes, yes. That would be fine."

Tina Merrick, her emotional armor in place once again, babbled and wept her way back out of Helen's office. After ushering her out, Helen looked down at the manila folder in her hand, opened it, and glanced at the contract. Tina's graceful signature curved across the bottom of the page with firm swooping lines. Helen had no doubt that Tina's copy was about to find its way to the attorney previously mentioned.

Tina's copy of the *Times* remained on Helen's desk. Seeing the newspaper there jarred Helen's memory, and she stood by the desk thinking for a moment. After she'd switched on her computer, Helen remembered. Yes, only a month ago in the local paper there had been a series of articles on the revitalization of Oakland's downtown financial district. Maybe she could go on-line and find something there —

No, wait. Helen glanced over at the stacks of newspapers, waiting to be recycled, in a corner behind the office door. Just minutes ago she'd hoped Mrs. Merrick wouldn't notice the moldy piles of newsprint cluttering the office. Somehow Helen's increasing dependence on the Internet for research and information hadn't resulted in a tidier office free of the clutter of newspapers. Turning her back on the terminal sitting on her desk, Helen sighed and kicked at the heap on the floor. Maybe, she reasoned, digging through this would force her into lugging the pile downstairs to the bin in the basement.

Yes, there it was. Helen managed to get a grip around a week's worth of the *Oakland Tribune* and yanked them from their place in the stack, toppling the rest. With a curse and a swift kick at the offending papers, she went back to her desk with the smeared sheaf of newsprint.

She found the remembered article about halfway through the stack. DOWNTOWN OAKLAND TAKES A HIGH JUMP INTO THE FUTURE, the headline screamed. Of course, no one could have known just how appropriate that caption would be. In the article, the Centurion building was the focus of the big color photograph that took up most of the front page of the business section. Helen recognized it — she'd driven by it often enough on her travels into Oakland. Standing at the corner of 12th and Broadway, the triangular-shaped building sported an Art Deco façade, complete with slender angels languishing amongst the faux-tropical wilderness carved into stone. The interesting shape of the building distracted the onlooker's attention just enough to prevent the bas-relief from being vulgar. For a couple of years, the building had undergone an earthquake retrofitting, as well as extensive repair and remodeling. On the second page of the business section, Helen found a photograph of the building taken in 1925, when it had first been erected.

The *Tribune* quoted Jason McFarland, CEO of Centurion's Administrative Division, which would be housed in the building. "We're very proud of the way Centurion stands at the forefront of preserving historic sites," he said. "We believe that our move from Santa Clara to Oakland will be a positive one, both for Centurion and for the city of Oakland."

Helen flipped back to the front page. That was McFarland, standing in front of the building, shaking hands with the mayor, who beamed with pleasure. And with good reason. Oakland had been trying for years to upgrade its horrible reputation — undeserved, Helen believed, and largely the fault of mass media feeding suburban paranoia — and to attract new businesses downtown. The move of a big corporation like Centurion from Silicon Valley to Oakland was certainly a step in that direction.

Apparently the reporter who wrote the article agreed. "The relocation of their administrative offices will, the mayor hopes, encourage other Fortune 500 companies to follow Centurion's example," stated the reporter.

Helen looked at the color photo again. Leslie had fallen from the eighth floor, the top floor of the building. Helen shuddered at the inescapable image of the woman's body hitting the pavement in front of the nice new shiny office building.

Forcing that mental picture aside, Helen went to the most recent newspaper in the pile — dated Saturday, the day after Leslie's death. Once again, Centurion was news.

The article about the downtown tragedy which occurred a month after the original piece about the building, had been written by the same reporter whose byline topped the Centurion building story. Helen noted down his name, Harold Glenn, on the same notepad she'd used for Tina's interview.

This time there were no photographs but Helen remembered most of the details. How Leslie's department had been "rightsized" out of existence, how her managers claimed she'd been pleased at the idea of starting up her own consulting business (which Helen interpreted as a euphemism for unemployment, at least temporarily), and how she'd been depressed for a long time. Several of her co-workers were quoted anonymously, confirming the suspicions of the police that it was indeed a suicide.

There was an interesting twist to the article, however, that had escaped Helen's notice when she'd first read the piece. The reporter, Glenn, mentioned that the apparent suicide came on the heels of an investigation into Centurion's business practices, specifically the way it treated employees both in the United States and in Korea. "Several consumer and human-rights groups have repeatedly accused Centurion Sportswear of gross negligence toward safety issues in their factories and assembly plants," Glenn wrote. "Father James Hitchcock, head of the Oakland chapter of NAFTA Watch and rector of St. Joseph's Catholic Church in Berkeley, has on several occasions made claims of inhuman treatment of Centurion employees." The priest had been unavailable for comment.

Helen smiled. She hadn't talked to Father Hitch in quite a long time — not since that case a few years back, the one out at the resort hotel, that had brought them together. While it looked as though he had no connection at all to her investigation of Leslie's death, it would still be interesting to hear his comments about Centurion. Who knows? If they had a reputation for treating workers like shit, it might conceivably have some bearing on Leslie's death. Besides, it would be good to talk to him again, and —

Her thoughts were interrupted by the telephone. "Helen Black Investigations," she said crisply, piling the newspapers back neatly on her desk.

"Helen? It's me."

"Hi, me." As always, her girlfriend's voice made something melt inside Helen. It was irritating, Helen thought, to be so affected by Alison Young's voice on the phone. It wasn't as if they were kids, or anything. Maybe it was just because of the way they'd met, with Helen playing fiercely protective butch dyke to Alison while she struggled to free herself from an abusive husband.

"How are you?"

"Okay. Tired."

"I know. Me too." A brief silence followed. "Look, Helen, I'm sorry things got a little weird last night."

"I'm sorry too. Let's both pretend it didn't happen, okay?"

"Okay. Listen, I was thinking — want to go to lunch?"

Helen thought. She had nothing else on her agenda for the morning beyond doing some homework for the Merrick case. Besides, she had an idea. "How much time can you take?" she asked as she slid the notebook she'd been using into the manila folder.

27

Helen listened to the muffled bits and pieces of a conversation taking place in Alison's office. Then, "Marty says I can take an hour longer today if I come in early tomorrow morning. Why?"

"Well, I was just wondering if you'd mind meeting me in downtown Oakland. There's a good sandwich place on Fourteenth Street, right on Broadway. And it won't take me more than ten minutes to get from Berkeley to Oakland."

"Oakland?" Helen always swore she could hear Alison's facial expressions over the phone. At the moment, she was willing to bet Alison's nose was crinkled in her standard Look of Astonishment, which Helen thought was really very cute. "Why Oakland?"

"Good news. I got a case this morning." She quickly described her meeting with Tina Merrick. "This will give me a chance to take a look at the place where it happened."

"I'm not sure I can get away that long. "

"Of course you can! You're a temp, working for an agency! You can do whatever you want."

"Come on, Helen! It's a real job and a real paycheck that pays the rent. Why can't you take my work, my livelihood, seriously?"

Lord, here we go again, Helen thought. "I'm not trying to belittle your efforts, Alison. Just relax, okay? You'll get a regular job soon — I'm certain of it."

"You know it's not that easy." She sighed. "Being a temp has its ups and downs, you know? Hey, I found out my mom is temping, too. Weird, huh?"

"Look, meet me for lunch and you can explain it all to me."

There was hesitation on the other end. "Well, I was really hoping we could talk about last night."

"We will, sweetheart, I promise."

"Cross your heart?"

"And hope to die," Helen answered uneasily. Probably

not the most tactful thing to say, considering the case, but it seemed to reassure Alison. Helen hung up vowing to herself that she really would talk to Alison and not just look out the window at the Centurion building and try to figure out where the body had landed.

Still, she reasoned, this might turn out to be her biggest case of the year, and she couldn't afford to lose an afternoon on it. Grabbing her jacket, she put the file in her cabinet, locked it, and hurried down the stairs to go meet Alison.

Chapter Two

"Hello! Earth to Helen Black. Scotty, beam her down to the planet surface."

"All right, all right." Helen grinned at Alison and returned to the remains of her sandwich. "Guess I keep hoping to find signs of intelligent life out there."

Alison glanced out the window of the restaurant. No Free Lunch had recently changed ownership — the third time in just a couple of years — and the menu had undergone another overhaul. The thick greasy fries and juicy hamburgers Helen remembered were long gone, replaced by a variety of brightly colored healthy entrees that were heavy on bean sprouts. The clientele matched the upscale menu. Not two blocks away stood Oakland's municipal buildings, and Helen bet that a good third of the people jammed into the small café space were attorneys. Peering uncertainly at the rest of the cucumbers and peppers poking out from under wheat bread, Helen wondered what had happened to the hard-hat guys and dock workers who used to come up from Jack London Square for lunches heavy on fat and cholesterol.

Just across the street, on the other side of Broadway, stood the Centurion building. From her perch at the counter Helen could see yellow police tape stretched from the front of the building across a triangular wedge of flagstone that limned the side of the building. The wedge narrowed as it led away from the street, matching the three-sided design of the Centurion building, which had its apex facing Broadway and sides that widened as the building reached back toward the alley behind.

Alison, cramped between Helen and a very large woman at the counter, picked at her chicken salad. She craned her neck to look out the window. "Jesus, look at all the people hanging around over there. My God, what do they think they're going to see now?"

Helen sighed. The sandwich wasn't all that good. She thought she remembered better food at this place, but then she hadn't been much in downtown Oakland lately. "It's been five whole days since the woman died. I'll bet a lot of them are just checking out the new line of sports equipment Centurion's putting out this year and wondering if they can afford the shoes and tights and so on."

"So the police are finished with the investigation?"

Helen shook her head. "I'm not sure yet. Tina Merrick certainly thinks so. If she's right, it was wrapped up pretty fast."

"Too fast, do you think?"

Helen shook her head again. "I won't know until I do a

31

little digging." She regarded her girlfriend's bright-eyed interest with surprise. "Why? Do you feel like snooping around with me today?"

"Not me. Anyway, what did you want to do out there today? You'll be going to that thing tomorrow with her mother, right?"

"It helps to take a look at things — try to get a feel for the place." Helen was suddenly reluctant to go into detail. She knew she had to study the scene, learn where the body had fallen and how, the layout of the building, which window — a lot of things Alison might feel very squeamish about. Besides, hadn't Helen's profession been a point of contention in all of her relationships? She was positive that her last lover had ended their relationship of many years precisely because Helen's work brought her — brought them both, actually — in direct contact with violent death. And now she wanted to protect Alison from exposure to the ugliness of what she did everyday. "I'm sorry, sweetheart, I didn't catch that," Helen said, dragging her thoughts away from Leslie Merrick and girlfriend troubles.

At hearing the term of endearment, Alison blushed and glanced around the crowded café. "Not right now, okay?" she murmured.

"Alison, no one gives a damn. There are dykes all over this place. This is Oakland. Come on, look around you." Helen did her best to put humor into the words but kept her voice low. "Anyway, isn't it better for me to call you sweetheart than to put my tongue in your ear?" she teased.

Alison rolled her eyes and dropped her fork on the counter. Apparently the chicken salad was as tasteless as Helen's sandwich. "Please, Helen. Promise me you won't do this at my parents' house, okay?"

Helen stared at her, ignoring the elbow jammed in her back by the man next to her. "What are you talking about?"

"You really haven't heard a thing I've said, have you? I've been talking for twenty minutes about the barbecue my

32

folks are having this weekend. They want me to bring you along."

Helen shook her head, surprised at herself. For the past year, ever since she'd considered herself in a real relationship with Alison, Helen had never really imagined Alison as part of a family. She was just Alison, herself, a lovely young woman with beautiful green eyes, long dark hair and thin sharp features. Helen had seen those same distinctive features reflected in photographs lining the walls of Alison's apartment for several months now, but she'd never connected her lover with anyone besides herself all this time. It was an uncomfortable realization, and Helen guiltily tried to remember if Alison had ever talked about parents or siblings in her presence. Either she hadn't, or Helen had conveniently deleted any such comments from her awareness.

Alison blushed again under Helen's gaze. She picked up her fork again and tentatively prodded her salad, the long black hair falling forward over her cheeks and concealing her embarrassment. "Helen, what are you staring at?" she finally hissed.

"I was just wondering if your mother is as beautiful as you are. Or maybe you take after your dad." Whatever the case, Alison's parents had produced a beautiful daughter. Her shoulder-length black hair fell shining over her shoulders as she looked away from Helen, and her bright green eyes stared down angrily at the plate of food.

"For God's sake." Alison shoved a slice of green pepper into her mouth and crunched at it furiously. "I don't think my family would appreciate hearing something like that."

"Not appreciate hearing that their daughter is beautiful? Are you kidding? Parents live for shit like that," Helen countered, working hard to maintain a tone of light-hearted banter. After all, her own familial experiences — being kicked out of her home as a teenager by an irate father who couldn't bear the thought of a perverted daughter

33

beneath his solid Christian roof — seemed to have nothing in common with the fragments of Alison's past Helen had gleaned from time to time. Maybe that was why she'd blocked out the possibility that Alison had a family. Helen fought down a stab of jealousy at the picture-perfect image of Alison's youth she'd conjured up. She went on, "Besides, I'm feeling kind of guilty that I haven't made more of an effort to meet them before now. I'm flattered they've invited me."

"Yeah, you say that now," Alison muttered. She moved her plate away toward the edge of the counter and reached for her soda. "Just wait until you meet them."

"Wait a minute, wait a minute." Truth washed over Helen like a cold shower, and with an angry nudge she shoved back at the elbow that had been poking her left side throughout the dismal meal. The man she'd disturbed earlier sighed loudly and unwedged himself from the counter with a pointed look of disgust. "You haven't told them, have you?"

"Told them what?"

"Oh, no, don't play that one with me, Alison." With an effort Helen kept her voice down. Leaning close to Alison, she asked, "You haven't told them about our relationship, have you?"

Alison stared straight ahead, her fingers playing with the straw in her glass. The blush that had crept over her face moments ago faded to smooth ivory. "I haven't had a chance."

"Bullshit." The moment the word spat out over the counter Helen wished it back. Of course Alison was petrified — who wouldn't be? And Helen had sworn to herself, over and over, that she'd be supportive and loving and understanding of Alison's decision to wait for the right moment to come out to her family. Helen took a deep breath, avoiding Alison's eyes, and tried again. "I don't understand, Alison. "We've been seeing each other for a year now. As far as I'm concerned, this is a relationship. Isn't it?"

"Yes, Helen, of course. I — I just —" Alison broke off stammering as the waiter picked up her plate.

"You want to take this with you?"

"What? Oh, no thanks."

The waiter's eyebrows rose in surprise as he turned away from them, chicken salad still piled high on the dish.

"Helen," Alison said quietly as soon as the waiter left them, "I have to do this my own way. We're different, you and me. You go riding in like Joan of Arc, but I just can't do that. It's not me. And they're my parents."

"What, you think Ozzie and Harriet can't handle it? Sorry — that was out of line." Before Alison could say anything else, Helen said, "It's just that maybe you need to let them know about us, sweetie. I mean, they might be in for kind of a shock when they see me."

"What do you mean?" Alison took the check from the waiter before Helen could grab it. "No, no, I've got it. Tell me what you mean," she said as she rifled through her backpack for money.

Helen focused on Alison's hands, fumbling in the depths of the canvas bag. Damn, she hated these conversations. "All I'm saying is that it might be kind of obvious that we're more than just pals who have lunch together, you know?"

Alison was silent until the waiter took her money to the cash register. Then she mumbled, "They won't wonder about anything if you continue to do things like call me honey and sweetie and make dirty jokes." Now Alison face was flushed again, this time with the deep red of anger. "I mean, the way you act in public, it's like you think no one notices, or cares."

Helen sat back, her whole body cold and unfeeling. The half-sandwich she'd gotten down weighed leaden in her gut. "I embarrass you. That's what you're trying to say to me, isn't it?"

"No, it isn't. And you don't. Damn, I don't know how to do this, Helen." In her eagerness to be gone, Alison nearly emptied the contents of her bag on the floor of the café. Helen helped her to grab it and Alison struggled to run the big metal zipper along its track. "I really don't. I'm scared of this."

"Alison —"

"And I have to get back to work. I'm already late. Look, I'll call you tonight and we'll get this worked out, okay?"

"But — are you sure you want me to come to this barbecue thing? Can't we postpone it until we have a chance to talk?"

Alison was already pushing her way past the nearest clutch of customers hovering by the counter. "I'll call you tonight." And she was gone.

"Excuse me, are you finished? We've been waiting for twenty minutes." Helen barely noticed as a man and a woman, laden with briefcases and cell phones, edged next to her. The man, smelling strongly of spicy aftershave, shoved his face close to hers and gave her a toothy smile. "We've got to be back in court in another twenty minutes."

Without a word, Helen got up and let the crowd push her through the café and out onto Broadway. She still felt a bit nauseous from the shock coming right after a terrible meal, and anger stirred acid up into her throat.

The traffic light on the corner glowed red. Helen looked up at the signal, waited, willed her hands to stop shaking. Her own life, living openly as a lesbian in a community that was quite tolerant of who slept with whom, had not come easily. She'd had to rebel against a fundamentalist Christian upbringing that still caught her unawares, over and over again. Then there were her parents, who'd never, Helen was convinced, ever really loved her. Not to mention all the hide-bound conservatism of the narrow minds surrounding

her and shaping her own personality as a kid. A lot of years
— a lot of tears, too, and sleepless nights and loneliness —
resulted, for Helen, in a hard-won peace with herself.

"Bitch, get out the way!'

It took the collective insults of a group of kids —
probably on lunch break from school — to rouse her from
her blank-eyed stare. The light flickered green as the kids
shoved past her. One of them clipped her with his
skateboard, inspiring jeers and shouts of appreciation from
his companions.

Helen followed them across the street. She could feel
her mind clamping down on the emotions of the past half
hour, shifting into that strange high gear where she worked
as a detective. The sick feeling that threatened nausea faded
as she approached the Centurion building, and Helen
blessed whatever gods had given her the ability to distance
herself from her feelings while she worked.

"This is it, huh?"

"Yeah, I think she landed right over there. On that
paved part, to the right."

"No shit!"

"But it's only eight floors, right? You'd think maybe she
would have just broken her neck or something."

"I guess better dead than in a fuckin' wheelchair the
rest of your life."

"Do you think the place will have some kind of curse on
it? Because she, like, killed herself."

"Oh, that's a bunch of bullshit. I think a lot of people
do things like this when they get laid off. It happens all the
time nowadays."

"Bet their sales go through the roof now."

"Hey, they got the new shoes on display in the window
at the front. You know, the ones that baseball player wears
on TV, with the special cushions in 'em."

"How about their plant in Korea? They turn these kids into slaves, working twelve-hour days putting running shoes together?"

"Oh, that's a bunch of bullshit. I don't believe any of that crap."

It took Helen several minutes to work her way through the constantly moving crowd that passed by the Centurion building as if they were on a guided museum tour, shuffling through to the next exhibit. Patience finally brought her to the edge of the yellow police tape.

She stopped in front of a glassed-in display that took up the window area around the entrance. Against a black background of heavy, draped fabric, the passersby could view an arrangement of mannequins wearing Centurion sports gear. Headless alabaster female dummies with anorexic limbs had been clothed in the latest Athena line of running shoes, tank tops, sweats, shorts, spandex and halter tops, their long thin white fingers curved lifeless around fake weights and balls and racquets. Helen noted that most of the people who slowed down to get a good look at the scene of death also lingered at the window display. Their pale faces reflected back, ghostly and disembodied, in the black marble facade.

Helen caught a glimpse of her own face there. Was she really that angry? Did her brow really hang that heavy and menacing over her eyes, which were almost invisible? And the way she stood, her arms tight folded across her bulky torso, both defensive and aggressive, somehow. No, it had to be the conversation she'd just had with Alison. That, and the weird distortion in the black marble.

" 'Scuse me." The crowd sluggishly moved along, and Helen managed to brace herself against the wall, slightly pushing up on the yellow tape. The people passing by jostled her without forcing her to move with them.

Actually, the tape itself would no doubt be removed by the end of the day. The debris of police work — mud and dirt tramped over the polished flagstone, colorless dark stains splotched in odd patterns, bits and pieces of wood and plastic littered and blowing along the walls — littered the pavement. A plastic Baggie lodged itself by Helen's toe. She leaned over awkwardly, not wanting to lose her place at the building, to look at the thin film that lay along her shoe. Although it looked like nothing so much as the contents of someone's lunch bag, minus the sandwich, the block letters still spelled out EVIDENCE in slightly smeared red ink.

Before she could reach down and pick it up, the Baggie whipped away in one of those sudden gusts of wind that blow through the rows of tall buildings in any city, coming from nowhere to spend themselves in cold bursts through an invisible pattern of air passages. She watched its path, through the weak sunlight of the spring afternoon, until it landed on the street next to a man in uniform.

His armpatch read MASTERS SECURITY. So the police must have packed up their dog and pony show, she decided, and moved on to the next event. Well, what did they have to hold them there, after all? She watched idly as the guard's hulking presence kept the fascinated observers from lingering too long in front of the building. From the way his arms strained against the blue uniform shirt, Helen would guess that he worked out with some pretty impressive weights on a regular basis. His bull neck surged up and over the shirt's collar, but it was flushed an unhealthy-looking red. Maybe just the cold April wind blowing on him, though, she thought, remembering the wind's bite.

Realizing that the guard's presence would probably limit any chance she'd hoped for in checking out the place, Helen quickly turned her attention back to the wedge of pavement. Peering up, squinting against a fresh gust of wind, she saw more yellow tape outlining a window on the top floor. The window was very nearly centered in the side of the building, halfway between the front facing Broadway and the back of the building where the flagstone reached its apex. A nondescript window in a nondescript wall — apparently the developers had put all their efforts into making the front of the building visually striking — it now gaped, wide open, the old fashioned shutter-like panes flung outward. It was too far up on the wall for Helen to make out any details, but her knowledge of police work supplied at least some of the things she knew she'd see there. The windowsill and the sash would still show grimy traces of fingerprint powder, the gritty black dust that lingered no matter how much one washed the affected surfaces. There was probably a litter adhesive strips remaining from the work of the photographer called to the scene — depending, of course, on who they'd called in. The woman's office was more than likely in a state of utter confusion, not yet tidied up from the inspection of files and records and objects in the room. Maybe tomorrow Helen could somehow get into the office, and if things were still a bit of a mess —

"Uh — uh, lady, excuse me —"

At first Helen thought the guard was talking to her. Guilty conscience, she decided, when she saw his florid face turned toward someone who had ducked under the tape and made her way into the wedge. The guard's face belied that heavy bull neck. He couldn't be more than thirty, she thought, with those round baby cheeks and bright eyes. A glimmer of sunlight flashed his nameplate at her. B. Reilly lurched his stocky body under the tape and his hand went to his waist. Armed security? she thought, catching a glimpse of the holster at his side. What the hell was Centurion up to that they needed armed guards to check people in and out at the front desk? More than likely, Helen reasoned, they just hired him for the duration of the police investigation. Still, it was interesting that the powers that be found it necessary.

No — it was just a walkie-talkie.

"You're going to have to leave here, ma'am," B. Reilly was saying.

"Please, sir, this won't take a moment. It must be done before any more time goes by."

"Look, no one is allowed in here for any reason. They'll be cleaning the place up tonight after everyone goes home, then you can walk through here again, okay?" B. relaxed a bit and let his hands rest on his hips. "Come on, let's not have any trouble, lady."

The woman, who'd been crouched over the flagstone directly under the window, sat back on her heels. Helen got a glimpse of a lined and weary face framed by thick masses of dull brown hair that blew and tossed in the cold wind thrusting between the buildings. She was probably in her forties, although the plain face and dull brown eyes made her seem like a much older woman. Her brown clothing didn't help. The robe-like garment, made from some indeterminate rough fabric, fell in loose folds over a heavy round body. The only thing she wore that broke the earth-tones of her appearance was a thick leather cord strung with rows of cowrie shells and beads.

"Of course, you wouldn't understand." Amazing in all that dull brown, her smile was sudden and brilliant, completely transforming her from a drab eccentric into something at once more feminine and more vibrant. "But I really must complete this now. It's precisely because the area will be cleaned up tonight that I must do this now."

"Huh?" B. Reilly stared in disbelief, his hand dropping away from his forgotten walkie-talkie, as the woman in brown set a plain white canvas bag on the pavement. With the slow motion of ritual she drew out a tall brown candle, a small wooden box that fit snugly in her hand, and a silver dish that reminded Helen of the patens used in Catholic churches.

"Would you please stand over there?" Too taken aback to say anything else, B. took a couple of steps backward, his mouth agape. The brown-robed woman lit the candle and somehow, despite the wind, the flame flickered into strength and burned a bright gold next to the dark brick wall. Her lips moving silently, she opened the wooden box and pinched something from it. With circular gestures, she sprinkled whatever she'd taken from the box onto the silver paten she'd placed before the candle.

"What the fuck is that?" Helen heard someone whisper behind her. "Jesus fucking Elvis, looks like some kind of voodoo thing going on."

"Told you there was some kind of weird shit going on here, didn't I? Who knows what made that woman really jump from the window."

"I see her blood, I see her blood, I see her blood." She moved shaking hands over the flagstones as she muttered. A group of hard-hatted construction workers had gathered at the triangle's apex, watching the scene unfold. Behind them, a vast cavern of an old office building minus its facade — presumably the site where these guys worked — gaped out across the alley.

As the crowd stared, the woman in brown withdrew a thick length of some kind of broom or sticks tied together from the canvas bag. She held it over the candle until it began to smolder. Helen smelled the fresh bite of sage as the woman stood up and walked slowly in a circle around the pavement just beneath the window, her lips still moving, her eyes heavy-lidded and slitted almost shut against the stares of the people gathered near Helen.

B. had had enough. "Okay, lady, that's it. Let's pack up our bag of tricks and get out of here before I have to pack it up for you." With that he strode over to her canvas bag and yanked it up from the pavement.

"No!" She moved so quickly that Helen didn't even see her get to the guard's side, but she definitely heard the slap the woman administered to the man's face. Behind her, a few people burst into surprised laughter at the scene.

"Don't you realize how dangerous it is to interfere with this?"

"This is better than ringside seats."

Helen turned around slowly. She knew that voice, although it had been a very long time since she'd heard it.

Sure enough, it was the bright red hair and freckled face of Homicide Detective James Macabee. He was so close that she could smell the stale nicotine breath of his last cigarette. At the moment, however, the only thing sticking out of his mouth was a toothpick that jiggled and swerved between his lips when he talked.

"Think if I wiggle my nose like Samantha in *Bewitched* she'll go away?" He smirked at Helen. Before she could answer he'd pulled aside the yellow tape and gone to B. Reilly's side.

Chapter Three

"Shit, look out, here comes McFarland."

Thank God for ID badges, Helen thought, turning around to see who had spoken. The two women, standing close together, both wore nylon cords slung round their necks on which dangled laminated photos embossed with the Centurion logo of Roman letters atop three Ionic columns. Beneath the logo Helen could make out names — Christine Santilli and Donna Stethins. Both were blonde, thin, and perhaps in their late thirties. The one labeled Stethins, dressed in a pink raw silk suit, appeared to be a loyal customer of her local gym. She had a well-defined upper body with a wiry corded neck that would one day be skinny and stringy. Her hips were almost non-existent, and Helen wondered if she had been born that way or if she'd had to spend many painful hours achieving that effect.

After studying the other woman for a moment, Helen decided that Christine Santilli had, as her long deceased grandmother from Mississippi would have said, been rode hard and put up wet. It wasn't that she was unattractive — her wide blue eyes and long legs made her stand out in a crowd — she carried with her an air of having hung too long in a closet somewhere. Matching wrist braces, the kind worn by people suffering from too much work at a computer, encased both of her arms. Right now those arms were folded across a thin chest that shook with her coughs. And unless Helen was seriously mistaken, those pretty blue eyes that looked out on the world with the semblance of innocence and youth, rimmed with carefully applied makeup, revealed the tired faded edges of too much alcohol.

The man that came pushing up through the crowd had to be McFarland. He looked and smelled too much like the office golden boy to not be the boss. Younger than both women, he was good-looking in a bland sort of way, without being overly noticeable. The only thing out of place were the suspenders — they were just slightly passé, Helen knew, in office wear. Still, they exuded an air Helen was certain McFarland worked long and hard to create — successful and young without having a stick too high up his butt.

"Oh, God. He's going to try to get her out of there." That was Donna Stethins. Helen leaned back against the wall and kept her attention divided between the scene unfolding at the side of the building and the two Centurion employees.

"This ought to be good." Christine Santilli pulled a pack of cigarettes from her skirt pocket and lit one, sucking hard at the smoke.

"So who the hell is that?" Stethins asked. "You ought to know. You worked for Leslie."

Christine merely narrowed her eyes and blew smoke out into the cool air.

McFarland and Reilly had between them managed to lift the woman up off the pavement by her arms. Helen watched them guiding her carefully toward the far end of the wedge of flagstone, away from the crowd that surged forward from Broadway and threatened to break through the yellow tape.

"McFarland sure looks pissed," was all Christine said.

He did, too, Helen noted. Beneath the smile pasted on his mouth, McFarland's jaw was clenched. Through gritted teeth he said something to Reilly that blanched the security guard's ruddy features and stopped him in his tracks.

"Well, the idiot watched her jump from the window and did nothing, right? And now here he is letting any weirdo in off the street to make a scene. Not a whole lot of security, if you ask me," Donna said.

"I don't think McFarland is going to ask you." Christine dropped the cigarette to the ground as the last tendrils of smoke dissipated.

"Well, you'll have to wait and see about that." Donna Stethins smiled smugly. "I've been asked to sit in on the next managers' meeting."

"Oh, wow." Christine rolled her eyes. "Just think, I knew her when."

"So who is that freak out there? Ever see her before?"

"Well —" Christine fished another cigarette out — "Let's just say she looks like someone who knew Leslie really well. And I mean really well."

"You mean — you mean they were, like, girlfriends?"

Christine started laughing at the look on Donna's face. "If only I had a camera! Jesus, Donna, what is your problem? You know Leslie's a — I mean, she was — a lesbian."

46

At that moment McFarland ducked back through the crowd, nodding at the two women. Helen watched the guard as he cleared his throat and called out to the crowd. "All right, folks, there's nothing left to see. Time to get moving along. Come on, now." Helen could no longer see the woman in brown and figured she must have gone away through one of the alleys that mazed through the backside of Oakland. And by the time Helen turned around again, the two women from Centurion had also disappeared.

Helen debated trying to follow the woman but decided it would be a waste of time. She would only get lost, wandering around the complicated warren of alleys she didn't know all that well. Instead, she hurried back to her car and got on the phone. To her relief, Tina Merrick answered after the first ring.

At first she was confused. "A big red-headed man?"

"Yes, he used to be with the Lafayette police."

"But are you sure? I mean, that was a long time ago. Over a year, you said."

"Yes, Mrs. Merrick, I know — I mean, Tina." Helen rolled her eyes. The last thing she wanted was to be on a first-name basis with Tina Merrick. "But Lieutenant Macabee is not an easy man to forget." Although what the hell he was doing in Oakland, she had no idea. Macabee had shoved his way past Helen and grabbed the woman's arms, pinning them behind her back with expert speed. Oblivious to her protests, he'd then marched her across the pavement to the black-and-white waiting at the curb. "He wasn't the officer who spoke with you about your daughter, then?"

"Well, Helen, I just don't know for certain. There were an awful lot of policemen asking me all kinds of questions."

Traffic was frozen on Ashby at this hour. With increasing frustration Helen inched slowly west on the busy street, crossing Sacramento as the sun blazed in her face. Her left hand occupied with the car phone, she groped

47

around the front seats for her sunglasses, keeping her left
elbow propped on the steering wheel. Damn, they must have
slipped under the seat. Stifling a sigh, Helen strained to
hear Tina Merrick's voice as it cracked and sputtered over
their horrible connection.

"I don't see — problem — even if — there — morrow,"
she heard.

"Well, I'm certain he'll be there. It's just luck he didn't
really get a good look at me earlier today. By the way, Tina
— are you still there? Tina?"

"Yes, I'm here. My goodness, that's so much better!
What did you do, Helen?"

"Not a thing." For some reason the line cleared. Helen
gave up on the sunglasses and craned her head back as far
as she could to try to keep her eyes shielded with the sun
visor. "I just wanted you to know, in case Macabee questions
my presence at the memorial tomorrow."

"Well, if he is there, it will be a big surprise to me.
None of those police people seemed to give a damn about
my Leslie."

"Tina, sorry, I have to ask you something —" Helen
hoped she'd successfully cut off another speech about inept
police practices and gave a brief description of the woman
in brown. "Does she sound familiar to you, Tina?"

A lengthy silence followed. Great, Helen thought. Now
we've been disconnected. Helen muttered a curse at a
bicyclist who thought he'd weave a new lane through the
traffic, darting in and out of the line of slowly moving cars.
"Stupid fuckhead," she hissed as the cyclist passed her car,
slapping one hand against her hood.

"Did you say something, Helen?"

"Uh, no, Mrs. Merrick. No, Tina. I thought we got cut
off."

"I can't say I do recognize anyone like that, Helen. Well,
it sounds sort of like — well, no, it just couldn't be her. No,
I don't think that's anyone I know."

"Well, who did you think it might be?"

"Helen, dear, I think — yes, there's someone at the door. I'd better go now. Was there anything else?"

"Nothing that can't wait until tomorrow, Tina. Thanks."

Mrs. Merrick hung up without another word, and Helen shook her head. Terrific. Of course she knew who the woman was. Why wouldn't she tell Helen?

And Macabee was no fool. He'd get a good look at Helen tomorrow, Tina or no Tina, and he'd remember. Of course, if Tina said she was a friend of the family, who was Macabee to say otherwise?

As she finally pulled around the gentle curve that led down Ashby to San Pablo Avenue, Helen saw the blank streetlight sitting dead in the late afternoon sun. No wonder traffic was so backed up, she thought. An idea flashed in her mind while she waited her turn to cross the busy intersection, and cutting through a parking lot she turned back around on Ashby. Yes, she could get to Alison's apartment easily from here. No longer blinded by the sun, Helen reached for the phone again and dialed Alison's number. The call was answered on the first ring.

"Yeah, I just got home," Alison said. "Are you — is everything all right?"

"Well, I think we need to talk. Look, I'm calling from the car phone and I'm only a few blocks from your place right now. Can I stop by for a few minutes?"

"Well, sure, that would be fine. But you need —"

Damnit to hell. Helen tossed her dead phone into the back seat. It couldn't be the batteries — she'd just charged the fucking thing up last night. What was going on with it?

None of that mattered, she told herself as she sped toward College Avenue, against the heavy flow of traffic coming off the freeways. It didn't take her long to get to Alison's building, but her usual parking spot, in back of the dry cleaners' on the cul-de-sac, had already been taken by a huge Lincoln Town Car. The gas hog had actually used up enough space for two cars, and Helen spared an evil thought for the idiot as she found another spot in the next block.

The nausea that had threatened her stomach all afternoon was finally gone. Maybe in private the two of them could work this out, speaking calmly and quietly. Things looked even better when she saw Alison waiting for her at the entrance to the apartment building.

"Hi, Helen."

"Hey." What was the matter now? Alison stood, hugging herself tight, her face tired and tense. Helen's heart sank. "You okay? Maybe I shouldn't have come."

Then Helen saw the man and woman standing behind Alison. Oh shit, Helen thought, seeing the planes of Alison's face reflected on the features of the woman who stood in the doorway. Yes, and she had his eyes, too. Helen forced a smile onto her face and walked forward to meet her girlfriend's parents.

"Well, well, so this is the famous Helen Black!" Mr. Young's deep voice boomed. "You're all our Alley Cat talks about!"

Helen saw Alison flinch at the nickname. She bravely stuck her hand out. Mr. Young stood well over six feet tall, with only the very beginning of a paunch beginning to strain at the waistline of his golf pants. Helen noted the tiny American flag pinned to the lapel of his Hawaiian print shirt as they shook hands.

Mrs. Young was an older, plumper version of her daughter. Her disk earrings bobbed as she vigorously shook Helen's hand. "After we talked to Alison last night, we thought we'd just pop over and visit her new apartment," she said. "Honey, we would have been glad to help you move! All you had to do was ask!" Alison's mother straightened her sundress and ran a beringed and manicured hand through her thin blonde hair. "But I guess you gals did just fine on your own!"

50

"That's our Alley Cat!" boomed Mr. Young. "By the way, Helen — we can call you Helen, I hope, I feel like we already know you — you can just call us Jim and Vicky."

"Thank you." Helen moved with Alison to usher them into the building. Recalling the brief phone call a few minutes ago, Helen realized Alison must have been trying to warn her about the presence of the in-laws. Fucking car phones.

"I was just telling Jim, honey, what a lovely building this is! You know, Helen" — Vicky Young stopped them in their tracks a few feet from the elevator — "when she told me she was moving to Berkeley, I was just a little concerned. I mean, it's not as quiet as Orinda."

"No, no, it isn't," Helen agreed, remembering vividly how she'd rescued Alison from an abusive husband in the wealthy East Bay suburb of Orinda just over a year ago. "I think her life out here is very different than it was in Orinda."

"Well, since I'm working that temp job right now in Oakland, it just made sense to stop by and see how my little Alley Cat was doing," Vicky babbled on. She wouldn't look directly at Helen, and Helen wondered whose idea this surprise visit was. Vicky's eyes darted around, looking at the ground, at her daughter, at her husband, at the car, anywhere but at Helen. "I mean, Jim, he didn't even want me to go back to work, and especially since all the awful things that happened last week —"

"Now, sweetheart, these gals don't want to hear all about that! They've got other more important things to talk about, I'm sure!" Helen flinched at Jim's loud baritone. Everyone stood there for a few moments, shuffling feet and not looking at one another.

Helen ignored the glare Alison tossed her way and punched the button in the wall that would summon the elevator.

"Well, looks like you gals have some plans for this

evening," Jim intoned, putting an arm around his wife. "Vicky and I are going over to the country club for dinner — maybe round up some of the guys for a few holes on the green tomorrow. Oh, Helen, you're coming to our barbecue this weekend, right?"

"With bells on, Jim. Wouldn't miss it for the world."

"Are you sure we don't have to worry about a parking ticket, honey?" Vicky asked her daughter. Then, to Helen, "We actually found the perfect parking spot, over behind that dry cleaners across the street. Just enough room for the Lincoln. You know how your dad is about parking that old car!" She beamed at Alison.

After a couple of hugs, Mr. and Mrs. Young left the two women standing at the elevators. "See you Saturday," they called back over their shoulders.

As soon as they were out of sight, Alison leaned against the wall and closed her eyes. "Jesus, Mary and Joseph," she breathed. "Helen, I tried to tell you, but the phone —"

"It's okay. Nothing happened, did it? It's going to be okay, sweetie. What is taking that elevator so long?" Helen punched the button again. The doors finally slid open with their usual creak. "Did they give you any warning?" she asked.

"Not at all. I couldn't believe it! I mean, you know how parents are, but this is ridiculous."

"Actually, I don't know how parents are." Helen was surprised at her own reaction to the situation. Curiosity was the strongest thing she felt at the moment. "You know, honey, in one sense you're very lucky to have parents that will come out to visit you. Mine never gave a damn what happened to me. And not just before my dad kicked me out. They were always like that." She glanced up. Color was returning to Alison's face, and her green eyes were bright with some unreadable emotion. "I'm really glad you said I could come over tonight."

Tears welled up and spilled onto Allison's cheeks. "Helen, I'm so sorry for what I said this afternoon. I was so afraid, and I don't think I even knew what I was saying."

"Hey, hey, it's all right. Oh, sweetie." She took Alison into her arms. "Please don't do that. Please. It's okay. I know this is all really new to you."

Alison's voice was muffled against Helen's shirt. "I'll stop crying if you promise me something."

Oh, God, now what? "Yes?"

"Just don't ever call me Alley Cat."

The elevator door opened, and a skinny young man carrying an enormous pile of laundry overflowing his basket stumbled past them into the elevator with a mumbled apology. "Well," Helen said as they headed down the hall to Alison's apartment, "I don't know if that's a promise I can keep."

"What makes you say that?" Alison asked as she opened the door.

"Because" — Helen grabbed Alison around the waist and pulled her close as soon as the door was shut behind them — "you do have a pretty sharp set of claws once in a while."

"Yeah, and I can purr, too."

"I remember. I remember how to make that happen, too."

"Prove it," Alison whispered, challenge in her eyes.

Without a word, standing in the foyer of Alison's apartment, Helen gently held Alison by the shoulders and backed her up against the wall. "Not a problem."

She kissed her, deep and hard, thrusting her tongue into Alison's mouth. With one hand she kept Alison pinned to the wall while the other slid down her body, caressing the curves and planes she found there.

"Maybe —" Alison caught her breath, leaning her head back against the wall. "Maybe we should move to a more comfortable place."

"Oh, no. You're not getting away from me that easily. I never refuse a challenge." Helen leaned against her, continuing her exploration.

"What do you mean?"

"Well, when a woman tells me to prove it, I can't let that one slip by." Kissing her again, she pulled Alison's shirt out from the waistband of her skirt. The buttons loosened easily under pressure, and Helen bent down until her mouth found her breasts, small and soft, like a young girl's.

"What about you? Let me —"

"Not yet. Just be still." She gently put aside Alison's hand, kissing the palm as she did so. Alison relaxed, letting herself be supported by the wall while Helen lifted her skirt. "Bet I can make you come while you still have all your clothes on."

Alison giggled, her breath warm on Helen's neck. "Bet you can't."

Helen leaned back and looked into those bright green eyes. "Watch me." Suddenly, in one swift move, Helen reached inside Alison's panties, her fingers coiling into the soft curls of hair nestled between her legs. Helen smiled as she felt the warm, sweet liquid there. "Still want to place bets on that?"

"Don't — don't be too sure of yourself yet." But Alison had closed her eyes already, and a soft moan started at the back of her throat. Helen teased her, letting her fingers play with the delicate layers of skin hidden there. With gentle strokes, she soon felt the hard nub of the clitoris start to bud, emerging from the folds of flesh.

"Jesus," Alison whispered, her voice faltering as she gave herself to the rocking motion of Helen's hand between her legs. Helen felt her beginning to tremble, and she slowed down, forcing Alison to wait. "I guess you lose the bet, then."

"What's that? What did you say?" Helen asked, thrusting deep into Alison as she spoke. Helen felt her own body respond, warmth spreading between her own legs as they rocked back and forth. "I don't think I caught that, Alison." Her hand slid back and forth across the vagina, now slick and hot, soft and yielding. Briefly Alison struggled to shift herself so Helen's fingers would reach inside her again, but Helen laughed softly and pulled her hand away. "Just think — what if your parents had decided to visit right now? What do you think they'd hear over the intercom when they rang from downstairs?"

"They'd hear this," and suddenly Alison wriggled loose from Helen's grasp. Alison needed only the top two buttons of Helen's jeans undone in order to slip her small hand inside. Helen shuddered, her whole body leaning into Alison's hand against her clitoris. It was too quick, too much of a surprise. Helen came with a cry almost as soon as Alison thrust her fingers in. She could feel her body opening and closing and opening again as her orgasm surged.

As soon as she could get her breath, Helen sank to the floor, her jeans falling down around her ankles. Somehow Alison had shed her skirt and the stockings beneath, and she straddled Helen's mouth. Already wet and nearing climax, Alison rocked her hips slowly back and forth across Helen's lips. She moaned as Helen circled her clitoris with each stroke of her tongue. "Jesus, I can't wait," and Alison jerked once more, then twice, then came with a deep, tremulous sigh. Helen held her there, keeping her hips still, drinking in the taste and smell and sight of her lover.

Soon, though, Alison lay down on the floor beside her. "Well," she said finally, "looks like my clothes didn't stay on, after all."

"Damn." Helen got up slowly, then reached down for Alison's hand. "Have to try it again sometime."

"Maybe a different room."

Much later, in bed, Helen finally asked, "So why the hell did your parents show up?"

"I have no idea. They were waiting here when I got home from work. I tried to say something on the phone to you, but the line went dead." Alison snuggled down under the blanket next to her. "I'm just really grateful they didn't stay very long."

Helen stroked Alison's back and asked, "Are you really dead set against this barbecue thing? Because if you are we don't have to do it."

Alison lay silent on her side for a few moments before answering. "No," she said at last. "We may as well get this over with."

"What exactly is it that you're so afraid of?" Helen raised up on one elbow to look down at her. "Your folks? They might be just fine with it. Besides, I can take care of your folks. I won't let them do anything to you."

"That's not it!" Alison closed her eyes in exasperation. "You're not some knight on a white horse, Helen!"

"Hey, sorry. Really. I just hate to see you like this." She stroked Alison's arm. "You're still mad at me, aren't you?"

"No, Helen. It's not them, really. It's me." Alison lay on her back and looked up at Helen. "It's me. I guess I had it drummed into me for so long that my goal in life was to find a good man. God knows I really fucked that one up. Everything in my life is so completely — completely different from what I thought it would be. Everything. It's like I'm in some damned leaky rowboat in the middle of the ocean, and I can't see the shore." She turned again on her side, punching the pillow before settling down. "I'm tired of spinning around in circles, no matter how hard I try."

"So why don't you just try drifting for a while?" Helen smiled and stroked Alison's hair. "Maybe that's the whole problem, sweetie. Quit fighting the current so hard, and wait to see where it takes you."

Alison grinned. "One day at a time," she said.
"Today is the first day of the rest of your life."
"Stop and smell the roses."
"Time flies when you're having fun."
"The longest journey begins with a single step."
"*Carpe diem* — seize the day."
"How about if I seize your ass instead?" The short tussle that followed ended with Alison sound asleep and Helen nestled up against her back. The soft, even sounds of Alison's breathing lulled Helen toward sleep, but each time it seemed just within grasp she darted awake again. When she did finally drift off, it was with a disturbing image in her mind — a woman, falling from a great height, accompanied by the sound of shattering glass. Somewhere in the distance, a candle burned.

Chapter Four

The next morning, Tuesday, Helen stood near the entrance of the church reception hall, sipping sherry and nibbling at a tasteless biscuit and itching in the stiff wool of her one good black suit. She almost never wore skirts or dresses any longer, but experience had taught her that a private investigator was called upon to dress for almost every imaginable occasion — including memorial services.

She moved a bit closer to one of the windows. It was a cool morning, shrouded in thin fog from the bay that nestled up against the Berkeley hills. The fog would be gone by early afternoon, when the sun burned it off with the eerie dim light that marked the advent of spring in this neck of the woods. The room felt stuffy — too many people, too much food arrayed on the folding buffet tables spread with paper covers, too little air. Besides, it reminded her of her childhood in Mississippi, where church fellowships and covered dishes for the bereaved followed in the wake of death. It was exactly the same kind of fellowship hall — old stained linoleum floor, battered upright piano in the corner, garish crayon drawings by the Sunday School students adorning the walls. Even the folding chairs had the same beige uncushioned seats.

In those services, however, there would have been much wailing and gnashing of teeth and cries of the mourning — maybe a sermon, or just hymn-singing. And the body of the deceased would have been there, more than likely in an open coffin, to be viewed by the loved ones. If there had been children, they might have been lifted up to the opening of the coffin for one last look at the departed, maybe even a final kiss on cold stiff lips.

This California version, though, was more impersonal. For one thing, there were still a couple of reporters working the crowd, even though Leslie had died six days ago. Now, on Tuesday morning, only a couple of die-hards lingered, hoping for a good anti-corporate hard-heartedness story. Except for the arrival of Richard Drake, the president of Centurion, there hadn't been much for them to do. The cameras had focused on the small, dapper man as he bent toward Tina Merrick. Unlike the newshounds, Helen had found her attention drawn to the thick-necked man with the hairless scalp who hovered behind Mr. Drake, eyes constantly roving the crowd. A tell-tale black cord coiled around one ear. Now and then Drake's bodyguard put one hand to that ear, listening to something no one else could hear. Although Helen knew that more and more businessmen felt the necessity of personal bodyguards, it was a bit unnerving to see this display of corporate power acted out at the little inner-city church. It was even more unnerving when the bald man's steel-gray eyes fixed on her, looking her up and down. Something in the way he stood — not military, not a cop. What was it? Helen flashed back to the days when she was a cop in uniform, walking through lockdown on some errand. The shouts and jeers of the inmates had never gotten to her the way the stares had. And that was exactly how this guy was staring at her.

"I'm so sorry for your loss," Richard Drake had murmured to Tina, taking both her hands in his own wrinkled paws. Even the accent was too good to be true, Helen thought. Sounded more like Texas than Helen's own neck of the South, though. "I believe the funeral itself took place on Saturday?" When Tina nodded, he went on. "No one can understand the pain that comes from the death of a loved child."

Tina responded beautifully to his ministrations, melting even further than the liquor had taken her already. It was clear that Tina Merrick was completely overwhelmed by Drake's smooth charms. Standing a discreet distance away from them Helen noted his surreptitious glances down at his watch before he left. After his departure — the visit took all of ten minutes — the whole room seemed to relax, to expand with the release of tension.

Helen shuddered, relieved that Drake and his buddy were gone. Their appearance, she suspected, had mostly been good PR for the few cameras that still hovered on the quickly fading story of Leslie Merrick's death. A glance out the nearest window confirmed that all the on-the-spot reporters had drifted off. Only one van, blazoned with KPIX in bright red, lingered at the edge of the parking lot. Someone had sneaked into the reception area and pilfered some food, she saw, as the news team bit into sandwiches that looked a lot like the one on her plate.

Helen bumped up against one of the buffet tables and nearly upset Tina's framed photograph of her daughter. The picture Tina Merrick had shown her in the office was quite different — in that one, Leslie had looked younger, much happier. It could have been a high-school graduation picture, given Leslie's curly dark hair and sweet smile and sparkling eyes. This one, though, showed an older woman. The soft dark brown hair had been cut short and hugged her head like a cap. She sported heavy glasses with thick lenses, and the lines around the mouth told of both worry and smiles. Helen wondered if Tina still saw her daughter as the fresh-faced girl from the earlier photo.

As they'd sat in the car, waiting in the parking lot outside the church, Helen had asked, "Don't you think we should be going inside, Tina? They'll all be looking for us."

"Not — not yet." Trembling, Tina fumbled for a moment in her handbag, then fished out the small leather portrait case. It had been nestled up against the silver flask wedged deep in the purse. Tina handed the case over to Helen, who took it carefully. It was too shiny, too slick and uncreased, to be more than a couple of days old. And just who was this little display case for? Helen wondered as she opened it up. Dutifully she gazed down at the lined and worried face of Leslie Merrick, aware that Tina was unscrewing the cap of the flask and taking in a healthy swallow of the liquor — whiskey, Helen thought.

Apparently no one else could smell the tang of whiskey on Tina's breath as they made their way through the small gathering of Centurion employees. Helen murmured greetings as she trailed behind Tina, hoping to remember a few names and faces. She spotted Donna Stethins and Christine Santilli right away. Again, Donna looked like a model for Centurion, even in the tasteful gray suit she'd chosen to wear, her thin frame poised with sherry glass in hand. Christine, still sporting her wrist braces, looked vaguely bedraggled.

Helen finished her sherry. It wasn't her favorite drink, but it seemed de rigueur for every wake or funeral or memorial she'd ever attended. Briefly she longed for the clean, hard bite of good bourbon — would Tina notice if she swiped the flask from her handbag? — then took another bite of her biscuit as she surveyed the crowd once again.

Actually, the Centurion gang were difficult to distinguish one from another. The muted tones and sounds of the memorial distracted her. She could make out stereotypes of what she imagined all big offices employed. Donna Stethins was probably high on the middle-management ladder — wielding some authority but not too much. Helen watched her leaning over some man, listening to him attentively. Helen saw that the man was Jason McFarland — the same well-groomed gentleman she'd seen first in the newspaper, then in the grimy alley next to the Centurion building. Helen checked the crowd for Christine and saw her standing at the entrance, fiddling with her cigarettes, perhaps hoping for an opportune moment to go outside and have a smoke.

Judging by the introductions, the two women had worked closely with Leslie — Donna had been her immediate supervisor, and Christine was no doubt an assistant. Then there was that other guy, Bob Tyrell, the one whose eyes were puffed and reddened, as if he'd been crying. Helen spotted him standing opposite her at the end of the long buffet tables. He hunched over a tray of sandwiches, his flabby pale figure slumped with exhaustion, grief, or some other strain. From the glazed look on his face, Helen didn't think he even saw the food arrayed before him — or noticed that he was already holding a sandwich. His pasty complexion might have been due to too many hours in front of a computer, or perhaps he'd been more affected by Leslie's death than most of the others in the room. Interesting, Helen thought. She'd have to talk to him soon. Helen glanced away only to confront Donna Stethins, whose eyes were fixed on Helen with an unreadable expression.

A very pretty young Asian woman came over to Bob and placed a hand on his arm. He jumped, startled, then relaxed and even managed a weak smile for her. Helen thought her name was Lily, and recalled that she'd been pointed out as the first-floor receptionist. Lily led him away from the table to a chair out of Helen's sight.

And where was the security guard? Nowhere to be seen — and it would be hard to miss his bulky muscular presence here.

"Enjoying yourself?" Lieutenant Macabee smiled at Helen as he reached behind her for a biscuit. "Quiet crowd today."

"What a surprise." Helen was certain her tone didn't indicate that it was a nice one, and she set her empty sherry glass down on the buffet table. "Watch out for the sandwiches — cucumber's not bad, but the chicken salad doesn't taste right."

"Thanks for the tip. Any other information for me?"

He carefully arranged biscuits, sandwich and a sliver of pastry on his paper plate. He'd dropped the Colombo look for today — besides, it didn't work with that bright red hair and those freckles. Instead, he'd opted for a plain brown suit, the jacket buttoned tight over a paunch straining to get out into the light of day.

"Why?" she asked. "Are you investigating something? What brings you here to Oakland, anyway?"

He nodded, intent on his food, which he consumed with surprising delicacy for someone so ham-handed. "Things change. I was about to ask you the same thing."

Helen shrugged and crossed her arms, noting that the two of them were receiving quite a bit of attention. Assuming he was working out of Oakland now, everyone here had probably already talked to Macabee. "I'm here with Tina Merrick."

"Friend of Leslie's, then?"

"Actually, I do have a tip for you. Stay away from Tina Merrick. She's not exactly thrilled with the police around here."

Helen was surprised to see him flush a deeper red. "Can't say I blame the woman. Got kids of my own."

Helen stood away from the table. What was this all about? "So the verdict is suicide, then?"

He snorted, dropping a half-eaten sandwich back on his plate. "Should have listened to you about the chicken salad. Yeah, that's the official verdict."

"Official. Do you agree with the official verdict?"

He shrugged. "Let's just say there are certain unresolved issues about the case. Doesn't look good for Oakland, you know, to have their latest corporate golden goose under investigation."

"So word was handed down from on high, then, to call it quits?"

Macabee smiled. "Hell, they gave it just about one whole week, didn't they? Not bad, considering the pressure all that money puts on a police force."

Before Helen had a chance to ask him anything else, Tina Merrick spotted them. One accusing finger, trembling beneath heavy rings, flailed out at them, nearly spiking Jason McFarland as he stood hovering over her. "You! How dare you come here? After everything you've said about my Leslie? You shame her memory, you horrible monster!"

"Tina, Tina, calm down, now —" In vain, Helen tried to put herself between Macabee and Tina, but McFarland beat her to the punch, with Stethins trailing close behind.

'I won't have that — that monster anywhere near me," she slurred, sinking dramatically into McFarland's arms. With one loud hiccup, Tina finally subsided.

"Jesus." Macabee let his paper plate fall onto the buffet table and Helen saw another deep red flush creep up from his shirt collar into his cheeks. "For God's sake, I'm on her side."

"Yeah, well, I guess she finds it hard to believe, since you guys dropped the investigation."

"Damnit, I didn't drop it!" Macabee hissed. "I did everything I could."

"Bob, would you give me a hand?" McFarland, a sheen of sweat breaking out over his face, was struggling to get Tina into a chair. Bob scuttled over from Lily's side and gingerly took Tina's arm, leading her across the room and away from Macabee.

"Christ, it wasn't my idea!" Macabee sighed and leaned against the wall. His small blue eyes stayed fixed on Tina Merrick, and anger creased his reddened face. "I wish I could tell her."

"Tell me. No, I mean it," Helen said in response to the disbelief on his face. "She might listen to me."

He snorted and ran a hand over his face. "It's hot as hell in here. Nothing much to tell, I guess. Except that the city of Oakland doesn't want some two-bit cop telling them their golden boys have been playing some nasty poker." He glanced at her. "Why do you think they fixed up that old building downtown? Purely aesthetic reasons?"

"Maybe they wanted to deal themselves into the game. Pretty high stakes, with a big name like Centurion. That's a hell of a lot of money a company like that would bring in to the city." Helen watched as Tina fluttered her eyes, staring at Bob Tyrell and McFarland as if they were complete strangers. "Look, I need to see if Mrs. Merrick is all right, and neither one of us has time for these little verbal tennis matches. What are you trying to say?"

He shrugged. The color had faded from his face. Rubbing his palms together, Macabee smiled at her. "You're the private eye. Do some investigating. You'll find out — there's plenty of dirt on Centurion."

Helen walked over to Tina, refusing to say anything else to Macabee. She didn't see him leave as she bent over the distraught woman. "Tina? Tina, it's Helen."

"Oh, Helen, that dreadful man —" She clutched at

Helen's hand, her red-rimmed eyes suddenly blazing alert. "Is he gone? Thank the Lord." With a heavy, tremulous sigh Tina slumped back into the metal folding chair, rattling it against the wall with the force of her considerable weight. "I don't know if I'll ever recover from this. Ever."

"It's quite all right, Mrs. Merrick. I understand — that is, we all understand. You've gone through quite a lot lately," McFarland said lamely. He stood up and looked around with a desperate hunted expression. As soon as Donna Stethins approached he relaxed visibly. "Donna, would you take Mrs. Merrick —"

"That's all right, Mr. McFarland. I think we should just go home now." Helen started to reach for Tina, who persisted in her vague Blanche Dubois imitation.

"Perhaps they should go," she heard Donna murmur behind her. "We could just send Leslie's things along by courier, or something —"

"As a matter of fact," Helen said, turning around, "we wanted to ask you about that. Mrs. Merrick and I spoke about this earlier. Didn't we, Tina?"

Please God, let her go along with it. In a liquor-fogged daze, Tina nodded blankly. Helen doubted if she knew what was going on around her.

"What do you mean? Call me Jason, by the way." McFarland offered her a dazzling smile that didn't quite reach his eyes. She saw him glance over her shoulder at Donna.

"Well, Tina and I thought that perhaps I could go over to Leslie's office tomorrow — take out her personal things, you know." She leaned over and continued in a low conspiratorial voice. "I don't think Tina is in any condition to do it herself, do you?"

"Oh, yes, please. Helen can do it. I couldn't face — no, I just couldn't do it." Tina sat up, sniffling and wiping her eyes. "I think that would be best."

"Well . . ."

No doubt feeling the pressure of a couple dozen of his employees staring at him, hanging onto his every word and memorizing the scene for future office gossip, Jason relented. "I suppose that would be all right. Lily?"

McFarland smoothly handed over the entire operation to the young Asian woman Helen had seen talking to Bob Tyrell. After agreeing to a ten o'clock appointment the next morning, Helen led Tina from the room.

"Thank you, thank you. No, please, Helen will take care of me. Thank you so much." Helen fought the urge to roll her eyes and grimace in disgust. What the hell did the woman think this was, a royal procession?

"Tina Merrick! Do you have any comments on the investigation into your daughter's death?"

Helen jerked away from the big microphone that suddenly lunged up toward their faces. She heard Tina's gasp and knew she wasn't faking her shock at this attack. Fortunately, Tina was too surprised to say a word, and Helen hustled them as quickly as she could through the parking lot. The car seemed awfully far away, though, and she heard the slap of feet behind her as the reporter and the camera crew hurried after them.

"What do you have to say about the way the police have dropped the investigation?"

"No comment," Helen spat out through gritted teeth. Gracelessly she shoved Tina into the passenger seat of the car and slammed the door.

"Are you a friend of the family? Do you have anything to say about the recent demonstrations against Centurion Sportswear?"

Helen looked up, arrested in the act of opening the car door. Demonstrations. Did this have something to do with what Macabee was talking about earlier? That there was plenty of dirt to dig up on Centurion?

The reporter saw her hesitation and waved his microphone back and forth between them. She could see herself reflected in the camera lens. "Father Hitchcock's planning another demonstration for the end of the week. Do you think there's a connection between Leslie's death and the protests?"

Without a word, Helen swung her door open, striking the microphone. The loud *whang* of metal on metal had a satisfying sound to it, she thought. As she pulled out of the parking lot, she could see the reporter shaking his head and herding the other members of the crew back to their van.

"Helen? Who were those men?" Tina sounded frightened. Helen felt a wash of sympathy. No matter what kind of woman Tina was, she'd still just lost an only child.

"Reporters, Tina. Don't worry. They shouldn't be bothering you anymore."

"But what did they mean about a demonstration? I don't understand." Now Tina was crying — real tears, Helen was sure, not the whipped-up sorrow she'd been working on all morning at the memorial.

Before Helen could answer, she saw a dull brown blur at the side of the car. Heart pounding, Helen slammed on the brakes and the car slid, screeching, to a halt in the middle of the street. The woman, that same haggard face, and dressed in the same ragged clothes she'd worn yesterday, pressed both hands against Helen's window. Although Helen and Tina were safely sealed inside the car, Helen could have sworn she felt the woman's panting breath on her skin, smelled the dirt and stale sweat accumulated on her wasted body.

"Fuck," Helen muttered, willing herself to calm down.

"Mrs. Merrick! Mrs. Merrick, I have to talk to you!" The words, muffled and indistinct, filtered through the thick glass. "It's about Leslie!"

"No!" Tina literally screamed and slapped her hand

against the seat. "Helen, get out of here! Damnit, get going!"

Slowly at first, then picking up speed as soon as the woman in brown backed away from the car, Helen turned off the street toward the freeway. They drove in silence until stopping at a red light just before the on-ramp.

"Tina, you have to tell me. Who the hell is that woman? She was at the Centurion building yesterday, and now here she is today, hanging around the church. Who is she?"

Tina mumbled something.

"Say that again?"

"I said she was Leslie's lover! Yes, my daughter was with that — that person! She had sex with her! They slept together! All right? Happy?"

Helen eased the car onto the freeway. Both women sat silent for a few minutes as they neared the tunnel that would take them away from Oakland and into suburbia. Tina, all tears and wailing over, was frozen into the seat, staring out at the green swath of grass lining the asphalt.

As they entered the tunnel, Helen finally said, "Tina, if you want me to do my job, you have to give me a little help here. What's her name and where can I find her?"

"Good luck finding her. She's probably living in some shelter these days." Tina sighed. In the shadow of the tunnel Helen couldn't see her expression. "Her name is Amelia Wainright."

"Tina, I just can't see Leslie involved with a woman like that." Helen looked over at the woman sniffling in the seat beside her. "She's clearly in need of medical help, and she appears to be homeless. How in the world did she and Leslie get together?"

"She wasn't always like that," Tina muttered. "She used to have a job, nice clothes, an apartment. An apartment where my little girl stayed for weeks and weeks, never calling me or anything. As soon as she started going to that awful coffee shop in Berkeley she met that bitch." The snuffles threatened to turn into wailing sobs as she went on.

Helen attempted to stave off further sounds of mourning with another question. "Do you know where she lives?"

"Look, all I know is that my daughter was taken over by this crazy pervert! Amelia Wainright used Leslie, took her for every penny and then went nuts! Leslie gave up her family and friends to take care of her. Nothing mattered to her but Amelia. I don't know where she lives and I don't want to know!" Tina shrieked.

"Thank you. And you really don't know where I can find her?"

"No idea at all. Honest." The outburst seemed to leave Tina drained, and she sank back, exhausted, on the seat.

"Okay." They emerged from the tunnel into blazing sunlight. The grass lining the hills of Orinda was still bright green with the spring rains. "One other question, Tina."

"What is it now?" Tina sighed.

"Is there anything left in that flask?"

Chapter Five

"Make yourself at home, Helen, I just have to lie down."
Tina Merrick rambled off through the suburban mansion she called home, her voice trailing off.

Helen was left standing near the front door. She sighed and leaned back against the wall. That illicit shot of whiskey she'd taken from Tina's flask caught up with her, and she found herself feeling fuzzy around the edges. Too bad she hadn't eaten more at the memorial. She glanced at her watch. Although it was past lunchtime, it was too much to hope that Tina had any provisions in the house — beyond her own liquid diet, of course. Helen groaned with the realization that she'd have to wait until she got back to Berkeley to eat.

She pushed herself away from the wall and started to poke around the house. Tina was nowhere in sight, and Helen wondered if she was all right. "Tina? Where did you go?"

As if in response to her question, Helen heard sobs emanating from behind a closed door at the other end of the hall. The door was ajar, and when Helen peered into the dimly lit bedroom she saw Tina sprawled on an unmade bed, one hand clutched at her breast and the other fixed on the sheets in a death grip.

Helen, realizing that Tina hadn't seen or heard her, backed out and walked quietly away from the bedroom. The house was dark and silent. Helen felt a sudden urge to fling open every window and door she could find, letting sunlight and warm summer air into the cold gloom that surrounded her. Here and there a shaft of light speared through drapes pulled tight against the outside world, and Helen stood still a few moments by one window, staring at dust motes dancing through one of the narrow beams of sunshine.

Helen detected a faint odor throughout the house, like a gentle but insistent undertow that pulled her in. It was untraceable and indecipherable, and Helen decided it must simply be the house itself, shuttered against the world.

She made her way back up the hall, into what she presumed was the living room. She fumbled for a light switch, and a second later the dusty overhead lamp sparked into a dull yellow glow. Aside from the dust that coated all available surfaces, the room was tidy. Tina probably spent very little time here, Helen thought. It was difficult to imagine visitors in this house, anyway.

The fireplace was a gaping black hole in the chintz and paisley room, a soot-filled cavity that did not appear to have been scrubbed down or used for a long, long time. The framed photograph display, however, arrayed on top of the mantel and framed by gilt candlesticks, caught Helen's attention.

She moved through the settees and love seats and oddly shaped tables toward the fireplace, stopping to open the French doors that faced the hearth. She glanced out onto the patio.

The hot tub had seen better days. It was more than likely bone-dry. A few chipped tiles had crashed and broken on the cement slab that ran the length of the house. And that was either a bird family or some clan of other small wild creatures making a home in the barbecue pit. Grass and weeds poked up through brick and concrete here and there, and a few shrubs that had probably once been well-tended were flourishing in wild growth that threatened like some primordial tribe to creep over the barbecue into the living room. She couldn't hear any traffic, this far away from the freeway and the main streets of Orinda, but somewhere in the distance a lawnmower roared. What sounded like a day-time television show echoed off beyond the Merrick house. A dog barked, a couple of birds chattered, but except for those small sounds, complete silence fell over the house and yard. In the midday sunshine, blanketed in late spring warmth, all seemed well in the vicinity. It was just the image of Tina, splayed across the bed on a crying jag, that broke the serenity of the day.

Taking a deep breath of air and savoring the scent of honeysuckle coming from somewhere in the tangle of weeds, Helen turned back to the mantel. Like everything else in the room, there was a fine-grained layer of dirt on the frames. She spotted a box of tissues — perhaps the last tangible result of some halfhearted attempt at hostessing or housekeeping — placed next to the biggest sofa. Grabbing a handful, she set to work wiping down the glass in the frames. Gathering up a few of the photographs, she took them to the sofa and studied them in the light that blazed in from the outside.

That had to be Tina, of course, wearing the gauzy white wedding gown. She stood, smiling, younger and slimmer and happier than Helen would ever see her, beneath a trellis woven with pink and white roses. Her hands held a tightly cinched bouquet of tiny white and pink flowers trailing white and pink ribbons. The man, whom Helen assumed was Bob Merrick, showed the flushed face and incipient paunch beneath a pink cummerbund. How had she gotten him to wear a pink cummerbund? Maybe the late fifties? Certainly no later than 1960. Leslie was thirty-five when she died, so that year would be about right. And it had the bright candy-colored tones of early color photographs.

Then there was a family portrait, the kind people carefully staged and packaged and sent off to relatives in lieu of more costly and troublesome holiday gifts. Against a deep blue background, Tina perched between her husband and daughter, her hair shellacked into place and tasteful pearls draped around a neck that was just beginning to show signs of age. Bob Merrick, positioned behind the womenfolk, had put on quite a few pounds since his wedding day. His face, redder than ever, puffed out over his white collar. The styling of his dark blue suit bespoke the mid 1970s, when wide lapels and double-breasted jackets hid a multitude of midriff sins.

But it was Leslie's face that tugged at her attention in this picture. She was sixteen or seventeen, no doubt still in high school. Her dark hair lay shining and feathered across her brow in one of the styles popular then, and her brightly patterned dress shrieked polyester. Blue eye shadow was smeared on her eyelids — too bad it matched the print in her dress, Helen thought. The scowl, barely concealed for the camera, seemed typical of teenage boredom and impatience with family conventions. Leslie stood with her hands behind her back, almost as if she were somehow bound and forced to stand still for the photographer. The taut lines of her body betrayed equal measures of tension

74

and unhappiness. It really wasn't too hard, Helen decided, to make out the stern features of an adult Leslie Merrick from this picture.

Helen brought the picture into the light and looked closer. Yes, there was something on Leslie's dress. A pin or brooch of some kind? What was that, anyhow? She smiled when she realized that she was looking at a button with the letters "N-O-W" printed on it in the stylized form that had become a symbol for the National Organization of Women. Had Leslie been wearing it before the Merrick family had walked into the photographers' studio? Or had she been carrying it tucked away in a pocket or purse, out of her parents' sight, then pinned it on as the photographer arranged them for the portrait?

Sitting there in Tina Merrick's musty living room, bathed in a patch of sunlight, Helen remembered a family portrait she herself had suffered through many years ago. She could still see the plain white walls of the studio where her father and her father's parents had gathered that humid Saturday in August. They'd gone all the way over from Vicksburg to Jackson, in sweltering Mississippi heat, for the portrait, and everyone, including the photographer, had looked a bit wilted.

"Now, Helen, quit fussing." Grandma turned that hawk nose in her direction. Helen had always been afraid of her grandmother, and she could still recall feeling that inner tremor whenever Grandma turned her way. "And I thought I told you to wear some lipstick, young lady. Do you want everyone to see you without makeup on?"

Dutifully Helen had retrieved the silver tube from her purse and applied the red gloss. Nestled in the purse, in the same pocket where she'd hidden the lipstick, was the tiny gold locket on a delicate chain. With trembling fingers, while everyone else in the group was involved with last-minute adjustments to their own appearances, Helen quickly slipped the charm over her perm.

"Aren't you ready yet, young lady?"

"Coming, Grandma." Without pausing at the mirror hung at the back of the studio to check how it looked, Helen hurried back to the others, savoring the feel of the heart-shaped locket like a cool drop of water on her chest. She knew it was real gold, too — there was something about the soft buttery glow of the locket in the sun. If she had to do this, Helen reasoned while listlessly obeying the photographer's orders, at least she could wear her girlfriend's gift to her.

She and Beth had just made love the evening before. They lay close together, their clothes still mussed, on the cool green grass beneath a cluster of trees where they could hear if someone tried to sneak up on them through the creek. They were sheltered here beneath the boughs. Just beyond the trees and the creek was a hill rising up at the edge of Grandma's property. Kudzu, thick and wild, rustled in the evening breeze that sometimes came in during the summer.

"It's gonna rain," Helen murmured. "Smell it?" As if in answer, Beth dropped the locket on her chest. "What's this?" she'd asked, amazed.

"Just so you'll remember me when you go off to college."

Another round of lovemaking had followed the presentation of the gift, and Helen could still remember the trembling in her legs and the warmth between them as she thought of that afternoon.

Grandma was the only one who noticed the necklace. Her sharp eyes, perched dark and angry over the beak of her nose, fixed on the gold chain glittering beneath the hot lights. "That's not your mother's, is it?"

"No, Grandma. I mean, it's her chain. I got the locket myself," Helen lied, her heart thudding painfully in her chest. She should have known better.

"Thought you was saving money from that job at the five-and-dime for college. What made you spend it on a piece of cheap tinsel like that?"

"They, uh, they had a sale on costume jewelry at the store. And with my discount and all, I just wanted to look nice," she faltered. Confused, unused to lying, Helen had glanced around the studio, at the photographer's bald shiny head, her father's gut that threatened to burst through his belt, Grandma's talcum powder that had caked on her dress. Of course, there was no help anywhere.

"Come on, y'all, this costs me money. Let's just get this thing over with," her father muttered, rolling his eyes at the fool women he had to deal with. With Grandma's questions forestalled for the moment, Helen took her place at the edge of the group, inching in closer at the photographer's direction, waiting for the blinding flashes of light.

Only a couple of weeks later her father had beaten her and thrown her out of the house — just when she was hoping to use that savings and maybe a couple of student loans to go to Ole Miss, just when she was hoping to persuade Beth to move away from Vicksburg and live with her up in Oxford while Helen went to school. Everything had fallen apart then.

Helen could still see Beth standing under the full moon, her gold hair shining, cicadas screaming in the hot still air. She'd met Helen one last time, at their special place under the trees near the kudzu-covered hill. "I won't go live with you, so just quit asking!"

"It doesn't have to be like this — we could go away from here, maybe even out to California! Tell me why you won't go!" Helen's whole body had hurt, ever since her father had finished with her. Lord only knows what Beth's family thought, the way Helen came pounding on their door at suppertime and then stood in the shadows asking to see their golden-haired daughter. "Please, I'm begging you. Let's be together somewhere else, where we can have a life, where we can meet other people like us."

But Beth had refused to answer. Instead she turned and ran quickly through the field lit by the moon, disappearing into the woods. In the same way the locket had gleamed in Helen's hand just before she threw it out over the trees and waited for the gentle sound of the gold heart dropping into the creek.

Helen glanced back down at the photograph of the Merrick family. She wondered if Leslie had defied her parents' wishes in order to wear the button for the portrait, or if she'd sneaked it into the studio and slipped it on surreptitiously while no one was looking. Had Tina Merrick cared? Had she even noticed what her daughter was wearing? And was Leslie's defiant expression just boredom, or some deep-held anger?

"You know," a familiar voice said over her shoulder, "people are, going to begin wondering about us if we keep this up."

Helen sprang up from the sofa, pictures spilling out of her lap and landing with dull thuds on the thick carpet. Macabee was standing just outside the French doors. "Jesus fucking Christ, Macabee!" she hissed, startled and angry. "What the hell are you doing here?"

"Mind if I come in?" Without waiting for her response he stepped over the threshold and into the living room. "Kinda warm out there."

"You haven't answered my question." Helen watched him as he slowly perused the room. Under one arm he carried a beige-toned parcel marked with large black lettering. In the gloom of the living room Helen couldn't make out what it said.

"Damn, she keeps it dark in here," he muttered. He

stopped by the fireplace, out of the sunlight. "Is Mrs. Merrick around, by the way?"

"She's unavailable." Helen hoped her tone was as icy as she felt at the moment. "Why are you here, and what is that you have with you?"

Macabee eased his bulk into an overstuffed armchair. Its plastic protective covering squeaked under his weight. "Shit, it feels good to sit in a real chair for once. Nobody has chairs like this anymore, you know? They're all little and plastic and modern and you can't sit in 'em."

Helen opened up another window, forcing more sun and air into the room. Macabee squinted in the sudden change of light. "Is that for Tina?"

"After the little drama we acted out earlier today," he said, resting the parcel on his knees, "I got to feeling really bad. I mean, the lady has a point about the way the police handled the whole mess."

"So?" Helen sat down on the sofa, facing him directly.

"So." He picked up the parcel and let it fall to his lap again. "So, since the official word is suicide, there's a lot of stuff we gathered that isn't evidence. Personal stuff, I mean." He looked up at her, his face blank. "Like what we found in her purse, in her pockets, shit like that. You know what I mean."

Helen gestured at the package. "You followed us here? With that?"

He shrugged, rustling the plastic slipcover. "It doesn't really make any difference to the case. Just a bunch of papers and shit that don't mean anything. It takes up space to keep garbage like this around." He handed her the parcel.

"What the hell is going on here, Macabee? You know as well as I do the kind of trouble you can get into for doing this."

"Hey, not me, kemosabe! It's all signed, sealed and delivered." He held up one pudgy freckled hand as if to ward off her suggestion of wrongdoing. "Signed it out myself as soon as I left the church. I told 'em I was going to hand-deliver it to the mother myself."

"So you just snuck around the back of her private residence, and if I weren't here you would have let yourself in?" She shook her. "Not too kosher."

Macabee snorted and got up from the chair. "Depending who you talk to these days, you'll get more than one opinion on how 'kosher' I am," he said. "I saw your car parked outside, and I saw the doors over here wide open at the side of the house when I walked up to ring the door bell. So shoot me."

"You're not going to tell me, are you?"

"Tell you what?" He was already out on the patio, loosening his tie and sloughing off his jacket under the midday sun. "Thought that's what I just did."

Helen followed him outside, sidestepping a rusted lawn chair. "I mean why you're working downtown Oakland these days, not the cushy 'burbs out here. What the hell happened?"

He folded his jacket over his arm and squinted at her. "It was time to move on. I'd gone about as far as I could out there in Lafayette."

Helen smiled. "You mean they got tired of you and invited you to consider transferring, right?"

"Drop it, Black." Despite the warmth of the day, Helen felt the chill in his voice. "You haven't earned the right to that story. Not yet."

As soon as he was out of sight, Helen went back inside and contemplated Macabee's offering. Should she wake Tina to tell her? Reluctantly, she headed for the bedroom. Tina lay snoring on the bed where she'd fallen earlier.

Relieved, Helen went back to the living room and unceremoniously ripped off the tightly wrapped packing tape. As she spread its contents across the sofa she reassured herself that Tina wouldn't mind if she went through these items first.

Then her heart sank. Why the hell did she imagine that the Oakland police would release anything of major importance? The real evidence — if there had been any — was still logged and filed deep inside the hallways of the station downtown. Sorting through the banal receipts and scraps of paper Helen wondered again at Macabee's sudden and inexplicable appearance in Tina Merrick's backyard.

He wouldn't have brought the package if he didn't think there was something worthwhile in it, Helen reasoned as she sorted through the various items. Or was this his way off trying to keep her off the case by tossing her a stray bone of meaningless information? Did Macabee follow them? Wait for an opportune moment to get these things to Helen, not Tina? He might have had the parcel with him the whole morning, tucked away in the trunk of his car while he watched Tina put on a show at the church.

Then why not just bring it to her office in Berkeley? Maybe, since he'd apparently made some sort of official request for the things, he had to put on at least the appearance of bringing it to Tina's house. That way he could say he delivered it to the Merrick residence. Although she hated to concede anything to someone as irritating as Macabee, Helen had to admit to herself that at least he appeared to be following through on the case. Maybe he hadn't fucked up out there. Maybe he really did want a change. She wondered if she'd pry the story out of him one day.

Helen started at the sound of coughing from the bedroom. Tina must be waking up. Helen bent back over the ragged bits and pieces from Leslie's pockets, hoping to see something of value. If Macabee's hands were tied — if he was prevented from pursuing the case since its official closure — perhaps he was doing his best, in a backhanded

81

sort of way, to make sure Helen had every scrap of information he could get to her. And Helen knew he had to be careful how he involved her in the Merrick case. Too bad she still couldn't trust him.

"Helen? You still here?"

"In here, Tina." Helen barely looked up when Tina leaned into the room, hanging onto the door jamb for balance. "You just had a visitor."

"Oh? Listen, I'm getting hungry. Want a sandwich or something?"

"No, not right now, thanks."

Tina wandered off with a heavy sigh, and Helen picked up a piece of paper from the pile on the sofa. The announcement had been printed on bright pink paper. Helen recognized the logo blazoned across the top — she'd been to this particular place many times. The event had taken place almost a year ago.

NOW PLAYING AT MOTHER HUBBARD'S
SATURDAY SLAM
HOT NEW DYKE GROUP
BE THERE OR BE YOU-KNOW-WHAT

Chapter Six

"Nope, those guys working on the building behind Centurion say they didn't really see anything before she landed. They wouldn't be looking that direction, anyway."

"Yeah, that's what I figured. But thanks for checking it out for me, Manny."

"Sure." He grabbed the paper sack, redolent of grease and fish, from the dashboard and tore it open, then wolfed down a piece of fried cod and started on the fries.

"So you haven't heard anything about what happened with Macabee? Why he's not in Lafayette anymore?"

Manny Hernandez, Helen's former partner from the bad

old days when she was a cop, leaned back in the car seat and rubbed his face. "How do you put this seat down?"

"The lever's on the side." She watched him struggle with the handle for a moment, then the seat snapped down and he lay almost flat. His handsome face, the one he used to get information out of people — especially women — was lined and pale. "Manny, what the hell is the matter with you? You look terrible."

"Why, thank you, Helen. That black suit makes you look like something the cat dragged in, if you want to get personal about it."

"Jesus, Manny. If you didn't want to talk to me all you had to say was No."

He sighed. "I'm sorry, Helen. It's not that — you know it isn't."

"Then what?"

"I'm just tired, okay?" He glared at her, and Helen turned away to look out at the customers of the seafood restaurant near the Berkeley Marina, where Manny had agreed to meet her. "Some stuff at home. Nothing to do with you."

"I'm sorry to hear it. Anything I can do?"

"Get me a new set of in-laws." He laughed. "Look, it'll blow over. I'll tell you all about it one day. And hey, thanks for the lunch."

"You growing boys need to keep your strength up," Helen joked lamely as he downed another piece of cod.

"And," he said around a mouthful of chips, "in answer to your question, no. No word on Macabee. I can give you an educated guess, though."

"Wait, let me try. He pissed off someone important."

"Exactly! So you do remember some shit from your cop days."

Helen looked at him. He'd been losing weight. His suit hung on his lanky frame a bit more loosely than it used to. "Okay, who got mad at him?"

He shook his head and wadded up the empty bag. "You'll have to get that out of him, Helen. No one's told me anything beyond Macabee leaving Lafayette with a bad rep."

"And the Merrick case? Has anyone in Berkeley heard why they shut it down?"

"As someone said earlier today, when I brought up the subject, 'The broad took a nose-dive and didn't come back up for air.' "

"Thank you — you're so sensitive. Seriously, that's the word?"

He nodded, took a long swallow of soda. "My guess is they're just putting off giving the mother the final details, you know? Nasty job. What mother wants to know all that? Easier to blame someone else out there."

"So, suicide while of unsound mind. Meaning, because she's an unbalanced pervert who can't get a man, and she'd just lost her job, which was all she had to keep her going, she tossed her shriveled-up old self out the window in despair."

"Helen, you're preaching to the choir, here. You know that."

"I know. Sorry."

"Where's your lunch? This isn't bad at all."

"Tina Merrick's whiskey kind of made me lose my appetite." She told him the events of the morning, including the attack from the television news team.

He snorted and took another fistful of fries from the bag. "Doesn't surprise me. In fact, I would have thought they'd all gotten tired of the story by now. No news there, not anymore."

Helen hesitated. Should she repeat anything that Macabee had said? She knew she could trust Manny — she'd trusted him with her life for many years — but it probably wasn't good policy to spread it around. "Maybe," she started cautiously, "maybe the city of Oakland doesn't want the Merrick case investigated. I mean, if Centurion has been up

85

to something shady, or if somehow they were implicated in Leslie's death, it sure wouldn't look too good after Oakland went to all that trouble to get them to move there. Bring in a big Fortune 500 corporation, then bam, lock 'em up for their evil deeds."

Manny finished his soda, then sat in silence for a few moments. "Possible, Helen," he said. "I can't say for sure, but I also can't count it out. I'll ask around, here and there, but I'm not sure I'll be able to get anything else for you. Not on this one."

"Hey, no problem. It's good to see you, anyway."

"Yeah, you too."

"Listen —" Manny was almost out of the car, but he stopped, waiting for her to go on. "I can see something is bugging you. Call me if you need to talk, okay?"

"It's a deal." The door slammed shut.

She sighed as he disappeared around a corner. What did that remark about in-laws mean? Manny and his wife, Linda, had been married for ten, no, twelve, years. This was the first time she'd ever heard him talk about family like that.

Now that all the food was gone, she was getting hungry. It was just after three o'clock. Even though she had one more stop to make before calling it quits, Helen decided to get another order of fish and chips before heading off downtown. Her final destination wasn't far away, but the rush hour traffic was beginning to pick up. Cursing as she stuffed food in her mouth, Helen made the crawl up University Avenue, past the downtown rapid-transit station with its maddening circle of traffic lights and heedless pedestrians, toward the relative open spaces away from the campus.

Mother Hubbard's Cupboard nestled between a barbecue stand and a laundromat on Telegraph Avenue, not far from UC Berkeley. That afternoon only one couple huddled together at a corner table. Another woman was leafing through the free weekly papers displayed near the entrance.

No matter how many times Helen walked through those doors into the inner sanctum of women-only space, she always remembered her arrival in Berkeley in the early 1980s and her first hopeful foray into the Cupboard. She'd been a cop, then, still in uniform. Uprooted from Mississippi, unsure of herself in what felt to her like an unfriendly big city, it had taken Helen a while to feel at ease in Mother Hubbard's. Still, Annie's friendliness had done a lot to coax the others to give Helen a chance. Tina Merrick had referred to "that awful coffee shop in Berkeley" where Leslie met Amelia. Maybe she'd meant Mother Hubbard's Cupboard.

"Hey, Annie," Helen called out, slinging the black wool coat over her shoulder as she sauntered to the coffee counter. Her black pumps clacked on the names of patrons etched on the tiled floor. Helen knew her name was there, close to the cash register on a tile she'd "purchased" at a benefit held to support the lesbian-owned café.

"Helen! It's been ages! Damn, it's good to see you!" Annie herself was running the espresso machine this afternoon. Helen always wondered how someone as tall and gawky as Annie could maneuver behind that narrow counter jam-packed with coffee-making equipment without constantly breaking something. Annie squeezed out from behind the counter and gave Helen a hug, almost knocking over one of her prized high-school basketball trophies perched against the wall. It was easy to make out Annie's six-foot-three lanky frame playing center in the black-and-white photos. "Look at you, all dressed up. Who died?"

"Well, actually, someone did."

"Shit. Hey, I'm sorry. I didn't know." Annie frowned. "Sure sorry to hear it. How about a freshly brewed cuppa joe on the house?"

"I'll arm-wrestle you about that on-the-house crap later. But yes, that would be great." Helen took a seat at the counter.

Amplifiers and microphone stands took up a good portion of the floor space. Stuck to one of the wooden posts in the room was a notice about a local band scheduled to play that evening, and Helen wondered if Alison would be interested in hearing them. She'd try to call her later.

Annie set down a cup in front of her, waving a farewell to the young woman who'd been scanning papers near the door. Helen smiled and set her cup down after one sip, then pulled out the leather photograph case she'd borrowed from Tina. "Actually, I'd like to ask you something, Annie. Ever see this woman around?"

Annie picked up the case, squinted at it, then pulled a pair of bifocals out of her shirt pocket. Once the glasses were settled on her nose, she gave a sharp intake of breath. "Good lord, Helen. You're involved in this?"

"You knew her, then?"

Annie slid the glasses off, sighed, shook her head. "Not exactly knew her, no. She used to come in here once or twice a week — get the papers, get a cup of coffee."

Helen pushed her cup aside. "You know what happened, then?"

"You mean about her jumping off a building? Yeah, sure. It was in all the papers, on TV." She leaned back from the counter and folded her arms over her chest.

"Any word around here?"

Annie, looking uncomfortable, glanced around. The couple was still in the corner, and still had eyes only for each other. "Well, Helen, you know I can't tell you names or anything."

"Of course not, Annie. I wouldn't ask. I'm really just after the gossip."

"Shit, I hear lots of that. Well, like I said, she used to come in here for the papers. I could tell by her clothes she was a corporate type. But don't get me wrong, I don't mean anything by that — just that you could tell, you know?" Annie pursed her lips then blurted out, "I think she was kind of a closet case. Not in or out — sort of in between. I mean, she'd come in here, get the papers like I said, but she'd hardly even say hello." Annie shrugged and smiled. "At first I thought maybe she was really stuck up or something, but finally I figured out she was scared to death. Kind of sad, I guess."

"Yeah." Helen glanced back down at the case, which still lay open on the counter. Folding it shut, she asked, "Did you ever see her with anyone else?"

Annie began to shake her head, then said, "Wait a minute. Yeah, I do remember one time. I guess it stuck in my mind because most times she'd just sort of run in, grab her coffee and run out again without saying anything to anyone. But this one time there was somebody with her."

"What happened? Anything?"

"Not really, not that I remember. I think they weren't too happy with each other, but they didn't really talk. Not in here, anyway."

"What makes you say they weren't happy? Anything at all you can remember, Annie."

Annie frowned, then came around to sit on the stool next to Helen. "You know, thinking about it now, it wasn't that they fought or anything like that. No, this woman — her name is — was — Leslie, right? I can see her walking up the sidewalk on Telegraph" — Annie gestured toward the picture window that faced the street — "with this other woman. Leslie starts to come in, but the other one won't come with her. So they're standing out there, talking back and forth, then Leslie comes by herself. I can see her friend standing under the awning in the shade, watching her."

"Then what?"

"Nothing. Leslie gets her coffee to go, grabs the papers. Oh, wait, one other thing — she got a couple of bagels. First time she ever got anything in the way of food here, I think. As soon as she gets outside she hands the bag with the bagels to the woman standing there waiting for her."

"That's it?"

"That's it." Annie swung around on the stool, facing the window and leaning her back against the counter. "They walked off. I never saw that other woman again, and Leslie went back to cup of coffee and the papers a couple of times a week. Say, how'd you get into this, anyway?"

"It's called money." Helen sighed, sipping her coffee which was cooling fast. "I needed the job."

Annie regarded her for a moment, then looked down at the tiles beneath her feet. "Thought it was all sewn up," she finally said. "Everyone said it was suicide."

"Who's everyone?"

Annie held up her hands in mock surrender. "Well, as soon as it was in the papers, people were talking about it. The women who work here remembered her, and you know the way those newsdogs went after her 'perverted' lifestyle. It upset people, you know? Yet another homo kills herself, all because she didn't have a husband and two-point-three kids and a station wagon."

Annie went to the cash register as the two lovebirds in the corner finally got up to leave. Helen pushed away her cup and stood up.

"Want a refill?"

"No, thanks. Oh, hi, Terry. Did you just get here?" The young woman standing next to her with the coffee pot smiled and nodded. "Is that a new tattoo? On your right arm?"

"Yep. I thought it was about time I got the woman symbol done. Like it?"

"Nice work. Seems like every time I come in you've done something new."

"Wait'll I get my next piercing." Terry looked down at

the open photograph case. "Holy shit, it's that woman who took a high dive in Oakland," she whispered, handing it back to Helen reverently. "Didn't they fire her because she was a dyke, or something like that?"

"The official word is suicide, Terry." Helen quickly put the case away and dug for her wallet.

Terry turned to Annie, who'd finished at the cash register. "You remember her, don't you? The icebox, they called her."

"Terry, stop it. She's dead, and —"

"Well, they did." Terry's brow wrinkled with worry. "Not me, but some of the others did. I mean, she never opened her mouth. Except to that weird woman."

Annie and Helen exchanged glances. "What weird woman?" Helen asked.

"You know, Annie — remember? The one who wore that brown dress."

Helen sat down again, pulling Terry down next to her. "Talk to me, Terry. What about her?"

Terry repeated the story Annie had already told her — how Leslie made silent visits to Mother Hubbard's, the way the woman in brown stood on the sidewalk and refused to come in. "And this woman, she seemed to get weirder and weirder. I mean, at first she didn't wear just that brown thing — at first she'd have on jeans, a T-shirt, you know. Then I'd see her looking all sick and torn up, her hair everywhere. I guess things went from bad to worse. Finally she just had on the brown dress, like, every time." Terry paused. "It was like she slowly lost her mind, or something. Like those poor people out on the streets that don't get their medication, you know?"

The front door opened, and Terry stood up to greet the group of laughing women gathered by the door. "Sorry, Helen, that's all I know," she said over her shoulder as she hurried to grab menus.

"You've seen this woman in brown, I take it?" Annie asked. "No, put that money away. I said on the house and I meant it."

"Here, take that, then." Helen stuffed two singles into the can marked TIPS and put her wallet away. "I sure have. Terry's right — she's probably in dire need of medication." Helen sighed and closed her eyes. "Guess that means the free clinic and the shelters. Jesus, I don't want to do that."

"Not a pretty sight, I agree."

"Thanks Annie. You've been a big help. By the way, the band playing tonight — any good?"

Annie laughed and shut the cash drawer with a clatter. "Oh, you know me, Helen — I cut my teeth on Meg Christian. Things have changed a lot since then."

"Yes, thank God — no more platform shoes for me. And don't bother to remind me that they're back in style. The phone still back there?"

Annie pointed toward the rear of the café, where the restrooms were, and Helen went back to give Alison a call. Damn, too early — she must putting in some overtime today. Helen waited for the message machine to recite its patter, then left a message that she'd call her later.

Someone had switched on the minuscule television set mounted on the wall behind the cash register. Annie, counting the till, had the sound turned nearly off.

Helen was about to give a final wave at Annie when something on the screen caught her eye. "Annie, could you turn that up a minute?" Sure enough, it was KPIX Nightly News at Five. And there was the van she'd seen earlier.

"Oh, my God," Helen murmured. A glimpse of Tina Merrick sitting in her car, with Helen at the wheel, flashed across the tiny screen. Helen tried to console herself that her own face was just a blur on the camera — no one would know it was Helen in the car.

The camera cut from the young blonde anchor to the

man who'd thrust his microphone into Helen's face. "It was a quiet gathering here today in downtown Oakland," he began. Helen breathed a sigh of relief. Looked like they didn't get any good footage out of the confrontation, so she was safe for now. All she needed was to get on the news with this.

Suddenly a familiar face popped onto the screen. It was Father Hitchcock, identified as "Berkeley's most famous religious activist."

"And we plan," Father Hitchcock was saying, "to organize another protest this week against Centurion Sportswear. Their business practices in Mexico, where hundreds of children work for sixteen to eighteen hours in the Centurion factories, need to be brought to light."

"Father, do you think there's any connection between the death of Leslie Merrick last week and the protests by your PAN group?" the reporter asked.

The priest, pale and drawn, flinched as the microphone came near his face. "We at the People Against NAFTA committee have nothing to say regarding the tragedy that took place last week. We mourn the death of Leslie Merrick, but our protests began long before this happened, and they will continue to take place until corporations like Centurion Sportswear behave in a humane and responsible manner toward their employees, both here in the US and abroad."

"Thanks, Annie." She said her good-byes and headed for the door.

Chapter Seven

Lily Mapa sat, a small lone figure, at an enormous reception desk that faced the front entrance to the Centurion building. Helen leaned over to sign in on the visitor's log, noting that except for the log and a telephone with an impressive number of lines, Lily's desk was completely bare. Behind Helen, the front of the building extended out like the front of a flatiron in an increasingly narrow apex that jutted into Broadway. She waited, a smile fixed on her lips. It was just past nine-thirty on Wednesday morning, and people were filing in past Lily's desk to the elevators. Some faces seemed familiar from the memorial service, but many more were unknown to her.

Helen got a glimpse of Bob Tyrell lurching quickly down the hall. Behind him, over to Helen's left beyond the elevators, a door slowly swung shut. She could read the plate engraved COMPUTER ROOM. A small steel box protruded from the wall by the doorjamb of the computer room. There was a slot where a key-card would fit, allowing the initiated into the room. If all the doors in the building had similar barriers to entrance, then surely only Centurion employees had come near Leslie before she died.

"Here." Lily handed her a peel-off-stick-on badge labeled simply GUEST. "Please keep this on at all times in the building, okay?"

"Sure. Thanks." Helen tried smiling at Lily — no response. What happened to the concerned young woman at the memorial service yesterday? The one who'd tried to comfort Bob Tyrell and who'd helped calm down Tina Merrick? Perhaps, Helen reasoned as she turned to the elevators, Lily shut down on herself when she walked through those doors. The real Lily Mapa was a well-kept secret, safe from the prying eyes of her colleagues.

"Right this way, Ms. Black." B. Reilly — Lily had called him Brian — held out one hand to guide her, and Helen got the hint to keep close to him. "See ya later, Lily."

The elevator doors slid shut on Lily's farewell. Brian cleared his throat and Helen looked at her feet, wondering just how much it had cost Centurion to upgrade the old building — with luxurious elevators, for example. After punching the circle marked "five" on the floor selector, the guard slouched against the wall of the elevator. The silence was irritating, and Helen couldn't even tell if they were moving. "I don't think I saw you at the memorial yesterday, Mr. Reilly," she said, her voice ringing out flat and loud.

He started at her comment, and Helen watched him pull

himself up a little straighter in the blue uniform. "Uh, no, I stayed here." Helen averted her eyes so she wouldn't have to see him suck in the tummy that protruded ever so slightly over his belt — perhaps a portent of too many beers, she thought, and not enough exercise. His face burned a dull red that looked more a habitual color than mere embarrassment. "The, uh, the security company didn't want me taking time off."

"I see." The elevator jerked to a halt at last, and Brian followed her out into a hallway lined with rows of cubicles. They varied in height and size — the blocked-off spaces around the perimeter had taller walls than those in the center of the floor — but they all conformed to the same pale gray color scheme. A few plants poked green fronds over the sides of some cubicles, and as she drew closer she spotted a framed photograph here, a small figurine there. It was a relief to see a few personal touches permitted in that sea of gray.

"There's Ms. Stethins," Brian said with a sigh. "Guess she'll take over from here."

"You're not taking me up to Leslie's office?"

"No, ma'am. Ms. Stethins still has the key to it. She wanted to keep it." He shrugged.

Donna Stethins, a point of sharp-edged color in her red suit, trotted over to the elevators. "Thank you, Brian. How are you, Ms. Black?"

Helen took her hand, careful to avoid getting stuck by her nails painted a bright red that matched the suit. "Fine, thank you. Oh, and thanks, Mr. Reilly," she called to the receding blue back of the security guard.

"Now, I just have to drop off this memo, and then — Yes, what is it, Carol?"

"Oh, Ms. Stethins, I'm sorry, but the sales logs from upstairs haven't come down yet, and I don't know how I'm going to finish my report if I don't have them." The young woman named Carol stared curiously at Helen and kept rattling off a long string of phrases in corporatese that made absolutely no sense to Helen.

Donna sighed and shook her head. She said to Helen, "I'm sorry, but I really have to make a phone call to take care of this. It won't take a moment."

"Not a problem." Helen refused offers of coffee, tea or water and settled herself down on a chair by the water cooler to wait.

Telephones issued a few muted beeps, but for the most part the air was filled with the clattering of keyboards as the processors in their cubicles tapped away, keeping the foundations of Centurion Corporation solid and sure. People milled about, many clutching stacks of computer printouts or sheaves of paper or piles of envelopes. The way everyone kept their eyes down, looked around them nervously, and scurried about like hamsters in a wheel built up a tension thick enough to cut with a knife. No one favored Helen with more than a passing glance. She shuddered at the muted colors and muted sounds, thanking her fates that she'd never had to work in such a place. She wondered how Leslie Merrick had liked being at Centurion.

Something bright and red approached her from behind. "There, that's taken care of!! It's amazing how I get anything done around here! That's what I tell Mr. McFarland, anyway," Donna cooed.

Helen smiled blandly. "I'm sure it is." So Donna Stethins was obsessed with the boss, she mused.

"Well. Shall we go?" Helen got back into the elevator and Donna punched at the number "seven." Helen stared, puzzled. Wasn't Leslie's office on the eighth floor? "Why I'm the one to keep keys, I don't know." Donna sighed. "I guess no one else wanted to take responsibility."

"I don't know what they'd do without you," Helen murmured. She earned a sharp glance from Donna for that remark, but Helen simply smiled. "I mean, it sounds like one crisis after another."

Apparently Donna decided that she meant no sarcasm. "Well, there's always something going on that has to be taken care of. I mean, Mr. McFarland is so busy, with his meetings and all, he just can't manage it on his own."

Which meant, Helen thought, that Donna was a hell of a control freak.

The elevator stopped and the door slid silently open. "Right this way." Donna led her through a short foyer toward double glass doors. "This is going to be our customer service area in a little while. Unfortunately, the elevator here doesn't go all the way to the eighth floor." She rattled off some explanation having to do with how the penthouse floor had a private elevator. Whatever the reason, then, anyone going up to the top floor would have had to take either the stairs or the private elevator Donna mentioned. "The stairs are just through here." Donna pushed through the glass doors and turned to give Helen a brilliant smile. Following her, Helen saw the stairwell at the other end of the room, tucked away in a corner to her left. "There was only the one office up there, anyway — and now we don't need that anymore." Donna bit her words off and motioned Helen in ahead of her as she held the door open.

They passed the person sitting at a bank of telephones and various kinds of office equipment — Helen recognized a shredder and a fax machine. The woman sitting at the front desk whipped around when she heard them.

"Oh, she's a temp. She'll only be up here to answer phones a few more weeks, until the customer service people start coming in," Donna said breezily.

Helen stopped dead, shocked. Vicky Young, Alison's mother, was sitting at the desk. Helen shut her mouth, which had fallen into an amazed gape, realizing there could be no mistake. This was indeed the same woman she'd met two nights ago, at Alison's apartment building. Same thinning blonde hair and disk earrings, same features she recognized in Alison.

Apparently Mrs. Young was just as shocked as Helen was.

"Ah — Ms. Black?" Donna was looking at her watch, impatience creasing the layer of beige makeup that smoothed her narrow face.

Helen took a deep breath. "Sorry. I was just — I saw the view."

"The view?"

"Isn't that Lake Merritt? I thought I could see the lake through those windows." Helen took a couple of steps closer to Mrs. Young. "Please don't say anything," she muttered, leaning slightly toward the befuddled woman. "I'll explain later."

Mrs. Young said nothing. She turned back to her telephone, cradled the receiver on her shoulder and began pressing numbers on the keypad.

"You can see Lake Merritt through those windows? Are you sure?" Donna squinted.

"Well, maybe not. It just took me by surprise," Helen said truthfully.

"Hm. You could be right. I wouldn't know." Mrs. Young sighed. "I'm too busy to look at the view."

Obediently Helen trotted after Donna toward the stairwell to their left, feeling Vicky Young's gaze on her. The short flight took them through yet another door and into a short hallway. The stairway ended in the center of the hallway, and there was a door at either end. A brass plate on the polished oak door to their right announced the location of Mr. Drake's office.

"Oh, Mr. Drake isn't in town today," Donna said as she

steered Helen in the opposite direction. "We just keep that suite available for him. There are just the two offices up here, and Mr. Drake's rooms take up most of the floor."

"Impressive." Helen smiled and submitted to Donna's guidance. They went instead to the left, toward a small plain door with no name plate. A man emerged from Drake's office just as they started down the hall.

"Why, Mr. McFarland!" Donna turned almost as pink as her blouse. One hand flew to her chest as she gasped amazement and — Helen would swear — pleasure. "I didn't expect to see you up here all alone!"

McFarland coughed and cleared his throat elaborately. "I, uh, I was just looking something up." He peered at Helen first in confusion, then in barely concealed disapproval. "That's right — you're here to get her things."

"That was the agreement, right?" In false innocence Helen looked from Donna to McFarland and back again, enjoying their discomfort. She doubted, though, that Donna's excitement at seeing her well-built boss had even a remote connection with McFarland's embarrassment at being caught snooping around Leslie's office.

"Oh, right, of course. Excuse me." He headed with deliberate slowness to the stairwell.

Blushing, Donna watched him go. "I don't believe anyone else has been in here since — since it, uh, happened." She fumbled briefly with a huge ring of keys, then opened the office door. "Except the police, that is."

Because the window had remained open since the moment Leslie had plummeted to her death, the air in the office felt fresh and clean. Eight stories up, the office was high enough to avoid most of the street smells and sounds. A thin film of dust layered the surfaces, and Helen saw a few traces of black fingerprint powder around the window itself. Packing boxes were stacked by the window, and Helen remembered that the Centurion building had only been open for business a few weeks. Clearly Leslie was still just moving in when the word had come down from on high about her termination. Squeezing her way past one precarious column of boxes, Helen took a couple of steps over to the open window, placed her hands squarely on the grimy ledge and looked down.

Eight stories didn't sound like such a big deal until you were looking down. Someone had been scrubbing the flagstones where the woman in brown had enacted her private drama, only two days ago. Unable to see any traces of where Leslie landed, and beginning to feel dizzy, Helen stepped back away.

"Are you all right?" Donna was standing right behind her, and Helen could smell the strong floral scent of her liberally applied perfume.

"Yes, yes, I'm fine. It just gave me a little vertigo, standing there like that." Helen tried not to inhale the perfume too deeply and made a move to get away from the window.

But Donna stood exactly where she was, almost touching her. Confused, Helen eased her way awkwardly around the boxes piles waist-high, past the window toward the desk, bumping up against it.

Donna was staring at her with an odd expression. "Um, everything is right where she left it. Of course, anything related to her work here at Centurion should stay here."

"I understand." What was she staring at?

"Do you need any help? Any help at all?"

"No, thanks." Suddenly realization dawned, and Helen flashed back to the last time she'd gone out bar-hopping, in the bad old days between relationships. Even then, for some reason unknown to her, the straight types had been drawn to her. Feeling a growing sense of panic, Helen went to the door and stood there, holding it open for Donna. "I think — I think I need just to be alone for a while. This will be harder than I thought." She tried to act pained, hoping she hadn't overdone it with the little catch in her voice.

"Well . . . if you're sure." With one last lingering glance Donna left. Helen closed the door behind her and held it there firmly for a moment, praying she was wrong. It was too much for one morning — first Alison's mom, staring at her in shock, then Donna Stethins, staring at her in what Helen feared was lust mingled with curiosity.

She leaned against the door, gathering her thoughts, grateful for privacy. Since she didn't know how much time she had to herself, though, she'd have to work fast.

It was a small office, an odd space, really. No wonder Drake hadn't wanted it, and she was sure his suite just down the hall was palatial in comparison to this overgrown closet. Since the building had been built at a time when square functional boxes were deemed appropriate offices, Helen guessed that every floor might have a few similar nooks and crannies. Three even, straight walls contrasted with a fourth curved one. Leslie had kept a few plants there, along with an uncomfortable-looking sofa that faced the desk. Except for the chair behind the desk, the sofa provided the only seating in the room. A bookshelf took up the rest of the space on the curved wall.

So why did they put her up on the eighth floor, so far away from everyone else? Leslie would have had to go back down to the seventh floor just to use the bathroom. Maybe she'd wanted it that way. And what about Christine? Perhaps they'd already put her back in some corner somewhere. It was possible, of course, that Leslie was more easily dealt with when out of sight. Certainly she would have been cut off from everyone else. But it was difficult to know if the apparent isolation was a reprimand or a reward.

The walls were blank. Helen found herself wondering what Leslie Merrick might have put on those walls. A calendar? Memos? Photographs or art prints? Announcements from the local lesbian newspapers she'd picked up every week at Mother Hubbard's?

Then there was the desk. Helen sat down behind it. There was no sign of a computer terminal anywhere in the room. She found it hard to believe Leslie hadn't used one. Perhaps the police had removed it, or someone else in the office must have claimed it for their own use as soon as it was available. At her back stood a long credenza with lockable file drawers. She tried them — open, the drawers empty, and not a disk in sight. Then she tried all the drawers in the desk — also unlocked. Pens, paper clips, yellow legal pads, rubber bands, a stapler — all the minutiae of office work, and absolutely nothing of interest beyond a wind-up toy of chattering teeth mounted on a pair of sneakers. So the Icebox, as Terry called her, had had some kind of sense of humor, hidden away somewhere.

A few knickknacks were scattered on top of the desk. At least she could get these back to Mrs. Merrick. But what to put them in? With all the boxes around, there had to be something she could use. She found one that was nearly empty and decided to use it. She'd just stack the papers in another box.

Then it struck her. Leslie would have had to clamber over the boxes to get to the window and make her fatal decision. While not impossible, it would have involved some struggle to reach the window. Helen set the empty box down on the desk and looked back and forth from the window to the door. What about Brian Reilly? Hadn't he stated that he'd tried to stop her? He'd accompanied her to her office, seen her rush from her desk and jump.

It made no sense at all. There were easily two dozen boxes stacked up. To struggle through them would've taken time — time that the guard could have used to stop Leslie from taking her life.

Helen squeezed through the boxes to the window ledge, thinking hard. To take one's life in that way — going through a difficult scenario of rushing through unwieldy obstacles, when a strong young man was doing his best to stop the sequence of events — didn't make any sense at all. Not when the guard was standing right there.

Unless he wasn't standing right there like he said he was.

Helen looked down to the street again and shuddered. Someone was lying, she was sure of it. It didn't mean that Leslie hadn't killed herself, but it might mean that Brian Reilly lied about his own role in the matter. But why would he do that? And why would he not be in the room, anyway? No doubt someone saw him accompany Leslie back to her office. Helen idly watched the crumbling edifice across the alley, where the construction crew shouted and gestured to one another. Probably the same guys she'd seen two days ago, she thought, when she'd first taken a look at the scene. What would it have looked like to them? Would they have been able to see anything inside Leslie's office?

Helen pushed herself away from the ledge and worked her way back to the desk. Maybe she'd have time, before Brian Reilly or Donna Stethins showed up, to take a quick look around the floor.

She swept a few baubles into the box, then glanced around the room. Maybe some of the books on the shelves? There was one that looked like a photo album, wedged between computer manuals.

With an effort Helen yanked it out. Unfortunately the Centurion company hadn't seen fit to supply its employees with well-made bookshelves, and she got a splinter in her palm for her trouble. "Shit," she muttered. A drop of blood welled up, and pain knifed through her hand. It was a deep puncture. She looked back up at the bookshelf — there were more splinters ready to come loose in someone else's hand — and saw the thick envelope hidden behind a computer manual.

Pain forgotten, Helen used her other hand to dislodge the envelope. She dropped the photo album into the box along with the paperweights and pen set, then stuffed the envelope into her handbag.

She had just located a tissue to dab at her palm when she heard voices at the other end of the hall. Brian Reilly's heavy steps resounded down the empty hallway. A moment later he appeared at the door of Leslie's office.

"Jeez, what happened to you?"

"Just a splinter. Is there a restroom I can wash up at?"

"Sure thing. We'll go down one floor, to seven. It has a first aid kit in it, too, with peroxide."

"That would be great." Helen cradled the box under one arm and left Leslie's office.

She followed him downstairs, around a bend in the hall, leading farther away from Mrs. Young's section of the floor, past empty offices and a storeroom. He pointed out an unmarked door. "I'll wait right here for you."

"Thank you." After setting the box on the linoleum floor she shut the door and turned on the tap. There was a first-aid kit, a square metal box, fixed to the wall. She poured peroxide on the puncture left by the splinter and tried to fix the layout of the floor in her mind.

There were a couple of other places the guard could have gone to on the seventh floor — this very bathroom, for one — but why? If he had done so, no one would have noticed. Mrs. Young's desk was cut off from Leslie's office by the door and the hall, and as far as she could tell no one else worked on this floor.

He was leaning against the wall as when she came out of the bathroom, the box tucked under her arm. He was bent over, crouching down, his head hanging close to his knees. "What is it? What's happened?"

He started, then jumped back up. His ruddy face burned

a bright, deep red, and his eyes glittered as if he had a high fever. He blinked twice, breathing heavily, then said, "Nothing. Fine. I'm fine."

"You don't look so fine. Are you sure you're okay? Maybe I should call Ms. Stethins, and —"

"No! No, don't do that." His voice came across breathless but angry. Or was it afraid? "I told you I'm fine. Really."

"Okay. Let's go."

As they went by Mrs. Young's desk, Alison's mother looked up. "Oh, are you Helen Black?" she asked, her eyes gleaming.

Before Helen could respond, she said, "Someone called. There's a message for you," and she handed Helen a slip of paper.

"Thank you. Thank you very much, for everything." Helen nodded awkwardly. As they went to the elevator, she stole a glance at Brian. His color was a little better, but he was still breathing heavily. Something was very wrong here, and she was briefly reminded of her conversation with Manny yesterday afternoon. Helen decided to call him again as soon as possible

Speaking of calls, Helen looked at the note Mrs. Young had handed to her. YOUR SECRET IS SAFE WITH ME it read.

Helen sighed and folded the note into her jacket pocket, hoping that this wasn't a prelude to cloak and dagger excitement on the part of Alison's mother. Maybe decoding rings and secret meetings would be next. Still, it would be good to hear her version of life at the office.

Unlike the smooth trip going up, the elevator ground to a resounding thud as it stopped on the first floor. "Thank you," Helen murmured to Reilly, repositioning the box more comfortably in her arms.

With a final smile for Lily, Helen was ready to go when she heard a familiar high-pitched voice behind her.

"Oh, wait! Ms. Black!"

Helen had almost made her escape but she turned around and put on a smile for Donna, who was hurrying around the side of Lily's desk. Lily, her eyes bright with amusement at Helen's predicament, pretended to pay attention to the file in front of her.

"I was just wondering, could I take you to lunch?"

Chapter Eight

"Have you ever been here before?" Donna asked her as she toyed with her pasta salad.

Helen wanted to say she'd just had an argument with her lover, day before yesterday, in this very restaurant — but she settled for the banal. "Once or twice. Not regularly."

"Usually I bring my lunch — some cottage cheese and celery sticks, you know? But I wanted a chance to talk to you. Without anyone else around."

Helen nodded and tried to attend to her own lunch. Why the hell did she order a Caesar salad? She fumed inwardly. She hated Caesar salads, she thought. Her mind kept going back to the box in the trunk of her car outside the café. She bit into the lettuce speared on her fork, letting Donna continue. She'd agreed to this lunch and insisted on the location, hoping that its proximity to Centurion would keep any weird ideas out of the woman's head — although Helen was beginning to suspect that those were the only ideas she ever had. Still, it might be possible to turn the conversation around to Leslie Merrick and glean something from this occasion.

Donna clicked her nails on the table-top, fidgeted in her chair, and twisted her water glass around and around. She avoided Helen's eyes every time Helen looked up from her plate. Finally Helen asked, "What was it you wanted to talk to me about, Ms. Stethins?"

"Oh, no, please! Donna. Call me Donna. And I'll call you Helen, all right? After all, how well can we get to know each other if we can't use our first names?"

Lovely. "What was it you wanted to talk to me about — Donna?"

"I was just thinking about what a lot of people are saying. People at Centurion, that is."

"Yes?" Helen gave up on the greens and drank some water.

"About poor Leslie." Donna sighed and dabbed her napkin at her lips. Her bright red fingernails looked like daubs of blood on the white cloth, and Helen was reminded briefly of the splinter of wood from Leslie's office. "Maybe I shouldn't be telling you this. It's office gossip, after all."

Please, you idiotic woman, tell me, tell me. Helen clamped down on the longing and made herself relax in the chair. "That's your decision, of course. Donna."

"It's just that — well — I feel you would understand this better than they would." Donna leaned over, staring into Helen's face with wide eyes. Her perfume drowned out the spicy smell of their meals in a weird clash of odors. "Leslie never quite fit in, you know. Oh, she was competent, don't get me wrong. Well, let's say adequate."

"What do you mean — she didn't fit in?"

Donna licked her lips as if savoring a juicy morsel. "She was different. In a way I think you and I would understand." She raised her eyebrows to convey special meaning. "Her lifestyle — her preferences, let's say. They were a bit unusual."

"You mean because she was a lesbian. Is that it?"

Donna smiled. Her eyelids lowered, giving her an addled sleepy appearance, although Helen was certain this was the woman's best seductive expression. "I knew you'd understand. You know, not everyone at Centurion liked Leslie. Some of them were prejudiced against people like her."

"But not you."

"Just the opposite. Some of my very best friends are like that. My very, very best and most intimate friends."

Helen forced herself to remain calm. She could handle Donna easily. Too bad she still had to try to get some information out of her. "So people said things about Leslie's being gay? Sounds like she might have had some enemies."

Donna shrugged. "Not what you'd call enemies. Besides, I figured she would have told you about it."

"Told me about it? No, Donna. I was — I'm a friend of her mother's. I never really knew Leslie all that well."

"Oh. But I thought — you mean, you and Leslie weren't — close?"

"No, not really."

"But you have certain things in common?"

Helen smiled. Clearly Donna wasn't going to be a good source of information, so she might as well give up on questioning her and give her a taste of what she was after. "Are you asking me if I'm a lesbian, Donna?"

Donna's face slowly turned almost as red as her suit.

"No, of course I'm not. I wouldn't ever ask anything so personal about anyone."

"Well, here we are, sitting here having lunch and calling each other by our first names. And I only met you yesterday." Helen leaned forward and saw Donna flinch. "I guess I was wrong, then," she said with a sorrowful sigh.

"Wrong about what?"

"That maybe you wanted to get to know me better. A lot better."

It was a gamble, but it worked. Donna immediately froze, no longer in control of the situation. Her face bleached from embarrassed red to white. She crumpled her napkin and threw it on the table.

"What's the matter, Donna? Did I say something wrong?"

Donna stood up, yanked her shoulder bag from her chair and pulled out a couple of bills. "Nothing. Nothing's wrong. I just remembered — Mr. McFarland wants me to prepare some reports for his meeting tomorrow."

"Gee, that's too bad. Maybe some other time?" Helen debated touching her, perhaps on the arm as she walked by, but decided that would be overkill.

"I'll have to see. I'm terribly busy —" Donna fled as fast as her red stiletto heels could carry her.

Before Helen could turn back to finish her salad, she heard laughter coming from the booth on the other side of the barrier next to her own. With a sinking feeling she raised herself off her seat enough to look over the barrier and see Bob Tyrell, Lily Mapa and Christine Santilli in the other booth, trying hard not to laugh again.

Helen shook her head, picked up her plate and Donna's cash and carried it around to their booth. She slid in next to Lily and tried the salad one more time.

Bob cleared his throat and asked, "How's your appetite?"

"Better. Too bad I didn't know we had an audience — I would have tried harder."

"No, you were terrific." Christine picked up a breadstick and took a bite. "Much better than Leslie ever was."

Helen looked around at the others. They had suddenly become very quiet. Lily spoke first. "Damnit, Christine, you shoot your mouth off too much."

"Yeah." Bob took his glasses off and rubbed the bridge of his nose. "Listen, I'm sorry," he said to Helen. "That was really rude."

"But amusing. So, Lily must have told you that Donna asked me to go to lunch and you all followed us here." The three Centurion employees looked sheepishly at one another, then down at the table. The waitress made a welcome interruption as she set down plates in front of them.

"No, I'm just fine here, thanks," Helen said in response to the waitress' worried questions. "Could you just keep my check separate? Thanks."

Bob looked at Christine and Lily, then blurted out, "It was a bet. Christine bet us lunch that Donna would — she would . . ." He mumbled something Helen couldn't hear.

"What was that?"

"That she'd make a pass at you." Christine picked up another breadstick, leaving her lunch untouched. "Wouldn't be the first time she pulled something like that."

Helen put down her fork and stared at Christine. "You mean she made a pass at Leslie. And you all knew about this."

"She didn't exactly keep it a secret." Lily said. "I mean, God, she would always ask her to go to lunch, and visit her upstairs. Even at the old building she was always on the phone to Leslie about something." Lily blushed and glared at Christine. "They don't even really work together, you know?"

"But don't you think Donna would be worried that people would talk? Or that Leslie would complain about it?"

Bob snorted. "Donna Stethins has a serious reality problem. Or didn't you notice that over lunch?" He took a huge bite of his sandwich and spoke around the food. "I think McFarland lets her get away with anything she wants because he'd fall apart without her."

"Donna Stethins is McFarland's personal assistant, right? And Leslie was — what, exactly? I mean, I know her title was project manager, but what did that mean?"

"Basically she was McFarland's troubleshooter. It's easy — you take anything that doesn't look right, call it a 'project,' and bring in the dynamic duo of Leslie and Christine to sort it all out."

Christine still hadn't touched her lunch. She'd finished all the breadsticks and looked around for their waitress. "Excuse me, could we have some more bread, please?" She idly scratched at her arm under the wrist brace. "Guess I should count myself lucky to still have a job right now," she went on. "Lord, these things itch!"

"I don't know why you wear them, anyway," Lily said, glaring as Christine slammed an elbow into the other woman while scratching beneath the brace. "You don't even use a computer that much — I'm the one always typing up your stuff."

"But now you don't have Leslie's work to do, do you?" Christine asked, turning a sunny smile toward Lily.

"Do you think they'll get someone else to fill her place?" Bob wondered aloud.

"You mean, since I've obviously been passed over?" Christine spat out.

Helen decided it was time to say something, if only to prevent a fight from breaking out. Besides, they might be able to help her. "Why was Leslie terminated? Was she doing that badly at Centurion?"

"God, no! No one could figure it out. It was a total shock to everyone," Lily said, looking to the others for confirmation. "I guess to Leslie, too." Tears welled up in

113

her eyes. "We should have seen it coming, I know we should have!"

Bob patted Lily's arm awkwardly. "Come on, no one ever sees anything like that coming! Don't start blaming yourself."

"But ever since that time she went away —" Lily stammered, then shut up when she caught Helen staring at her.

"She went away? A business trip?"

Lily shrugged and looked at Bob. "I don't know. You don't know, either, do you, Christine?" he asked. Christine shook her head. Bob went on, "About the time we were relocating to Oakland, Leslie took vacation time. Normally no one would have paid a whole lot of attention, but to take time off then was pretty strange. It was so busy, you know? All those boxes, all that stuff to organize. So it was pretty weird for her to go away."

"And right when she came back," Lily said, "that's when she had that big fight with McFarland. Well, it was in her office, anyway. I don't know who was in there with her." She sighed. "That's when it got really bad. Leslie would just sort of walk around all angry and not talk to anyone. Not that she ever said a whole lot, anyway."

"Christine, you were her assistant, or partner, or whatever. What do you think happened?" Helen asked.

Christine shrugged. "God only knows. Lily's right. Leslie took time off and came back in a terrible mood. She never said why. Maybe something happened then."

"But why would she be fired? For being grouchy?"

Christine laughed. "Obviously you've never worked in an office like ours. People get canned for a lot less. No, McFarland said it was a reorganization. My guess is it came down from higher up. Maybe even the president."

"Oh, Christine, don't get started on your conspiracy theory stuff again," Bob moaned. "Why the hell would

Drake want to get rid of Leslie? He barely knows any of us exist."

"We don't know that. I certainly don't know it. Where the hell is that waitress?"

Lily folded her arms and stared down at the table. The tears Helen had seen a moment ago had spilled over and streaked her face. "I think you're awful, Christine. Saying things like that. It's like you think Drake pushed her out the window himself." She sniffled and grabbed a napkin to wipe her eyes. "I can still see her on the ground — God, it was worse than anything in the world!"

"Well, if you were all the way down on the first floor when she landed, then at least your alibi is safe, right?"

"You're disgusting, Christine."

"Yeah, well, where were you, then?" Bob demanded of Christine, his face growing red with anger.

"Shredding all morning, honey." Christine made a ripping motion with both hands in front of her. "Got to get rid of the evidence, you know. And what about you, Bob?"

"None of your damned business."

"Oh, I know — the john, right?" Christine pealed out ringing laughter at his grimace. "Don't suppose there were any witnesses?"

"What about Drake? Was he in the building that day?" Helen asked.

Christine shrugged. "Ask Bob. Maybe he was in the john, too."

Lily said, "Shut up, Christine!" Then, to Helen, "I don't think so. I didn't see him come through the front."

"Huh. You should probably be asking about that bodyguard of his. What's his name? Howard? Hal? Something like that." Bob had recovered a bit of composure. He leaned his beefy arms on the table and pointedly ignored Christine.

A silence descended over the table. Bob put down his

sandwich. Christine finally began to eat. "Okay, maybe Drake didn't have anything to do with it. Maybe she jumped, after all. What do you think?" she asked, turning to Helen.

Helen toyed with her fork and watched the others as she spoke. "I think there are a lot of questions still unanswered about this whole thing. If Leslie jumped, why did she jump? The job? Something in her personal life? What was it?"

"Well, you're the old family friend. You must have some idea."

"I have to be going." Lily stood up. "Are you coming, Bob?"

He nodded, tossed money on the table and followed Lily. "Look, Ms. Black, I'm really sorry about all this. And I'm sorry about Leslie."

"Thank you. I appreciate that." Helen watched them leave, then moved to the other side of the booth so that she was facing Christine. "You seem to be the only one with an appetite today."

Christine glanced down Donna's twenties beside Helen's plate. "Well, as long as it's a free lunch, why not? Poor Leslie. She never even got a free lunch out of Donna."

"Well, I doubt Leslie killed herself over that."

Christine leaned back in the booth and studied her. "Who are you, anyway? You sure don't seem like an old friend of the family to me."

Helen smiled. "Are you close to Leslie's family?"

"That's a laugh. Leslie barely talked to dear old Mom. I think moving back home was her biggest mistake." Christine looked bleakly out across the café. "How would you like to come home to Tina Merrick every night?" She sighed, put down her fork and rested the wrist braces carefully on the table. "Look, since you seem so damned curious, it's no big secret. I think Leslie was depressed for quite a long time. Frankly, I think she did jump out that window. It was all just too much for her — first her girlfriend, then living with mommie dearest, then McFarland and Drake cook up this ridiculous excuse to get rid of her." She picked up her fork again and stabbed at her food. "So, yeah, I think it was suicide. And if you think that makes it any better, then think again."

"So you knew that much about her life, then. You knew she had a girlfriend."

"I saw them once, together. You could tell, the way they kind of leaned in at each other. Leslie wasn't exactly in the closet. She just kept her life to herself. And I worked with her every day. I got to know things."

"So who was this girlfriend?"

Christine smiled. "Well, if I were you, I'd look for a crazy woman who wears brown. Brown, brown, brown — and nothing else." She slid out of the booth and dropped a ten on the table. "Kind of like that freak who tried to get herself run over by your car at the memorial service."

Helen ordered coffee and sat alone in the booth, savoring the heady aroma of French roast and thinking hard. She'd been handed quite a few pieces to the puzzle today, but she couldn't seem to put the fragments together into anything recognizable. An ex-girlfriend who was, literally, insane. A supervisor who'd harassed her sexually. Disgruntled company presidents. Confused co-workers who found Leslie's life an enigma. A security guard who lied about his whereabouts at the moment of Leslie's death. Mysterious journeys resulting in depression and suicide. Envelopes hidden in office bookcases —

Helen grabbed her shoulder bag and sighed in relief at the sight of the plain brown paper. She debated going through the contents, but the arrival of the waitress decided her against it. Donna had left enough for a healthy tip. Helen didn't feel the slightest twinge of guilt at taking Donna's money, since she believed she'd more than earned it during their conversation.

117

After paying the cashier, Helen stopped outside the restaurant and looked over at the Centurion building. Remembering she'd left her cell phone in the glove compartment, she walked over to a pay phone and punched in a few numbers.

"Centurion? Yes, can you put me through to the seventh floor, please. Yes, I'll hold. Hello, Mrs. Young? It's Helen Black. No, no, you were wonderful. Listen, I can explain everything. What time do you get home? I have to be in Orinda for a meeting this evening. Would it be all right if I stopped by your place?"

After getting directions to the Young residence, Helen hung up the phone and hurried over to her car. It was just after two p.m. If Helen remembered correctly, the Berkeley Free Clinic should be open. Although it was probably a big waste of time to search for the woman in brown, the clinic was as good a place as any to start. If her behavior was an indication of her mental state, she might be on some sort of medication program there. She was unique enough that someone might remember her.

Helen swung the car off Broadway over to College Avenue and followed it into Berkeley, swinging over on Durant. Traffic, as always on the narrow streets of Oakland and Berkeley, was sluggish. An hour later, after a long wait at the clinic, Helen got the answer she was hoping for.

The woman wore a lab coat too large for her and had thick red hair pulled back in a ponytail. It should have made her look severe, but it only highlighted how young she was. Her name tag read KIM FARRADAY and identified her as an RN.

"Oh, yeah, that's Amelia Airhead."

"Amelia what?" So, Helen thought, that name again.

"Sorry, that's what everyone calls her." The clinic attendant had to shout over the noise of toddlers and adolescents running in and out of the building. Apparently Helen had the good fortune to arrive there on a scheduled vaccination afternoon, and dozens of families herded their offspring into the clinic. "She wanders in here looking like hell, but refuses any help. Just hangs around talking to herself. Manic depressive behavior. She told me one day her name was Amelia. 'Amelia, like the aviatrix,' she said. So some of the people started calling her Airhead. For Earheart." The attendant blushed and smiled wryly. "I know it sounds cruel."

"Yeah, well, this woman's flying days are over."

"No kidding. She's out there. I'm certain she ought to be on some kind of meds, but we get so many street people that need meds and won't take them."

"Does she come here regularly or anything? The same time each week, or any other pattern?"

The young woman shrugged and jammed her hands into the pockets of her lab coat. "No, nothing I can think of. Except — wait a minute." She stepped around a cluster of young girls sitting on the floor and headed for a bulletin board. Pinned into the cork were rows of apartment listings, requests for roommates, baby-sitting services, and offers of used merchandise. Kim stood in front of the board for several moments, then she took a small card from its place between a flyer advertising yard work and a note asking for used clothing.

"Here. I thought I remembered her putting this up there."

The card was torn and stained, but the words were still legible. "She was an accountant," Helen said. "Her office was in Berkeley."

Kim nodded. "God knows how long since her business folded. Every once in a while, when she comes in, she goes over to the board to check on her card. It's like something she holds onto, somehow. A memory of what she used to be."

Helen fumbled in her bag. "Look, I know you're completely swamped here, but I'd like to leave my card. If

119

you see her and get a chance to get to a phone, would you give me a call."

"Sure."

Helen left her rounding up a set of youngsters for their shots. This was not going to be easy. There were a limited number of places to look for a woman like Amelia, a woman who'd fallen through the cracks of society, but there certainly weren't any limits on the number of doorways where she could try to sleep. Or on the horrible things that could happen to someone living on the streets. Helen tried to shut out the images burned into her memory from her days as a Berkeley cop, but pictures of Amelia plastered to the pavement, bruised and bloody, haunted her as she drove toward her office on Shattuck.

The traffic got worse the closer she came to the Caldecott Tunnel. She had to sit in the tunnel for a few minutes — there was no doubt some sort of accident up ahead. It was odd, Helen reflected, that the tunnel led to a completely different world from Berkeley. Both heat and cold got trapped throughout the year just beyond the Berkeley hills, making the climate changes of each season more intense than it ever became closer to San Francisco Bay. But it wasn't only the temperature that had caused a paradigm shift. Helen always told herself it was only an illusion that the very air was thicker and heavier when she emerged into the sunlight of Contra Costa County. It was all her imagination, she mentally recited, that she felt hemmed in, cornered and trapped by everything the place represented.

Still, it was a good sign that Alison's mother had sounded excited to have her come for a visit. Of course, it was all business, but it might be a good start to building a comfortable, congenial relationship with the Young family.

Surprised, Helen pulled up in front of the enormous three-story house on a quiet, secluded street of Orinda. She'd always known that Alison's family had money, but because Alison herself lived so simply and frugally she'd never considered the wealth Alison was used to.

"Yoo-hoo! Hello!"

Helen climbed out of the car into the warmth of late afternoon. All Mrs. Young lacked to make the picture complete was a plate of cookies and a pitcher of milk.

"I told them I had a dentist appointment so I could get out early. Come on in. I can't wait to hear about the case!"

Chapter Nine

Vicky Young picked up the last cookie on the plate, then put it down again.

"No, please, you take it. I've had plenty," Helen said.

Vicky shook her head. "I really shouldn't. You should see my desk at work — candy bars and muffins and chocolate hidden away everywhere! And I wouldn't want to answer for the state of my purse, either."

Helen smiled. "Indulge. Why not?"

"You're sure?" When Helen nodded, she picked it up again and broke it apart. "At first, after that crazy meeting when Leslie smashed the bottle, I was surprised that no one said anything about it. But of course, I'm just the temp — no one would say anything to me, anyway. And offices like Centurion are just like dysfunctional families. No one talks about anything, and there's massive denial going on at all times." She sighed and popped half the cookie into her mouth. "Every day at Centurion has been like the first. I go up to my little sanctuary on the seventh floor and never see anyone."

"No one?"

"Well, maybe once in a while someone will come up to use the shredder or the fax or something. They're still getting fax machines and stuff like that set up throughout the building, so there's always people fighting to use them. That's when they make the journey up to the seventh floor. For the most part, I'm by myself." She smiled and took a bite of cookie. "A whole floor, all alone! Very weird. Donna Stethins plopped me down at that huge desk and left me alone to play computer games. Until —" Her face darkened and she put the remaining half of her cookie down on the plate. "Until that guy came upstairs, yelling about Leslie."

"And that's the first you heard or saw of it, Vicky?"

She nodded, popping the last portion of cookie into her mouth. "Unless someone wants to shred something, I almost never see a soul. I just sit there and put information into their computers — names and phone numbers of potential customers to call once they get their toll-free system put in place." She grinned. "Haven't seen your name yet, Helen, so I guess you're not on the list to get one of those annoying phone calls during dinner, trying to get you to buy something."

Helen, propped up on her elbows at the kitchen table, marveled at Mrs. Young and at her own ignorance. Here they were, sitting in an enormous, color-coordinated, All-American kitchen. It had everything — a huge butcher's block in the center of the room, polished copper pots and pans hanging from hooks in the ceiling, an oversized refrigerator that rumbled away making little ice cubes throughout the conversation. Mrs. Young's kitchen glorified the epitome of consumer goods and material comforts that Helen, after years in Berkeley, associated with complacent middle-class "family" values. Yet Vicky sat across the scrubbed pine table, eating homemade chocolate chip cookies, talking easily about the shortcomings of the corporate lifestyle.

As the descendant of dirt-poor Mississippi farmers, carrying a heritage of racism and ignorance, Helen had never quite gotten over her timidity around wealth. No matter how many times she had come into contact with rich and powerful people, no matter how often she'd been able to hold her own quite well with them, Helen still felt as if she'd come in by the wrong door whenever she was in a situation like this one. It was the emotional equivalent of checking under her fingernails for dirt from the fields. And it was even harder when the people involved were quite naturally nice and friendly.

"What made you take up temp work?" Helen asked, suddenly curious.

Vicky laughed and got up, carrying the empty plate over to the sink. "My husband asks me the same thing all the time," she said over the running water. "Of course, he's worked so hard to give me and Alison everything we could want. Jim's doing his best to understand how I need a life, too." She turned and smiled. "He's even got past asking when dinner will be ready the minute he hits that door coming home."

"But why temporary jobs?" Helen got up, carrying her teacup with her, and leaned against the counter while Vicky rinsed the plate. "Why not go back to school, or interview for a permanent job?"

Vicky set the plate in the drainer and reached for the dishtowel that hung from a hook above the sink. "I don't really know what I want to do, Helen," she said. "At fifty-seven, I've done a lot of different things in my time. Housewife and mother, PTA mom, administrative assistant in my husband's firm. I headed the League of Women Voters for many years. I've taken computer classes and gone to management seminars and even," she grinned, "done some new-age kind of retreat work. I know, I know, hard to believe — this place looks as if the head of the Republican National Committee could walk through that door any moment, doesn't it?"

Helen laughed as they went back to the table. "I guess I've lived in the People's Republic of Berkeley just a little too long."

Impulsively, hesitant at first, Vicky reached over and touched Helen's hand. "I want you to know that I — that both of us — are very, very happy for Alison."

"Thank you," Helen murmured.

"The best thing that ever happened to that girl was to get away from her husband." Vicky shook her head, and a shadow of anger crossed her face. "There was nothing we could do — she kept going back to him. I think it might have been a reaction to Jim and me. We were so liberal, especially for Orinda, that it frightened her. She was looking for something rock-solid, I guess."

"Well, in my experience, the only things in life that are rock-solid are rocks."

"That's why you're good for Alison. Shake her up a little." Vicky's smile faded. "Of course, we had no idea that you were a private investigator. I was completely shocked when you walked in the door with Tight-Butt."

"Tight-Butt?"

"Oh, that's just my private name for Donna Stethins. You know — wants to sleep with the boss but he isn't having any? So she prances around on her high heels for him all day."

"I see. Tight-Butt. I'll have to remember that." Helen finished her tea and glanced at her watch. In another hour

125

she was due to head over to Tina Merrick's house to go through the personal items from Leslie's office. "By the way, did you ever meet Tina or Leslie Merrick? Tina, Leslie's mother, lives a few blocks away, and I know for the last couple of months Leslie had been living at home."

Vicky shook her head. "No, I don't think so. I may have seen Tina at the grocery store, or something like that, but I wouldn't have known her. And I certainly would have remembered seeing Leslie. I guess they kept to themselves."

"Any gossip about Leslie?"

Vicky frowned as she thought, then sadly shook her head. "Like I said, people don't talk much to me. Oh, they're nice enough, friendly for the most part, but I don't really count, you know? They come up and fax something somewhere, sometimes they say hello and sometimes they don't. Then they go back through that door and I'm alone again. Playing solitaire."

"Sounds pretty awful."

"Oh, no, don't get me wrong. Actually, it's given me a lot of time to work on my resume and set up interviews. I've decided after this to get out of temping and look for a real job. At a much smaller company."

Helen stood up. "I can't thank you enough, Vicky. For not giving me away today — and for the cookies and conversation."

"Are you sure you can't stay for dinner? Jim should be home from the golf course in just a few minutes, and I was going to whip up some stir-fry."

"No, really, I have to be going. Tina will be waiting for me."

But her exit was delayed by the arrival of Jim Young. Helen took his outstretched hand and studied him as he greeted her. To her immense relief, he gave every appearance of being truly pleased to see her.

"At Centurion?" He turned an amazed face to Helen when Vicky explained their meeting in Oakland that morning. "I can't believe it!" Then he sobered. "It's about that woman, then? The one who killed herself?"

"Now, Jim —" Vicky slid her arms around her husband in a quick embrace. "Helen can't talk about her cases. That's confidential." She winked at Helen.

After a few more promises of seeing one another at the family barbecue on Saturday — only three days away — Helen checked the directions Tina had written down for her and drove through the quiet streets to the Merrick house. She pulled up behind Tina's Mercedes, noting the Jaguar parked to the side of the house. Tina's dead husband must have left her off a lot better than she let on.

It was no surprise that she felt much more uncomfortable with Tina than she had with Vicky Young. The house where Tina lived was almost as large and spacious as the Young home, but there was no sense of welcome there. "Everything's such a mess — please forgive me," Tina babbled.

Helen smiled against the all-too-familiar scent of liquor emanating from her hostess. "Not a problem," she said as they headed into a sitting room filled with oversized, overstuffed furniture. Helen hadn't seen this part of the house when she'd brought Tina home from the memorial service. Plastic sheeting, firmly wrapped around every single chair and sofa, gleamed dusty and dull in the yellow haze of sunlight that crept in through the blinds drawn tight. Helen stepped carefully through the room, looking for a place to put the box of Leslie's belongings down. She settled on an end table that wasn't completely covered with magazines and knickknacks and gingerly set the box down next to a collection of dirty coffee mugs.

"Actually, Helen —" Tina stopped short and whispered. Helen grimaced and moved closer than she would have liked in order to hear. "I do have another visitor right now. This is sort of awkward."

Helen was glad the room was murky so Tina couldn't

see the anger she felt. "Well, we did make this appointment, Tina, and I really think this is important."

"Is everything all right, Tina?" The small wiry figure of Richard Drake appeared in silhouette at the doorway of the room just ahead. "Oh, I'm terribly sorry. I didn't mean to interrupt."

Tina blushed and stammered while Helen stared, hiding her anger and surprise as best she could. "Well, this is — I mean — you met Helen Black yesterday, I believe?"

"Of course. How do you do?"

Helen took his small dry hand in her own. "This is unexpected, Mr. Drake."

"I'm sorry to intrude. Tina didn't tell me she was expecting someone else." The faint Southern accent Helen had picked up on the previous morning was more in evidence today. He had turned on his best courtly behavior, all the while never taking his eyes away from Helen. "She was kind enough to allow me a visit this afternoon, so I took advantage of that."

"Maybe we should all sit down, or something." Tina moved hopefully toward the room ahead only to have her way, as well as most of the light, blocked by Drake's bodyguard. Helen couldn't see his face at all in the darkness, but he stood with the same motionless control she'd seen yesterday. And she was certain he was staring at her.

"Howard, perhaps you'd be good enough to get the car warmed up." Drake fished keys out of his pocket, and Howard moved noiselessly through the cluttered room, keys in hand, deliberately and slowly brushing up against Helen as he went. Recoiling, Helen turned back to Drake. She could just see his grim smile. Tina looked from Helen to Drake, confused. "Tina, I believe I left my coat in your front closet," Drake said.

It was a polite but firm dismissal. Tina scuttled out of

the hallway and Drake took a step closer to Helen. "Is that a Southern accent I hear, Ms. Black? I'm from Tennessee, myself. Many years ago, now."

"Mississippi. I'm surprised, Mr. Drake. Few people can hear it in my voice."

"Well, it's just a question of knowing what to listen for. Like so many things in life."

"And here I was, thinking I'd shed the accent a long time ago."

"Oh, things like that don't go away, Ms. Black. They just sort of" — he moved his hands in the darkness — "go underground."

"Like so many things in life," Helen responded.

"All too true. I have learned, however, that things underground often burst back out into the light of day. I suppose in your profession you find that to be the case."

Helen raised her eyebrows. "You do your homework, Mr. Drake."

His laughter rasped unpleasantly across the hall. "Well, it's important to know all you can about a subject. Especially if you want to be a success in this world."

"As you are with Centurion Sportswear. How do you like Oakland, Mr. Drake?"

He laughed again. "Oh, I rarely go to Oakland. I much prefer working at home. Why, thank you, Tina," and he took the thick wool coat from her. "I know it must seem odd, wearing something like this in the summertime, but both you ladies are too young to know how cold an old man can get, no matter how warm the climate."

"Are you sure you have to go? I think Helen was only going to be here for a few minutes," Tina said, eagerly following him out through the hall toward the front door.

"I'm so sorry, Tina, but I really have some things to do still today. Duty calls. Ms. Black, it was a pleasure seeing you again."

"It's mutual." Helen didn't trust herself to say more.

A few moments later, Tina reappeared with bottle in hand. "Want a drink? I could sure use one."

"No, thanks. So what the hell was Drake doing here?"

"Huh? Oh, he just wanted to offer his condolences. Nice man." Tina arranged herself on a sofa that wasn't covered in plastic sheeting, closed her eyes and leaned back, one hand pressed to her forehead. "He thinks there might be a small amount of money coming to me. Some kind of insurance thing that Leslie was entitled to."

Helen sat down on a footstool next to the sofa. It was the only other thing in the room not shrink-wrapped. "A lot of money? A little? Just how much was Leslie worth to Centurion?" *Or to you,* Helen refrained from asking.

"I don't really know. Mr. Drake — Richard — he said he would bring it by himself. Don't you think that was really a nice thing to do, Helen? I mean, since I have to wait for the insurance money and all." Tina raised herself up enough from the sofa to pour amber liquid from the bottle into a glass. She took a swallow and made a face. With a couple of vague pushes at her hair, she said, "I think he's rather handsome. You know — for an older man. Don't you? Oh, I forgot." Tina blushed and giggled.

"Don't you think it's possible that he's buying you off, somehow? It's not exactly common to get handed a lump sum by the company president when an employee dies." Helen took the envelope from her purse and began sorting through its contents, hoping she'd kept the bitter edge of anger out of her voice.

"Richard? Oh, Helen, how can you say such a thing? He's so sweet and sympathetic. And he understands how badly I need the money. Besides," she said, "I can pay you more quickly now than if I had to wait for the insurance."

Helen took a deep breath and tried again. "Mrs. Merrick — Tina — I brought these things from Leslie's office today. I thought we could go through them together. Why don't you take a look at them with me?"

"Oh, yes. I'd forgotten." She patted the sofa next to her. Helen sat down and laid papers out on the sofa between them.

Except for a stack of articles about the Centurion factory in Korea, the bulk of the envelope's contents consisted of bills and receipts. "Who are these girls?" Tina asked Helen, lifting a newsprint photograph of a group of Asian women.

Helen took it from her. "I think they must be the people who work in the Centurion factory in Korea." They couldn't be more than fifteen, she thought. Was it the work they did for Centurion that made them look so old and tired?

Tina handed her the remainder of the articles, refusing to look at photographs of mutilated hands, reaching instead for the pile of bills. "They look like just a bunch of receipts."

"Yes, that's what they are." Some were handwritten, some were printouts of the sort produced by credit card machines. Helen did some rough mental calculations and came up with an estimate. "It looks like Leslie — or someone — spent almost two thousand dollars doing something, somewhere."

Tina held up one of the receipts to the light. "What the hell — this isn't English."

"No, they're in Spanish. Well, most of them." One single sheet, handwritten, appeared to be a list of addresses. There was no indication of what city these places were — or what country, for that matter. "Tina, did Leslie speak Spanish?"

"Huh?" She put down the slips of paper she'd been leafing through and looked up at Helen. "Well, I don't know. I remember she took some Spanish in high school, like everyone does."

Helen picked up a torn piece of lined notebook paper. There were numbers scribbled on it. "These are flight numbers," she murmured. "Arrival times. 'MEX' would mean Mexico." Leslie's sudden disappearance, she remembered. Over lunch Bob had talked about the way Leslie took off suddenly when everyone else at Centurion was getting settled into their new home in Oakland.

Then Helen spotted a flimsy scrap. Much creased and lined, it looked as if it had been torn from a paper bag. Six numbers were printed on it. There had possibly been a seventh, but the edge of the scrap was torn on the left side, where an additional number might have been written. Helen could see faint ink smears along the edge. She read the numbers aloud. "Zero, one, eight, two, three, two."

"Is it an amount? Or a receipt for something?"

Helen shook her head. "I have no idea. It could be an account number. I think a number is missing, anyway."

"I don't know, Helen. None of it means anything to me."

"Leslie went away on a trip, right before the Centurion building opened up. Do you know where she went?"

"No. She never told me anything. I never knew what she was up to. It was always like that, ever since she was a little girl." Tina shook her head. Her eyes, bleared by alcohol, filled with tears. Helen collected the receipts back into the envelope while Tina wept. "No, Helen, you keep those. I don't have any idea what they mean. Maybe you can make sense out of them."

Helen stood up. "I brought a box in with me, Tina. Leslie had a few things in her office I thought you might want to keep."

Tina sniffled and wiped her eyes, tried to get up, then

132

sank back onto the sofa. "I — I don't think I could face it right now, Helen. It would just remind me that I'm all alone. My husband is gone, and now my little girl."

Helen turned away to hide her disgust. "I'll just put the box in Leslie's room. Behind the kitchen, right?"

"Yes, you'll find it. I — I need to be alone for a minute, Helen."

It struck her that Tina's kitchen was just as spacious as the one in the Young house, but Tina's kitchen was littered with trash, food-encrusted plates, and columns of ants tracking across the floor and up onto the counters. Helen went quickly to Leslie's door, wondering briefly why Leslie had chosen this room, unless her mother had chosen it for her.

But when she saw that it had a private entrance, leading out through the backyard, the choice made perfect sense. No doubt Leslie, for the brief time she'd stayed there, had wanted to ensure a quick getaway whenever she needed it. Or, possibly, she might have had visitors she didn't want her mother to know about. Except for the private entrance, however, the room had little to recommend it. Small and dark and dank, there was room only for a bed and dresser. Helen felt a wave of pity wash over her. Leslie's final days had therefore been spent in this depressing room or in the bleak offices of Centurion Sportswear.

In the gloom, Helen set the box down on the dresser and knocked off the telephone resting there. It bumped down to the floor, its bell sounding once on the carpet. As Helen bent over to pick it up she remembered the scrap of paper with six numbers she'd found in the envelope. Sitting on the bed, Helen rustled through the receipts until she found the scrap.

Six numbers, with a seventh missing. If it was a telephone number, then the missing digit was part of a prefix. And that prefix, even with only two numbers, looked familiar.

She hurried out of Leslie's room back to where she'd left Tina. "Tina? Could I use your telephone? I think I know what this set of numbers is, and I'd like to —"

Snores greeted her at the entrance of the room. Still clutching the bottle in one hand, an empty glass in the other, Tina slept it off while Helen went back into the kitchen. There was a telephone on the wall, next to the pantry.

Holding the scrap of paper before her, Helen keyed in the numbers, adding a six to the complete the sequence. It rang for quite a while. Helen counted ten pulses until a voice finally sounded in her ear.

"Hitchcock."

For a long moment, Helen was too stunned to speak.

"Yes? Who is this?"

"Father Hitchcock?"

"Yes. Can I help you?"

"Father, I don't know if you'll remember me. It's Helen Black."

A lengthy silence followed. Then Helen heard a chuckle. "I can't believe it. Helen Black! It's been — well, I can't remember, but it's been years, hasn't it? How the hell are you?"

"I'm fine, just fine. I'm calling — well, it's more a professional call, Father."

"Oh? What can I do for you?"

She sighed, not sure how to begin. "I got this phone number from an unusual place. Actually, I didn't know it was yours until I called."

"I don't really understand."

"Neither do I. I'm hoping we can figure it out together."

"Where did you get this number?"

"I found it among the personal belongings of Leslie Merrick. She died recently."

He sighed heavily. "You'd better come over. We have a few things to discuss."

Helen left without bothering to wake Tina. As she put the envelope in the trunk of her car, Helen promised herself she'd finish going through Leslie's papers as soon as she'd talked to Father Hitchcock. This conversation was too important to put off. She headed back through the tunnel to Berkeley.

Chapter Ten

"So how long have you been in this parish?"

"Oh, I got shipped out here about a year ago," Father Hitchcock replied.

Located in East Oakland, not far from the old Cypress Freeway, St. Ignatius had seen better times, Helen was sure. As she'd walked from her car to the rectory — an old Victorian with a sagging front porch, bars on the windows, and concrete for a low-maintenance front yard — she couldn't help comparing this neighborhood with the one where he used to live. Father Hitch had fallen on difficult times, it seemed. His previous assignment, St. Joseph's in

Berkeley, had been far from wealthy, but the working-class families who'd filled his church every week hadn't had the same air of despair she felt here.

To her surprise, he'd actually seemed quite happy to see her. Helen wondered if he had many visitors, even from his own parish, here at the crumbling rectory. In his tiny office, paint peeled and flaked from the walls in several spots, some of which had been artfully concealed with posters and tacked-up announcements. The single window, which was draped with a bedsheet, remained open to the cool evening air. Although the sun was sinking fast, Helen could see in its reflected light that the windowpane bore a thick layer of grime that was smeared, as if someone had made a recent attempt to clean it. The door to the office wouldn't stay shut. From outside came the sounds of loud music, cars revving, arguments and curses. Helen was certain that, if she stayed around long enough into the night, she'd hear gunfire as well.

"Why this particular parish?" she asked.

He laughed and shook his head. He looked exactly as he did when Helen first met him several years ago while investigating a case — average height, thin, with a prominent nose. He still wore his hair long and drawn back into a ponytail, which Helen guessed the local church authorities still had a difficult time tolerating. The biggest difference she could see in Father Hitch was that he'd grown more careworn, more tired and gray. "I think," he said, "that the bishop is trying to teach me a lesson."

"And what would that be?"

He shrugged, pushed back his chair and crossed his feet on the desk. "Probably to start minding my manners."

"So how's it going? The manners, I mean."

"Terrible." He laughed again.

"I saw you on the news the other night. Talking about PAN."

He sobered quickly. "Yes. Interesting. The pagan

acronym, I mean. That's something else the bishop doesn't like."

"What — that it's the name of a Greek god — or the politics?"

"Both, I suspect." He sighed heavily and took off his glasses, dropping them on the desk. "So what made you give me a call, Helen?"

She gave him a synopsis, leaving out Tina Merrick's name, carefully editing details and summarizing events up till that afternoon, when she'd discovered his phone number in Leslie's personal effects. "Basically, Leslie Merrick was depressed, I think. A breakup with this elusive girlfriend, just lost her job, had to move back home — I was just coming to the same conclusion as everyone else."

"That she committed suicide."

Helen nodded.

"But you changed your mind."

She fidgeted in her chair for a moment. "I don't think I can really say why. Just that some things have come up — some questions — that I'd like to see answered before I end the investigation."

"I see." After a moment of complete stillness, Father Hitch sprang up from the chair and went to a cupboard built into the wall behind Helen. "I'd like to show you something." He came out from behind her carrying a stack of what looked like newsletters.

"This is not exactly the weekly parish bulletin," Helen said after reading the headline. DEMONSTRATION TO BE HELD AT NEW CENTURION BUILDING, the front page proclaimed. "I take it this is one of the reasons you're tucked away in the corner here in Oakland now?"

He perched on the edge of his desk, still smiling. "I've been helping to print and distribute the PAN newsletter for months, but the bishop hasn't caught wind of it yet. I figure I've got at least the rest of the year before I'm officially asked to cease and desist." He pointed to a line in the article. "The protest happens two days from now, on Friday."

"And Leslie was involved in this somehow?"

He got up and moved back around the desk, sinking with a sudden alarming weariness into his chair. "I can tell you that Leslie was very disturbed by some things she'd recently seen in Mexico at the factory Centurion opened up there."

The receipts. The Spanish-sounding addresses. "What kind of things, Father?"

He grimaced. "Things like sixteen-hour work days for twelve-year-old girls. Things like women and young girls losing fingers in machinery and getting fired for getting hurt, with no medical attention beyond stopping the bleeding. Things like getting fired for saying anything about unions, then blacklisted everywhere else to make sure the troublemaker can't get work again." He picked up his glasses and placed them back on his nose. There was exhaustion and despair in his eyes. "And how many of the people running, working out or just walking around in Centurion Sportswear think about the blood and sweat and anguish that goes into every damn shoe they slip on?"

"Not many, I'd guess," Helen said softly.

"Sorry, Helen. I didn't mean to start preaching again." He sighed and shook his head. "You didn't come here for a homily. Let's see. Leslie showed up just about two weeks ago, I think — yes, that's right." He glanced up at the calendar hanging behind him. "I remember we'd just had a parish meeting about the Easter pageant coming up."

"So she approached you, then?"

"I'd never met her before, or seen her at the demonstrations. She sat right there, right where you're sitting now, and said she might have some information for me."

"Can you tell me what kind of information?"

Father Hitch shrugged. "I don't know for sure. She did

say that she would get me some answers about the new Centurion factory opening up in Chiapas. We — PAN members, I mean — we knew Centurion had a factory in the planning stages, but didn't know where it would be or when it was due to open. And if it was going to be run the way they did business in Korea, we needed to get the word out."

"But weren't you surprised? That someone in the company would come to you?"

He shrugged. "Not exactly. It happens, once in a while. The executives themselves often find they can't live with what they're doing. Not when they see the damage it does. Still, you're right, I didn't put too much stock into that first visit. I asked her to come back the next week to talk some more. I was planning on having someone check her out. Then, by the following week, it was too late."

"Did she have any photographs, any documentation of what she saw there?"

He shook his head. "Nothing she showed me, or told me about. I got the impression she mostly walked around and talked to people. It wasn't a professional investigation. It was more like she was sorting things out for her own conscience. Very unofficial."

"And you didn't trust her? You wanted her checked out?"

Hitch smiled and folded his arms across his chest. "Just a question here and there. Nothing to cause alarm. The Inquisition is long gone, remember?"

"So your spies are everywhere." Helen grinned.

"You never know. There have been other attempts to discredit our work."

"And you never saw her after that?"

"I'm sorry to say that's the case, Helen. I could see then she was very troubled. It looked like she hadn't slept in quite a while, and her clothes were loose on her, like she'd been losing weight. I should have seen something, I guess, but I put it down to her distress about Centurion."

Helen saw a wry smile tug at his face. "I get too caught up in saving the whole world sometimes. I wish I'd seen how bad things were."

"Well, I'm not at all certain she killed herself. Not anymore." Helen placed the newsletter atop the stack on the desk. "I found evidence that she'd gone to Mexico recently. Along with that information I found your phone number. Nothing else, though. No information about the factory, no indication of what exactly she was going to tell you."

"Did she tell someone else?" He leaned forward over the desk, looking alert for the first time since Helen had arrived. "Maybe she handed it on to someone else."

"I don't know. I might find other information, but I wouldn't count on it."

He sighed and tapped restless fingers on the desk. "If only I'd tried to get her to talk! None of this might have happened." A bleak smile played across his haggard face. "I've spent the last fifteen years of my life coming out swinging at everything in sight. It's painful to realize that my eagerness to engage the enemy may have cost that woman her life."

"I don't see how you could have done a thing," Helen said gently.

"No? But that's my job, Helen, to try to do things nobody can be expected to do." He clasped his hands together and looking at her. "Would you keep me informed? As much as you can, without compromising your client? I'd really like to know how this turns out."

"I'm not sure I'll ever be able to prove anything, but maybe I can get some things settled for my client — and for you, too."

"Will we see you at the protest on Friday?" he asked as she stood up and slung her shoulder bag over her arm.

"I hadn't really thought about it. Might be a good idea, especially after what you've told me this evening."

"Bound to be lots of excitement on Friday," he said, getting up to follow her out of the study. "Who knows, I might get on television again."

"Something else for the bishop's file."

"Oh, damn." He stood at the front door, hand on the knob.

"What is it?"

"I forgot. Someone shot out the streetlights a couple of nights ago. Actually, a rather quiet evening, for this neighborhood. Let me grab a flashlight and I'll walk you to your car."

"I'll be okay —"

He cut off her protests. "There's one next door in the church by the front door. Stay right there till I get back," he said, and with that he hurried out the door.

With a sigh — she really was tired and hungry — Helen sat on a hard bench in the front hall and waited. Glancing out the window, she was surprised to see how dark it had gotten.

A couple of cars drove by, boom boxes thudding with increasing resonance, then fading as they slowly cruised down the street. A sharp crack echoed from outside. It was probably just a car backfiring, Helen reasoned, or maybe a rock? A fleeting thought of her car went through her mind, but she forced it back out. She heard a group of people — they sounded like teenagers — arguing and shouting on the sidewalk outside. The shouts turned into laughter as they, too, passed by the church.

Another car drove by with what sounded like an identical pattern of bass thudding. She realized that Father Hitch had been gone for several minutes. Surely it shouldn't take this long to grab the flashlight and come back.

She opened the front door slowly. At least his porch light was working. Bathed in a yellow glow, the house looked even shabbier than it did in daylight. Helen's shoes, the same uncomfortable pumps she'd worn at the memorial, clicked loudly on the concrete slab that covered the front lawn.

The kids — she counted five of them — were standing on the sidewalk in front of the church. It was too dark to see their faces, but she could hear the anger in their voices.

With as blank a face as she could muster, Helen slowly walked to the sidewalk and around the low iron fence separating rectory from church. In order to do so she had to pass right beneath one of the streetlights — a black circle against the silvery evening fog — and right through the knot of angry teenagers.

Complete silence surrounded her. She didn't bother to excuse herself politely — just edged her way carefully past stolid figures that didn't move a muscle, even when she couldn't help brushing against them. One of them, a particularly tall and muscular young woman, muttered something under her breath as Helen walked by.

" 'Scuse you, bitch," somebody said to her back. Hooting laughter followed her all the way to the front of the church.

The church wasn't much bigger than the rectory. Lights burned over the double wooden doors of the entrance, dimmer than the rectory's porch light. The faux Gothic façade of the church presented a wild incongruence to its seedy surroundings. As she got closer to the church, Helen saw that one of the wooden doors was open — a sliver of complete blackness under the faint light.

She went up the stone steps as quietly as she could. She could read the wooden board that announced mass and confession times behind the cracked glass of the display by the entrance. "Father Hitch?" Although she'd tried to speak softly, her words seemed to reverberate inside the old building. "Hitch? Where are you?"

Poised at the top of the stairs, Helen listened intently for a moment. Not a sound came from inside the church.

Her gun. It was in the glove compartment, locked inside

a special miniature strongbox she'd had made especially for her car. She mentally kicked herself for leaving it. She could run back to the house and call the police from there. She was worried about Hitch. She didn't feel right leaving the church until she knew his condition, but getting herself hurt wouldn't help if Hitch was already injured somehow. She turned back around to head for the house.

Suddenly someone grabbed her from behind, pulling her so hard she fell down on the cold hard floor of the vestibule. Her head knocked against something — a table? holy water font? — and for a moment she literally saw brilliantly colored stars, forming and dissolving under her eyelids.

Stunned, trying to catch her breath, she wondered if the kids outside were watching this. Or if they cared. She lay flat for a moment, struggling to think against the pain.

A moment was all it took. Helen felt her arms lifted up over her head by the wrists. Her legs swung out, then straightened as her attacker dragged her across the floor into the church. She felt her clothing rip along her back as her body scraped across an uneven surface. The pain in her head was followed by searing pain in her back, and she could feel blood soaking through the thin fabric.

Just as her assailant started to drop her wrists Helen whipped a leg upward. She didn't care what she hit — she just wanted to slow him down long enough to have a chance to stop him altogether. She knew she must have clipped his crotch, at least, when she heard a sharp cry of pain bellowing out above her. Helen fell back, her head knocking against a pile of something that toppled with a series of thuds onto the floor. Books, maybe. Hymnals.

Before she could roll completely out of the way, she felt his foot slamming into her side. She yelled and, cringing from the pain, forced herself to move. Slithering across the floor in total darkness, she heard someone gasping for air. Helen estimated she'd landed her kick with enough accuracy to give her some time to maneuver. She still had no idea where Hitch was, or if he was all right.

"Bitch!" She heard the word hissed out from in front of her. "I'll fucking rip your fucking head off for that." He was leaning over her, still breathing heavily.

This time she was ready. Before he could hit her again she reached for one of the hymnals she'd knocked down. Her hand, still sore from the cut it had received earlier, closed firmly around the thick book. With a grunt she swung up into the black hole where, judging by his breathing, he hovered over her.

There was a crack, a sound of something splitting, and a sharp yelp of pain. The floor shook when he fell, and Helen managed to move beyond the reach of his legs that kicked wildly in her direction.

When she felt his hand groping for her she slammed another hymnal down on top of it and heard a satisfying crunch. Hopefully she'd broken at least a few bones.

Although he whimpered, he lay still after that. Helen pulled herself up, fighting off further visions of starbursts in her head, and started toward the door. If she could just get to a phone before he got up —

Just then the lights flooded on. Wincing at their brightness, Helen saw him at her feet. The book she'd heaved at his face must have landed right on his nose. Where Howard the bodyguard had recently sported an arrogant grin there was only a bloody pulp of tissue. He was trying to protect what was left of his nose with one hand. The other hand, splayed out against the maroon tiles of the floor, looked worse than his nose.

"Helen?"

She barely recognized the thick voice that sounded from the back of the church. Fortunately, Father Hitch seemed to have come off fairly easily in this confrontation. His glasses — missing one lens entirely, with the other lens cracked in a spider's web of fissures — hung askew on his beaked nose.

The ponytail had been yanked almost completely apart, and his gray-streaked brown hair cascaded over his black shirt.

"My God, Helen! You're hurt!"

"I'll be okay," she said, hoping to convince herself. Slowly, keeping her eyes on Howard the whole time, she eased herself onto the nearest pew. "How about you?"

"I think he must have knocked me out. I don't remember anything after looking for the flashlight. I always keep it here, right by the front door." Father Hitch waved vaguely at the upended table, now knocked over, that had held the hymnals. "Wait —" He rubbed his head and winced as his fingers found a sore spot. "He must have hit the lights, somehow. It was completely dark. Then I came to and heard you up here." A siren wailed in the distance, coming closer. "Cops," Hitch said. "On the way."

"Good. Our friend Howard here's going to have some explaining to do."

"His name is Howard? Who is he, Helen?"

Helen shook her head and immediately regretted it when the spots came back before her eyes.

"Long story," she said. "Tell you later." When Howard made a move as if to get up from the floor, Helen got back to her feet. Under the dull gleam of blood spilled across his shoulders Helen saw that he was wearing the same suit he'd had on at the memorial. She was surprised. It was hard to imagine Drake's not outfitting his bodyguard a little better.

"Come on. You need to sit down."

"Look who's talking."

A trio of black-and-whites screamed up the street to the door. She saw an unmarked, too, pulling right onto the concrete lawn of the rectory, its removable flashing light strobing the dark street with red.

Suddenly the room moved. Helen couldn't figure out if she was looking at the floor or the ceiling. A not unpleasant wave of vertigo swept over her, and she felt a hand on her arm. Her perspective shifted again, and nausea came up behind the dizziness.

"We got injured!" she heard a uniform yell.

Behind him she could see the kids who'd been on the sidewalk. They bunched up in the doorway, pushing past the officer who'd bounded into the church.

"Fuck, that woman beat the shit outta that dude!"

"What, baldie here? No shit."

"You go, bitch."

Hitch laughed weakly. "Take it from me, Helen. You've just earned high honors here."

She tried to smile but it hurt too much. Nursing her swollen face, Helen leaned back in the pew. Then she heard a familiar voice.

"Painting the town red again, Black?" Macabee's red-headed bulk lurched into view for a moment before she faded into oblivion.

Chapter Eleven

Alta Mira Hospital, one of the oldest hospitals in the San Francisco Bay area, was the only medical facility operating in Berkeley and Oakland that was prepared to take in emergency cases. With cutbacks across the board in trauma units, intensive and acute care, and staffing, the sick and injured of three counties had very few options in where to go when they needed medical attention.

Fortunately Helen was spared a long wait when she arrived that night — no doubt due to the presence of uniformed officers in attendance. She sat very still on a gurney wheeled out of the way in a hall, trying not to notice the pain in her head. At least Hitch was not in any immediate danger. The element of surprise seemed to have been a blessing of sorts. Howard was able to completely subdue the priest without rendering a merciless beating, leaving him in much better shape than Helen was.

"You sure you don't want me to wait?" he asked.

Helen studied him. A bandage swathed across one cheekbone and a yellow-purple bump forming over an eye were the only visible signs of injury he bore. "That's really a sickening color on that bruise," she said quietly.

"Alison is on the way and should be here in just a couple of minutes," Hitch went on. "But I think I ought to stay till she gets here."

"She won't be long. Oh — is it okay to leave my car there at the church until tomorrow?" Helen moved around to look at him and immediately regretted turning her head in that direction. She winced and went on, "That must have been a stone I heard hitting the windshield, before I went looking for you. The window's cracked pretty badly."

"Yeah, it looks almost as bad as I do." He rubbed a hand over his forehead, gingerly moving his fingers around the bandage over his right eye. "We'll get it moved into the garage, at least."

"Would you get the hell out of here and go to bed?" Helen said, grimacing as her words rang achingly in the white hallway. Lowering her voice again, she went on, "The entire police department is here looking after me, and Alison will be here in a little while to fuss and fume. I don't need you, too."

He tried to smile but gave up. "Well, if you're sure. I want to hear from you tomorrow, after we've both had a chance to rest. Or maybe I should call you."

"No, I'm not sure where I'll be. Let me call you."

"Home in bed, I hope."

"I can't take on Drake's thugs and you at the same time. Go away, you bother me."

He squeezed her shoulder and started to move away. Helen faded back and forth through pain and befuddlement. The shot given her by the nurse seemed to be taking effect — if the woozy edges the world had just acquired were evidence — and she had to fight hard to resist lying down on the gurney. Against the nurse's protests, however, Helen had insisted on waiting in the hallway, sitting up and at least potentially alert, so that she could see what happened with Howard.

The nurse's broad black face bobbed up and down in her memory. "No skin off my nose," she'd finally sighed, giving up on her entreaties. "Just don't go yelling at me when you slide right down onto the floor, all right?"

Alison's face melded for a moment with the image of the nurse, then Helen realized that Alison was actually standing right in front of her. "Jesus Christ, Helen, what did he do to you?"

"He beat me up." Helen gripped the sides of the gurney. Alison's appearance brought with it such a sense of relief that it almost overpowered her. Helen heard her voice thicken as she talked, and she wasn't sure how much longer she could keep sitting up and talking.

"No shit." Alison fumbled at her side for a moment, trying to support her and hold her without causing pain. "What did the doctors say?"

"Took some X-rays, told me they didn't think I had a concussion but needed to watch." Helen started to relax against Alison but pushed herself upright again. "Said I could go home but come back in a couple of days for more X-rays."

"So let's get going." Alison waited, then stood with hands on hips, watching her. "I'll get a nurse or someone to help us."

"No, not yet." Helen didn't even try to shake her head, but she waved one hand at Alison in a negative gesture. "I want to see what goes down with my buddy Howard."

Alison perched on the gurney beside her. "I don't suppose there's any point in trying to change your mind."

"None at all. Did Hitch tell you what happened?"

"Some of it. He didn't sound too good himself. Is he still here?" Alison craned her neck and looked up and down the hallway.

"I sent him home. I forgot, you haven't met him. This guy — I only know his first name is Howard, and he shows up with Drake everywhere —"

An angry voice from somewhere to Helen's right rang through the hall. Recognizing its rasp, Helen turned, cursed at the pain in her head and her side, and slowly moved to get up.

"Here." Alison took her by the arm.

"I just need to get down by the nurses' station. They're all standing over there." As if through a long tunnel Helen saw the red flare of Macabee's enraged countenance. He stood looming over the diminutive figure of Richard Drake, whose pale face had bleached even paler since Helen saw him last.

"Yes, I know all about his history," Drake was saying, the Southern accent even more pronounced as he fought to control his temper. "I'm a firm believer in giving a man a second chance. He's had no trouble since his parole ended over two years ago. I have no doubt that this is all a terrible mistake."

"Oh, really?" Macabee glanced in Helen's direction. "Maybe he thought he was swatting a fly when he took a swing at her head. Then he must have felt the need to stomp on it, as well."

Drake swiveled and looked at Helen with a cold stare, then turned back to Macabee. "You might ask her what she was doing with that instigator at the church. Those two probably provoked a fight, and Howard was forced to defend himself —"

Macabee shook his head. His ruddy complexion burned

with anger. "Well, I think Howard Mitchum is going to have to start defending his innocent little ass pretty soon, because there'll be a lot of guys in his cellblock who'd like a piece of it."

Drake stiffened and pulled his suit jacket tighter. "You'll be hearing from my attorney shortly. I hope that you and the Oakland police are prepared for a very painful experience."

Helen leaned against the counter of the nurses' station. Neither Macabee nor Drake had spoken a word directly to her yet. Alison hovered nearby, but she took a step back and watched the scene unfold.

"Told you, Mac." Helen managed to get the words croaked out, and Drake closed his eyes. Now that she was standing closer, she could see his pallor went beyond exhaustion. For the first time Helen wondered if he was seriously ill.

Drake walked over to her, ignoring Macabee as if he weren't standing there glaring, and Helen felt his papery dry hand on her own. "I'm so sorry, my dear," he murmured. "This has all been a dreadful misunderstanding. I just know that we can sit down like civilized people and get it all worked out satisfactorily. In fact," he said as he pulled out a small electronic notebook, "I'm prepared right now to set up a meeting with yourself and Father Hitchcock, so that —"

"Misunderstanding?" Despite the throbbing in her head, Helen could feel her mouth trying to smile. "You mean, Howard misunderstood your orders to keep an eye on me? Took things a little too far on his own." Raising her voice had been a mistake. Alison darted to her side, pulling a chair behind her. Helen sank down gratefully, slowly. "Maybe you've been having him keep on eye on Hitch, too. I guess getting the both of us together just overwhelmed his poor little addled brain, didn't it?"

"Now, Helen, let's not be too judgmental." Macabee

came to stand beside her, pulling a notebook from his pocket and leafing through its pages. "I'd say that Mitchum showed considerable restraint, seeing that his priors were all for rape, along with assault and battery."

Drake snapped his electronic notebook shut and slid it back inside his jacket. "There's no point in trying to be reasonable with y'all." He sighed. "You leave me no choice but to pursue legal channels." With a crooked smile he bowed slightly towards Helen. "I'm very sorry, my dear, that we haven't yet reached an understanding. Perhaps in a day or two I'll have my attorney give you a call."

"You mean, maybe I'll take some money and shut up and go away like a good little girl? Like Tina Merrick did?" Helen pushed herself up out of the chair, ignoring the alarms going off all over her body as she did so. "I think you'll find I'm very different from Tina."

"Is that so?" Drake's cheeks reddened — one small spot beneath each eye — which only emphasized the pale parchment look of his face. He stood up straight. "You know, the sages have all been wrong about death being the great equalizer, Ms. Black. The only thing in this wicked world of ours that puts all of us on the same level is money."

"Careful, Drake." Macabee rubbed his head with a pudgy hand and sighed. "You don't have Howard out here with you now, and there's witnesses who heard you talk about money to a cop."

"Guess it worked all right for you in Mexico, then, didn't it?" Helen spat out. The muscle relaxers and painkillers were giving her an edge of bravado she would have ignored under normal circumstances — but getting beaten up by the employee of the man who now stood calmly before her didn't seem to count as ordinary. "Just give the right people a bit of the profits and no one gives a shit. That's how it works, right? Same as in Korea. Of course, the poor girls who work in the factories don't see any money, but they don't matter. They never have, and never will."

In a fog of drug-induced euphoria, Helen barely realized that Drake had silently walked away while she was still talking. It wasn't until she was being helped into the car by Alison that she realized that Alison and Macabee were having quite a friendly conversation without her.

"Well, of course I get back to Orinda to visit my family," Alison was saying as she shut Helen's door and walked around her car to the driver's side. "But my life is pretty much focused out here these days."

"That's good. Brand new start on things, after what happened a couple of years ago," Macabee said.

"Well, the one good thing from it — I met Helen."

Helen didn't hear Macabee respond to that comment since Alison shut her own door and started the car. Easing her head back onto the cushioned headrest, Helen saw Macaque's round face peering in her window. He gestured with his hand, and Alison rolled Helen's window down with the control switch in her armrest.

He rested his hands on the open window, and Helen got a whiff of cigarettes from his clothes. "You going to be able to get to the station tomorrow? We'll be bringing Mitchum over a.s.a.p. and we'll need that statement. If not, someone can come over and take it."

Helen made one last extreme effort — it was getting harder and harder to talk as the drugs and the aftermath of the fight washed over her — and said, "I think I can get in there under my own steam."

"Don't worry, I'll keep an eye on her for you."

"Hey, Mac, hold on." He turned back around and leaned into her window again. "How the hell did you get the word on what was going down at the church? I thought the whole Merrick issue was closed shut."

"It is." He grinned and fished a pack of cigarettes out of his coat. "I just keep my eyes and ears open. When I heard where this was happening, I talked my way in for a ride."

"Glad you could make it."

The rest of the night was a complete blank for Helen. She woke after a deep and completely dreamless sleep — a blank stretch of time that lasted for almost twelve hours. What woke her was a piercing shriek that thrust her up out of unconsciousness with a painful jolt. She sat up quickly — too quickly — and felt the now-familiar throb return to her head. Still, the pain had lessened since the previous night, and she was incredibly thirsty. The shriek dissolved into the whine of her pager as her vision cleared. Where the hell was it? She struggled out of a tangle of sheets and fumbled through the pile of clothing on top of the trunk at the foot of the bed. When she stopped the beeping, Helen focused blurred eyes onto the completely unfamiliar number that flashed red on the pager.

Damn, where was she? It took a moment to register that she was in Alison's bedroom. Turning slowly around the room, gathering up clothes, Helen saw the readout on the digital clock beside the bed. Twelve o'clock — obviously, judging from the daylight streaming across the room, twelve noon. "Fuck," Helen muttered. She'd slept all morning and still had to make a statement for the police. "There goes Thursday."

She found a pen and notepad next to the clock and wrote down the number on her pager. Before she called, she needed a shower.

Helen positioned herself carefully under the stream of warm water, avoiding splashing the cuts on her head. The heat helped to ease some of the ache in her side, and by the time she emerged and got into Alison's bathrobe, she was beginning to feel human again.

The note Alison had taped to the bathroom mirror curled at the edges from the steam that puffed out of the shower stall. "Hi sweetheart," it read. "There's plenty of coffee and breakfast stuff in the kitchen, so make yourself at home. I don't want you to drive yourself, so I'm taking the afternoon off so we can go to the police station together. Call me at the office when you get up. Lots of love, A."

First, though — who'd paged her? Taking Alison's note with her, Helen went to the kitchen. She called the number while coffee brewed.

"Berkeley Free Clinic."

Helen sat up straight, surprised and pleased. "Kim Farraday, please."

Kim was hurried and harried. "I can only spare a minute," she said breathlessly. "We've got a bit of a crisis here — overflowing today —"

"Anything at all, Kim."

"Well —" Helen could hear shouts in the background, and something metallic at the clinic fell down with a clatter. "For what it's worth, Amelia came in here just before lunchtime."

"She's not still there?"

"No. I talked to her for just a moment, then she slipped away. What? No, I'll see them in room number one. Sorry, Helen, I have people waiting for me."

"She didn't say anything about where she was going?"

Kim sighed. "I don't know what this means, but she said she was going home."

"Home?"

"That's all. Said she was tired and going home."

Helen sighed. "Kim, thanks. I appreciate your time."

"Hope it's a help to you. Gotta go."

Helen dialed Alison's work number while she drank her first cup of coffee. "Well, do you know when she'll be out of the meeting? No? Okay, could you just let her know Helen called? Right, thanks."

Taking her second cup into the bedroom, Helen dug her bag out from under the clothes. She hoped she could fit into something from Alison's closet. Her own clothes were torn and bloody from the fight last night. Thank God she'd had the presence of mind last night to insist that Alison get the envelope from her car before they went to the hospital. Surely there was a receipt or form or something that had a return address on it.

She finally found what she was looking for on the tattered remains of an envelope. Helen couldn't tell what the envelope had contained — the return address had been smudged and ripped in half, and the rest of the envelope was smeared as if it had been plunged into mud and run over by a fleet of trucks. Even the name of the addressee was missing. Still, there was a street address. Helen wrote it down. It was in Oakland, a street that ran off of Lake Merritt behind the Grand Lake Theater. She knew there were rows of relatively inexpensive apartments, largely inhabited by lesbians, clustered in that neighborhood.

Helen was happily surprised to find she could fit into a pair of Alison's jeans. They were a little long, but she decided that they wouldn't look too bad with the cuffs rolled up. And had she left her sandals here last weekend? Yes, there they were, tucked into the front closet. A T-shirt completed her attire, and Helen took a quick glance in the bathroom mirror. She couldn't believe that she showed as little bruising as she did. Her side still felt like hell, but fortunately that nasty bruise was covered by clothing. Beyond looking as though she hadn't slept for a couple of weeks, and that ugly cut on her right cheek, she didn't look too bad.

The phone rang while she was still in the bathroom. Helen waited for the message machine to click on and run through its recording. "Helen? Are you there? It's Alison."

Damn. She was supposed to be at the police station. She picked up. "Hi, honey. Listen — could you do me a favor? Could you call Macabee and let him know I won't get over there until about" — it was one o'clock now — "maybe about four this afternoon?"

Helen's heart sank at the silence on the other end. "What's going on, Helen?" Alison finally asked.

"I have to be somewhere."

"Look, you have to tell me. I'm not going to let you run around town and get yourself beat up again, or maybe worse." Helen was taken aback by the tremor in Alison's voice. "Talk to me. Now."

Reluctantly, with one eye on her watch, Helen related the gist of Kim Farraday's call. "This may be my only chance to talk to Amelia Wainright. I can't pass it by."

"Oh, Helen. There's no way I can stop you, is there?"

"I don't think so." Jesus, what did Alison want? For Helen to sit around on her ass and let the case slip through her fingers? And then be forced to shut down her office? Helen tried to get a grip on her emotions.

Again a long silence. Then, "I'll be there in five minutes. I'll take you there to see her — if that's where she really is — and then we go to the police station. Agreed?"

"Agreed." Helen hung up, trying to calculate. Amelia had appeared at the clinic around noon, a few minutes before. She'd have to work her way from downtown Berkeley into Oakland using her feet, public transit, or — if she was incredibly lucky — a ride from someone. The last possibility, though, was remote. More than likely it would be a combination of buses and walking that would get her over to the lake. Assuming, of course, that the address Helen had deciphered on the envelope was indeed Amelia's "home."

She didn't have to wait long for Alison. "Did you break every single traffic law on the books to get here so fast?"

Alison was rigid with anger, her hands clenched so tight on the steering wheel that her knuckles were white. "Don't even ask me why I'm doing this, okay? I'm here, and I'm sticking with you the rest of the day."

Helen nodded. "Okay, I won't. But thanks."

"You're welcome. Tell me where I'm going."

They drove into Oakland on Telegraph Avenue, with Alison talking the whole way. "And this address is where Leslie used to live? Is that it?"

Helen shrugged. Her head was beginning to ache, and she realized she hadn't eaten yet that day. "I hope so. It's the only address in the whole mess I could find that didn't look like a commercial location."

Alison sighed. "Well, we should find out soon enough." They were driving by Lake Merritt now. The sunlight reflected off the water in bright shafts. Helen realized she'd left her sunglasses in her own car. She leaned her head back and closed her eyes.

Alison turned left and Helen opened her eyes. The apartment buildings were one of a kind around the lake — no two alike, and all of them crumbling at the edges. Years ago, when Helen had first fled to California from Mississippi, she'd dated a girl who lived in one of these buildings. After the tree-lined backroads and country lanes of the deep South, Helen had initially been charmed by the quaint look of pastel-tinted Victorians and oddly shaped homes — charmed, that is, until she'd seen the roaches that shared the apartment, rent-free, with her girlfriend. Alison slowed down, earning a couple of curses from other drivers. A utility truck, effervescing the unmistakable odor of garbage, blocked the way, and Alison muttered a few curses herself as she wove between a pair of garbage handlers who swung a dumpster around in the street as if they were performing a pas de trois. Finally she pulled to a halt.

"This must be it. Eighteen-oh-two."

"Can you park close by?" Fortunately most of the residents in the area must have gone to work for the day, and there were plenty of empty spaces. The garbage truck, however, pulled up right beside them just as Alison turned off the engine.

"Now what?"

As if in answer to her question, Helen heard an argument coming from the direction of the trash hauler.

"I told you, bitch, get out the way!"

"I live here. I have a right to be here."

Headache forgotten, Helen got quickly out of the car. Pushing her way past the garbage haulers, she looked into the face of Amelia Wainright.

Chapter Twelve

"I don't know what you're talking about. I moved in here three months ago, and the place was completely clean." The woman who'd answered the door refused to let Helen in. She stood, arms folded across ample chest, and glared up at Helen. Her hair was tucked up under a bandanna, and the stains on her sweat pants — not to mention the pungent odor of pine-scented cleaner — told Helen that she'd interrupted her during housekeeping chores. "I wouldn't have moved in unless it was spotless. You can take it from me, nothing was here from the previous tenant."

Helen nodded and sighed. She was sure that her own

bruised appearance did nothing to help her in trying to set foot inside the apartment. With a final thanks, Helen turned and went back down the corridor of the apartment building. She could feel the other woman's glare burning holes into her back with every step of the way. As Helen passed by the bank of windows next to the elevator, she glanced down into the street below. Alison and Amelia were still standing next to Alison's car, waiting for her to get back downstairs.

"Well? Anything?"

"Nope." Helen held open the back door on the passenger side of the car and motioned for Amelia to get in. She avoided Alison's gaze as she shepherded the woman in brown into the back seat. After shutting the door gently, Helen leaned against the top of the car and looked across to Alison.

"And just what the hell am I supposed to do with her now?" Helen hissed in an angry whisper. "You should have stayed at work. That would have been easier all around."

"Oh, and it would be perfectly all right for you to ask her a lot of questions and then dump her back out on the street, I suppose?" Alison stared at her in amazement.

Helen snorted. "Obviously you haven't lived out here in the 'hood too long. Start feeling sorry for these people and you end up getting nailed. And I speak from personal experience."

"Look, we're headed straight for the police station, right? We'll take her there, round up social services, get her at least to a shelter. We can't just leave her here, can we?"

Helen sighed, leaned her head down on her arm. "You're right. We can't. I don't have to be happy about it, though."

Alison started to respond, but before Helen could answer Alison had gotten into the drivers' seat and revved the engine. Helen slowly maneuvered her aching body into the passenger seat, and Alison put the car into gear.

That was the moment Amelia chose to make a run for

162

it. It happened so fast that Helen, already groggy from the events of the night before, wasn't able to react in time to stop her. There was a rustle of clothing, the slap of a seatbelt hitting the door, and Amelia was gone. The car door swung back and forth behind her, then slammed shut under the power of Amelia's thrust.

"Fuck!" Helen forced her sore muscles into action, ignoring Alison's exclamation. She knew she would pay for this later — both physically, with her overstressed body, and with Alison. Right now, though, she couldn't let Amelia get away.

Helen could feel shooting pains in her side and increased throbbing in her head as she pounded down the street. There was a smudge of brown at the side of the building, then nothing. Helen rounded the corner of the building and saw only an empty alleyway, littered with the usual urban rubbish of papers and bottles and cans. The ripe smell slapped her like a huge open palm in the face.

"Amelia? Amelia, please come out, now."

This was ridiculous. Helen turned at the sound of running that closed in behind her and saw Alison there, leaning against the building, panting and red-faced. "You probably just fucked up what remained of your health with that little jog," Alison managed to get out.

Helen scanned the alley again. "I saw her run in here, I know I did."

She took a couple of cautious steps deeper into the alley. The sunlight was cut off by the tall buildings on either side. Foul-smelling refuse heaps were piled haphazardly against the stained concrete walls, and it was difficult to make out anything in the stinking murk. Something glinted in the weak shaft of light that wavered through an abandoned shopping cart upended at the blank wall closing off the alley.

Helen darted forward. "Amelia, I know you're under there. Come on, now, come out and let's get away from here, okay?" Maybe behind the cart, she thought. It was so hard to see, and the cart was layered with grime.

There was no warning at all before the shopping cart flew up at her. Helen was able to ward it off, but she wrenched her side and was unable to suppress a groan. "Alison, stop her! She's right behind me!"

"As if I could miss her!" Alison yelled. Helen leaned against the wall and picked her way past the cart. At the mouth of the alley she could see the two figures. Alison had Amelia's arms pinned behind her back in a tight grip.

"Where the hell did you learn to do that?" Helen asked, her breath coming back as the pain began to ease.

"Oh, you know. Movies, television. My big bad butch detective girlfriend." Alison let up on her grip as Helen stood in front of Amelia. The woman in brown was crying, huge tears streaking through the dirt on her face in webbed tracks.

"This is what slowed her down." Alison let go with one hand and held up a plastic trash bag. Here and there on its gray filmy surface holes poked through, exposing unidentifiable bits of Amelia's shriveled life.

Amelia's silent tears turned into loud sobs as Helen took the bag from Alison. "This is your stuff, isn't it? No, don't worry. I'm just going to hold it for you. Okay? Promise."

Helen talked quietly to Amelia the whole way to the police station. Alison drove in stony silence, her gaze fixed on weaving through the downtown traffic. She finally asked Helen about going back to the hospital for a check-up.

"Right now, I just want to get finished with the statement and go home, Alison." Helen turned her aching head around from staring into the back seat, where Amelia continued to weep. The plastic bag rustled in her lap, and something near the bottom had pierced through and was sticking her leg painfully. "I'll get back to the hospital in the morning, before the demonstration."

164

"Demonstration? You mean, the one PAN is putting on at Centurion?"

"Right." Helen glanced over at her, then looked away quickly again. Perhaps Alison was just postponing the argument Helen expected to erupt the moment they got back home. Whatever the reason, Helen was grateful that for the moment she didn't have to talk about it.

Her gratitude faded as they went farther downtown. "Helen, we have to figure out something to do with her," Alison murmured.

"Like what? You're not asking her to be your new roommate, right?"

"You don't have to be so sarcastic." Her voice sounded soft and weak and she refused to look at Helen.

"Alison, if you're going on a one-woman crusade here, be my guest. Just don't expect me to carry a banner for you, okay?"

Alison didn't respond. They'd reached the station, so Helen focused her attention back on Amelia, hoping they wouldn't go through another chase scene. But the fact that Helen had a firm grip on the trash bag seemed to keep Amelia docile — whether from trust or from fear that Helen wouldn't release her treasures, Helen could not tell.

Positioned close to one of the ugliest freeways in the state of California, the downtown police station rose like a gritty gray wart among the brightly colored storefronts of Oakland's Chinatown. The overpass of the freeway lurched above, and just beyond it, at the end of Broadway, lay Jack London Square. Recently renovated into an upscale community of shops and restaurants, the area presented a safely enclosed haven, away from the dirt and desolation of urban blight nearby.

"Well! Haven't seen you here in a while, Amelia." The officer on duty at the front counter, a big man whose paunch swung over his belt, looked up with grim surprise. The gum he vigorously chewed snapped between his teeth.

"Looks like you found a couple friends out there, didn't you?"

"I'm here to see Lieutenant Macabee. Where can I find him?" Helen felt Alison staying close behind her, and she remembered that Alison's only memories of police stations were associated with her abusive husband and of that husband's death. "And we need to call social services, to find some help for Amelia."

"Oh, 'we' do, do we?" The gum snapped and popped ferociously as the big belly heaved out from behind the counter. "Well, why don't 'we' just park Amelia over there on that bench while I see if I can find the lieutenant?" He crouched down on his heels in front of Amelia. "Looking a little worse for the wear these days, Amelia." After peering at her with a blank expression, he stood up and sauntered back to the counter. Helen heard him mutter something under his breath about how Amelia smelled almost as bad as she looked, then his pudgy fingers punched at numbers on the phone.

"Jesus, Helen, how long is this going to take?" Alison looked small and frail, huddled against the beige concrete wall next to where Amelia sat.

Her head ached uncontrollably, and for a moment the scruffy wooden bench swam and danced before her eyes. "I don't know, honey. Not long, if Macaque's here."

"Helen, I want to go in with you."

"No, you need to stay with Amelia. She might run away again." Feeling a sudden stab of nausea, Helen slid down onto the bench next to the weeping woman.

Without a word Alison took the plastic bag away from Helen's weakened grip. "I doubt it — not while I'm holding this." She sighed and knelt on the floor before both women, her eyes turned to Amelia. "Okay, I'm holding the bag for you now. See? I'm going to hold onto it for a while. I promise to take care of it. Can you understand me?"

To Helen's amazement, Amelia nodded. The tears had subsided into sniffles. What the hell had happened? Helen wondered, despite the ringing pain behind her eyes. Perhaps being in the unfortunately familiar surroundings of the police station felt as much like home as anything else in her life. After all, the oaf at the front desk had recognized her. Maybe Amelia was accustomed to, even comfortable with, the fact that she knew what to expect — not like when Helen and Alison had forced her into the car, she realized with a twinge of guilt.

And the guilt went painfully deep. Since when had Helen herself been so callous? Sure, she could use the excuse that she was just burned out — burned out from her days as a cop, from her work on the streets as a private investigator, burned out from a string of stormy relationships. Staring at the terrified face of Amelia Wainright, through the layers of dirt caked on her skin, Helen wondered if her own mental and moral exhaustion were a prelude to something worse — to breaking the way Amelia had apparently broken. Given those thoughts, she was immensely relieved to see Macabee trundling toward them down the hall.

"Who's your new friend?" Helen had no doubt that the lit cigarette poised between Macabee's fingers was entirely against all the rules. He took a deep drag, turned his face away to blow out smoke, and peered at Amelia with curiosity.

"Long story. What's up with my buddy Howard Mitchum?"

He glanced over at the desk officer, who with a carefully blank countenance reached for the phone. "You're calling social services right now. Am I right?" Macabee asked, then steered Helen down the hall by her elbow. He paused as she winced. "Sure you're up to this?"

"Let's get it over with." Macabee nodded a greeting to

Alison, still holding Amelia's plastic bag, as she took a couple of uncertain steps behind them. "As you can see, I brought moral support with me."

"More the merrier. You'll have to wait outside the room, but you can see in through the window, okay?"

"I just — I just don't want her sitting in there too long."

"No problem." As they went slowly down the hall to the room Macabee had commandeered for the occasion, he related the events of the morning. "Except for that wounded pride of his, Mitchum survived the night quite well," he said. "He's even now enjoying the hospitality of the city of Oakland downstairs, as we speak. Your charges will make sure he gets an extended visit."

"And Hitch? Did he come in?"

"Been and gone."

Helen knew she had to reserve all her energies for the simple task of speech. She was irritated at how lightheaded she felt as Macabee prompted her through the procedure, but she refused his offer to finish up the following day. "No, let's get it over with." An entire century surely must have passed by the time she finally signed papers with a hand shaking the pen all over the paper.

"No, it's only just past five-thirty," Alison answered her question.

"What? I could have sworn it took us a couple of years in there. Jesus, I have a headache."

"Not only do you need to rest, I'm positive you haven't eaten since last night, either."

"Just coffee this morning."

"I knew it." Helen heard the plastic bag crinkle as Alison shifted it. "Where's Amelia?"

"Probably sitting right where we left her. Or maybe a social worker got here." They followed Macabee down the hall to the front desk. By the time they caught up with him he was speaking to the officer.

He must have inserted a fresh stick of gum since Helen had seen him last — this one didn't seem to pop between his teeth as much. "No, sir, I did call. Right when you left with them over there," he was saying, gesturing toward Alison and Helen.

"So where did they go?"

"Excuse me. I got a call from you people?" The nameplate pinned to her jacket flashed in the bright fluorescent light. Helen couldn't see the name etched on it, but the words *Social Services* were lettered beneath in black. She was tall and black, her long braids coiled on top of her head. Her expression was one of exasperation and tiredness. "You had someone here for me to see?"

The gum finally snapped, loudly, as the desk clerk said, "Well, uh, she's not here now."

"What?" Helen woke up with a painful start. "What are you talking about?" Refusing Alison's help, pushed through a knot of by the bench. Amelia was nowhere to be seen.

"Damnit." Alison hurried to her side. "I should have stayed here, after all."

"Shit. No, no, sweetheart, don't beat yourself up about it. I'm pretty sure she didn't really want the attentions of people wearing badges and uniforms, anyway."

"But, I was sure, since I was holding this . . ." Alison's voice trailed off. The uniforms made a path for them back to the front desk, then moved together again, shutting out all view of the bench.

The social worker, a clipboard tucked under one arm, rolled her eyes heavenward. "In other words," she said to the desk officer, "I wasted my time coming down here."

"Come on, Alison. Let's get the fuck out of here. Macabee, I'll talk to you later."

"Prob'ly see you tomorrow," he said, reaching into his pocket for a cigarette while the desk officer submitted, red-faced, to a harangue from the social worker.

Once they were back in Alison's car, Helen let herself

relax again. "Just like the old days." She sighed. "Thank God those are done."

"You worked for Berkeley, though, not Oakland, right?"

"I think it's the same everywhere you go." Without opening her eyes or lifting up from the headrest, Helen reached over to touch Alison. "I haven't even said thank you yet. Thank you, thank you, thank you."

"Oh, well, I had the whole afternoon off. I would have just been bored, sitting around, you know?"

Helen could hear the undertone of nerves in her lover's voice. She looked over at Alison, noting again the clean lines of her pale face, the green eyes that shone, even in this dimness, the way her hair kept falling into her eyes. "This is where it's always gotten tough, in the past. This is where the people who care about me have a hard time letting me do my job."

"You mean like Frieda." Alison made the reference to Helen's ex-lover of several years lightly, although Helen often wondered what Alison thought of Frieda. "Is that really what broke you two up? Your work?"

"I'd be lying if I said it didn't play a part." Helen looked back out onto Broadway. "How much of that was because I shut her out of it, well, it's hard to say."

"How about letting me in? For a change, I mean." They stopped at a red light and Alison looked at her. In the diminishing light, Helen couldn't see her expression. "Don't shut me out, Helen. I want to know what's going on. I might not always like it, but I do want to understand it." Alison's gentle touch on her hand turned into a caress that moved along her wrist, her arm, then softly stroked her cheek. Behind them, the blares of car horns sounded and Alison moved away and put the car back in gear. Watching Alison's hands on the wheel, Helen felt a wave of panic sweep over her. It scared her, to give up control even to the small extent that Alison was driving her around, Alison had taken charge of Amelia, Alison made sure that Helen got to her appointments. It felt so wrong, so uncomfortable, that she immediately flashed on an image of herself opening the car door and walking off down the busy streets of Berkeley — leaving Alison behind. At that moment the traffic light overhead switched from red to green.

"Fine detective I'm going to make — not even watching to see when the traffic lights change."

"Tell you what. Pick up some dinner for us and I'll talk about the case while we eat. Although I feel like I could sleep for a month, I'm also starving. Deal?"

"Fair enough." Alison turned off Broadway and they sped along a side street to a take-out restaurant close to Alison's apartment building. Helen waited in the car, willing the pain in her head to subside. Fortunately the delicious aroma of greasy fried chicken and even greasier French fries seemed to do wonders for her aches and pains.

She heard Alison chuckle. "It's not exactly like Nancy Drew, is it? Of course, you're kind of like the boyish sidekick — what was her name?"

Helen smiled, then grimaced. Damn, it hurt even to smile, let alone laugh. "Sidekick? Pardon me, but I'm the one with the expensive business cards and dingy little office with my name on the door."

"Yeah, you look pretty important right now." Alison was quiet for a moment then said, "Poor Amelia. We shouldn't be laughing."

Helen opened her eyes again. The sun was starting to go down, and cars were turning their headlights on. "Like I said, she left because she wanted to. I have a feeling she'll turn up again. They seem to know her, at the police station."

"That reminds me —" Alison steered with one hand and rummaged in the seat behind her with the other. "I still have the bag."

"Let me see." Helen took it gingerly, remembering how something sharp had sliced through the bottom. There was still enough light of day to illuminate the contents as she cautiously sifted through them, but it was too much to grapple with fried chicken and the bag at once.

"All right, hotshot, let's go on inside."

As they rode up the elevator, Helen bit into a drumstick she'd grabbed from the carton.

"Now, this is what I like — a girlfriend in bandages, covered with chicken grease."

"I knew you were kinky." They kissed just as the doors opened. "Just think, maybe your parents stopped by for a visit."

"Well, you and Mom are old friends now. Here, give me that." She took cartons of food from Helen as they got inside. "I'll grab some plates."

The relief that flooded over Helen was so intense it threatened to overwhelm her. To be safe inside, in a warm, clean home, with a wonderful woman she loved and food on the way — it was a painful contrast to the harsh reality she imagined to be Amelia's day-to-day life. Helen lifted the trash bag from the floor beside her. Yesterday's newspaper was still on the coffee table — that would do nicely.

"What are you doing?" Alison asked, putting plates on the coffee table.

Helen looked up. "Going over the case with you, and going over Amelia's things at the same time."

"Oh." Alison curled up beside her, watching but not interfering, while Helen spread out the contents of Amelia's bag over the sheets of the newspaper she'd spread out on the floor. "How about if we eat first? Then I'll help you."

"Well . . ." Helen relented and got up to wash her hands. "You know, sidekicks — even really cute ones like you — they don't get paid much."

"Is that so? As soon as that bandage comes off your face we can talk about what you can pay me with. Go wash your hands and get your butt back in here quick."

But when Helen got back, Alison seemed to have forgotten her. "Hey. Hello. Dinner? Fried chicken?"

"Sorry. I was just looking — here, take a look at this." Alison sat cross-legged on the floor, surrounded by Amelia's belongings. "This might be important."

Helen took up the much-creased and dirty piece of paper folded into a tiny, bulky square. Cautiously she opened up its folds. Settling down on the sofa she began to read.

Chapter Thirteen

" 'And so, even though I don't know for certain if you'll ever read this letter, I feel I have to give you something, Amelia, something that may really make sense to you one day. Maybe you'll hold onto it and be able to understand. I did everything possible, sweetheart. But when you started refusing your medication, things just kept getting worse and worse. I couldn't live with you any longer, not with the nights spent looking for you all over town, the days spent trying to persuade you to come home with me, the hours of crying myself to exhaustion because you were somewhere I couldn't reach, no matter how much I loved you.' "

"So that was where they lived together, then? In that building where we found her?"

Helen shrugged and carefully got down on the floor beside Alison. For the moment, hungry as she was, the food was forgotten. "I guess so. From this letter, it sounds like Amelia was slipping into mental problems all along." She picked up the letter again. " 'I hope one day you'll forgive me for doing what must seem like desertion. But it's the only way I could think of to manage. I couldn't leave you on the streets, and I couldn't stop my life completely to take care of you. So the program at the hospital seems like the best compromise. I've talked to the nurses there, and I think it will be good for you to be under their supervision. They'll keep track of your meds, and then when things settle down we'll work out some sort of job for you. We might even be able to get you your old job back. I know you'd love that!' She must mean the accounting business." Helen told Alison about the old business card Amelia had put up in the clinic.

"Then what happened?" Alison asked, moving closer. "If Leslie got her into some kind of program or something, and she was getting the medication she needed, how did she end up on the streets?"

"An out-patient program like the one Leslie describes, where Amelia could get all the supervision and personal care she needs, costs money. Hospitals are run just like big business, these days."

"You mean they just kicked her out? Like that?" Alison turned away, shocked. "But Amelia needs help."

"There might've been cutbacks, or maybe Amelia just walked away. She's an adult. They can't make her stay. I wonder what hospital? Maybe Kim, that woman at the clinic, would know." Helen picked up the letter. " 'So, sweet Amelia, until I can get it worked out where we can be together, which really shouldn't be too much longer, I'm going to move back in with my mother. Honestly, it'll just be a couple of months at most. I'm going to take that trip, remember, the one we talked about? Then as soon as I come back and sort things out at work I'll come and get you and we'll take care of everything. I promise you, with all my heart and all my love, everything is going to be fine.' " She paused. "Yeah, and then she gets thrown out a window."

"You're sure of that now? That it was murder, not suicide?"

Helen shook her head. "No, I'm not sure. But everything except the death itself points away from suicide. I mean, listen." Helen gestured to the letter. "She's talking about the long term here, isn't she? About the move to her mother's house being temporary, a stop-gap until she could — what did she say?" Helen went back to the letter and scanned its lines until she found what she wanted. "Here. She says, 'As soon as I come back and sort things out at work I'll come and get you.' " She refolded the letter and set it down with the other odds and ends of Amelia's life. "Now, does that sound like someone who wants to commit suicide?"

Alison remained silent as Helen described the arrangement of Leslie's office to her. "But, Helen," she finally protested, "things can change. Really fast. Look at my life. Believe me, suicide had been a thought, from time to time, for me, too." Alison picked up a stack of envelopes held together with a rubber band. "And look at all these. They're addressed to Leslie Merrick, at the apartment in Oakland."

"What are they?"

Alison slipped off the rubber band. "A mixed bunch. Some letters, a couple of bills, and this one's a come-on from one of those credit card companies that promise you the world." She tore an envelope open and perused the contents. After a moment she said, "This letter is from an old college friend. She's wondering why Leslie never

176

answers her calls or checks her e-mail anymore." She turned the page over. "Jesus. It's dated six months ago."

Helen opened another letter. "Same kind of thing here, too," she said. "Someone she used to work with who wonders what the hell is going on."

"So Leslie wasn't reading her mail or returning calls. She wasn't even paying some of her bills." Alison turned a puzzled face to Helen. "What the hell was going on?"

"I think that Amelia was becoming all of Leslie's world," Helen said, gathering up the letters and bills into a stack. "Tina said it, when we were leaving the memorial service. She said that Leslie gave up her family and friends to take care of Amelia."

Alison sighed. "Cutting yourself off from life is the worst thing anyone can do. I was acting the same way when my husband — when the abuse started. The isolation just made everything worse. That's when putting an end to my life began to look like a good idea."

Helen touched Alison's face. "I'm glad I came along when I did, then."

"Me, too." Alison held her hand briefly, then scrambled up from the floor. "Listen, let's get the food on the table, and we can go through the rest of her stuff later."

Helen followed her into the small dining area. "We'll have to try to figure out where Amelia is and get her back to wherever her program was — maybe Alta Mira. Kim might know."

"We?" Alison turned, her hands full of food cartons. "Did I hear you say *we*?"

Helen froze at the side of the table. "Unless you don't want to."

Alison set down cartons and came around beside her. "It isn't that."

"Then what?"

"Come on, sit down." She pushed gently at Helen's shoulders, then opened up cartons. Hesitantly, she said, "I know how hard it is for you to — to let people get close to you. I think I know at least some of the reasons things didn't work between you and Frieda."

Helen stiffened. "Go ahead," she said, spooning cole slaw onto her plate.

Alison sighed, ignoring the food. "No, I'm fine. You go ahead and eat, and let me talk for a couple of minutes. Deal?"

Helen nodded, taking a bite of chicken.

Alison folded her hands on the table, looking fixedly at her enlaced fingers. "Here goes. I know that Frieda was never happy about your decision to start up your business, that she kept hoping you'd give up the idea sooner or later. And I have to say I understand how she felt."

Helen looked up, her appetite waning. Not Alison, too, she thought. Not now.

"Now, take it easy. I said *understand*. I didn't say I agreed." Alison darted a glance at Helen, then looked away again. "How do you think it felt to see you at the hospital — to see you right now, sitting there all covered with bruises? And that's just what I can see. I know from experience, if you'll recall, what it's like to be beaten." She fiddled with a paper napkin, and Helen watched as Alison slowly and methodically tore it into small strips, then began to shred them. "You saw yourself what that monster I married did to me. And a lot of the damage happens inside, where no one can see it."

"Alison, last night was completely different. And taking some physical risks — usually not much, but some — is part of the job. In fact, it was worse when I was a cop. That was a daily invitation for any freak out there to take a shot at me, especially when I was in uniform."

Alison held up her hand to stop. "All I'm saying, Helen, is that if I can try to accept what you do — and believe me,

I'm going to do my best — then you have to understand how afraid I get."

"Is that all? You're afraid?"

She laughed out of exasperation. "Is that all? Jesus, Helen, you just got out of the hospital, you're going to go to that demonstration tomorrow and face God knows what — I think I have every right to be afraid!"

"Hold on, hold on." Helen took both Alison's hands and saw tears in her green eyes. "Look, it's hard to explain. I'm just not used to someone giving a damn. Not even after all those years with Frieda."

Alison looked up. Helen reached over and wiped tears from her cheeks. "Sometimes I worry whether I'll ever see you again. I know it's childish —"

"Of course it isn't childish. If there's anyone being immature, it's me. Not taking responsibility for how my life affects other lives. I just barrel on ahead, running all over town." Helen watched as Alison got up from the table to prowl restlessly around the room. "I guess it comes from a lot of years when no one gave a damn if I lived or died."

"Not anyone? Your family?"

"Especially them." The images that always came up when anyone asked about her family were undimmed by time and experience. First there was her father, slapping her all over their shotgun house in the Mississippi delta, hollering in her face that she was damned to hell for her perversions. After him, her grandparents, refusing to let her darken their door because of her sinful ways.

"Hey, Helen? Where'd you go?"

"I'm sorry. Guess I took a fast trip down memory lane."

"Not a good one, by the look of it." Alison sat down beside her again with a sigh. "All I'm saying is that I'm doing my best to understand."

"That's all I can ever ask."

179

"Would you — can you tell me about your work?"

Helen gazed at her, fighting off confusion. When Frieda had attempted to get involved, at least to the extent of listening to Helen talk about her work, everything started to fall apart. "Are you sure, sweetie?"

"Well, I think the question really is, are you, Helen Black, sure you're ready to open up to me?"

"I think so. Yes." With a sense that she was jumping right off a very high cliff, Helen wavered. Her own terror at committing herself to love again told her this was a necessary step to take. Her coldness, her reflex reaction of freezing people out, frightened her nearly as much as Alison did. "I have to, Alison. I have to get off this carnival ride of circling around. I have to let people in. I have to let you in."

Alison kissed her, gently, carefully. "I'm so afraid I'm going to hurt you," she whispered as she nuzzled at Helen's neck. "Look at you — you're still covered with bruises."

"Come on, let's eat." Helen backed away and put more food on her own plate, then handed a carton to Alison. "I forget — white meat or dark? And no smart remarks about how I ought to remember that detail."

Alison was just reaching for the mashed potatoes when the phone rang. "Oh, God," she groaned, "please don't let it be my parents."

"Why not? Vicky and I are old pals now."

But it was a completely different voice that sounded from the answering machine when Alison's voice finished on the tape. "Helen, it's Manny here. Listen, I heard through the grapevine about what happened, hoped I could get you at home —"

The words crackled over the speaker. "He must be calling from his car phone," Helen said, moving away from the table. "How'd he find me here?" She managed to pick up the receiver before he finished talking.

"It's me," she said.

"Are you okay?"

"Yeah, I'm fine. Won't win any beauty contests right now, but then my pageant days are over." Alison rolled her eyes and Helen smiled. "What's up? How'd you find me?"

For a moment she heard only crackling noises on the phone, then Manny said, "You're planning to be at that protest thing tomorrow, aren't you? The one your priest friend is planning in front of Centurion?"

Helen sighed. Not Manny, too. Was he going to start in on how she was always putting herself at risk? "It's just as an observer, and to see Hitch and make sure he's okay. Honestly, that's it, Manny."

"I wanted to ask you to do me a favor tomorrow."

His voice crackled again, and Helen strained to hear his next words. "I'm sorry, Manny, I didn't catch that. What did you say?"

"I said, my wife will be there at the protest tomorrow. Could you keep an eye on her?"

"You've got to be kidding." Then she remembered Manny's tired, strained expression a couple of days ago. Were he and Linda having some trouble around this?

"I only wish I were. She won't listen to reason. Or to me, or anyone else who tries to talk to her about this nonsense."

Nonsense. "Well, Manny, I'll look for her. I don't know what else I can do, but —"

"Just try to keep her from doing anything dumb, like getting arrested, you know?"

"Where are you right now, Manny?" Since he was only a few blocks away, Helen glanced at Alison and mouthed a request to have him stop by. Alison shrugged and nodded.

"Okay, but only for a minute."

By the time Helen had finished eating Manny had arrived. He looked just as strained and unhappy as he had two nights ago.

"Of course we've talked about it! I've talked until I'm

181

blue in the face, Helen." Sprawled across Alison's sofa, he refused offers of food or drink. Alison switched on another lamp in the living room, which only served to highlight his pale drawn face. "But I can't get her to stop thinking she has to do something at that fucking protest."

"What got her started in all this?" Helen asked, easing herself onto the sofa next to her former partner.

He rubbed both hands over his face. "Look, you don't have a beer, do you?"

"Sure." With a smile for Helen, Alison went into the kitchen.

"Sure you don't want something to eat first?" Helen asked. "I know you haven't had dinner yet."

"No, just a beer. Don't think I can eat anyway, and Linda is off at that church, setting things up with Father Hitchcock for the morning. She won't have dinner ready." He thanked Alison when she brought him the beer and took a long swallow, tipping his head back on the sofa. "Damn, that tastes good."

"How did Linda get involved in this?"

Slowly, reluctantly, Manny told Helen the story of Linda's last visit to her family near Chiapas. "When she found out her cousins were going to look for work in the new Centurion factory, she just went wild. I mean, crazy — like they were going off to see Satan himself. I tried to tell her, she can't tell them what to do. But like I said, she won't listen to me."

"Well, if Centurion does the same thing in Mexico that they did in Korea, I can understand it," Alison said quietly. Both Helen and Manny turned to look at her. Helen had almost forgotten her presence. Alison faltered under Manny's cool gaze. "I mean, if Linda really believes that — well, I wouldn't want my family involved in it, either." She blushed and averted her eyes.

Helen leaned back into the sofa, preparing herself for

the argument she was certain would now take place. Alison perched on the edge of an armchair, looking back and forth between them. "Manny, I happen to agree with Linda on this issue. No, wait, just hear me out," she protested when he made a move as if to spring up from the sofa. "Linda is an adult, and she has the right to make her own decisions. And it's her family. She's bound to feel strongly about things that affect them."

"But, Jesus, Helen — you know how these things can be! Did you forget all the shit you saw as a cop, for God's sake? I can't let my wife go off half-cocked into a crowd of idiot bleeding hearts and get herself hurt." He looked at her in astonishment, his eyes wide, the beer forgotten.

Helen felt the throbbing return to her head as she fought down the urge to shout at him. Instead, slowly and calmly, she went on, "You know as well as I do that she'll more than likely just get sore feet from standing for hours. Sure, a few people are going to yell at her, the cops may try to herd them somewhere, and her face might show up for a couple of seconds on the nightly news. I'll be there, and I will keep an eye out for her. I promise you that. But I can't join you in condemning her decision to do this."

Manny stared a moment longer, then slammed the half-empty beer bottle onto the coffee table. "You know, I don't know why the hell I even asked you," he said. "What is this, some kind of feminist thing, all you women stick together?"

It was Helen's turn to stare in amazement. "Where did my ex-partner go? Hello, you in there, Manny? Next thing I know, you're going to start accusing me of trying to recruit your wife."

He stood up, hands on his hips, his face flushed with anger. "You know me better than that. Jesus, we worked together for years. I've never been anything but tolerant of your lifestyle —"

"Wait a minute. Tolerant? You mean, you put up with it out of the kindness of your male heart? Isn't that white of you!" Helen stood up too quickly. Her head swam as if she, not Manny, had had that beer. "I'm going to try to convince myself that you're talking out of worry, and not saying things you really believe. Okay? Like I said, I'll see if I can find your wife tomorrow, but that's it. She's a grown-up, Manny, and she's a hell of a lot more than a wife and mother. The fact that she has the guts to go against your wishes and take a very public and potentially dangerous stand for something she believes in proves that to me. You should be proud of her."

They glared at each other in silence for a couple of seconds before Manny hurried from the room, almost knocking over a lamp in his haste to get away from them.

After the door had slammed, Alison let out a long, quiet breath. "Oh, Lord, Helen," she murmured. "I can't believe what I just heard."

"Neither can I." Helen felt hot and cold at the same time, and her head ached. She slumped back into the sofa and listlessly picked up the beer Manny had left behind. "What do you think? Did he really mean it, or was he just so afraid for Linda that he couldn't think straight? No pun intended."

Alison shook her head and came over to sit next to Helen. Outside they could hear Manny's car roar in the parking lot, its engine revving. As he tore off down the street, Alison said, "I couldn't say. You know him. You worked together. And you said yourself that he's been looking depressed."

"You know, right now I'm just too tired and sore to think anymore," Helen muttered. She slid down, resting against the warmth of Alison's body. "My head is splitting."

"What time is this protest tomorrow?" Alison asked as her arms encircled Helen.

"Starts at noon." Helen yawned. "Hitch is going to get there around ten-thirty, and everyone ought to be there by eleven-thirty."

"Including the press."

"Well, sure. That's the real reason to do something like this. Not because anyone believes Centurion will pay attention, but in the hope that people watching on the evening news will think twice before they buy another pair of running shoes from the company."

"That's enough." Alison took a good look at Helen. "No more talk. Time for you to get some sleep."

"I'm okay," Helen protested, but she yawned again. "It's not that late."

"Come on, even ace girl detectives need their rest. Quit arguing." Alison took both her hands to help her up.

"Okay, okay. So which one of the famous Nancy Drew sidekicks do you want to be tonight? Bess or George? Ouch, let go." Helen moaned.

"Oh, God, did I hurt something?" Alison hovered anxiously, waiting for Helen to get up.

"No, I don't think so." Helen carefully twisted her head around, then moved her shoulders. "No, I'm fine. I think I'm just going to have aches and pains for a while."

Alison shook her head and preceded Helen out of the living room. "We still have a date to go to the doctor in the morning, before the demonstration?"

"Right."

"I hope he doesn't recommend some kind of neck brace or anything. That bastard did a number on you."

"I can still do this." Helen planted a kiss on Alison's mouth before Alison had a chance to protest. Alison giggled and returned the embrace, but she pulled away as soon as Helen reached for the buttons on her shirt.

"Not tonight," Alison murmured. "I'm afraid I'd put you right into traction if I let you."

"But it's sure to put me right to sleep — you know how I am after —"

"Not another word. Bed."

Later, as they lay in the darkness, Helen listened to Alison's breathing. Helen lay very still, afraid to wake her. Maybe it was the events of the day, or the accumulation of stresses and strains on her bruised body — whatever it was, she lay wide-eyed, watching the bright red digital readout on Alison's alarm clock cycle through one hour, then another.

What was it? She should be sleeping like a damned rock. She tried to relax, and succeeded, finally, from sheer exhaustion, in putting herself in that strange state between waking and sleeping. The moment she felt sleep approach, however, her body surged awake from a variety of painful twinges.

Giving up, Helen slowly moved out from under the sheets. She headed for the kitchen, with the intention of making a cup of tea. It wasn't just aches and pains, she realized as she sat at the table waiting for water to boil. And it wasn't Manny's outburst, either.

Fiddling with the boxes of assorted teas stuffed haphazardly in the cupboard — did she really need so many types of herbal concoctions? — Helen grudgingly admitted to herself that at least in part she was relieved to be out of the bed, away from Alison's physical presence, for the time being. She was certain that her reluctance would pass, but after the emotional intensity of her revelations to her lover, coming right on top of a traumatic and painful encounter with Howard, it was all too much. Plus, she needed to get her car, which was still in Father Hitchcock's garage.

Alison had left their plates in the sink for the evening, and Helen poured boiling water into a mug for the tea, looking down on the remains of dinner. The red glow of her cell phone display, fully charged again, shone a tiny beam of light from the end table in the darkened living room Still, she knew, it wasn't completely Manny, or even Alison. There was something more. The feeling was familiar, from years of police and detective work. "Something happened today," she whispered. "Something important." Someone had said something, done something that would, once she remembered it, explain what had happened to Leslie Merrick.

But what? Helen stood at the sink for a long time, thinking, while her tea grew cold.

Chapter Fourteen

Something soft and warm and round pressed up against
Helen as she slept. She stirred slightly, the movement
changing the focus of her dreams. She felt her hands
following the curve of Alison's body beneath the sheets, and
soon she had roused herself from sleep.

"Mmm?" Alison murmured. Helen sighed and fitted her
own body to Alison's, ignoring the faint twinge of pain that
coursed along her shoulders. Alison pulled away for just a
moment, readjusting her position on the bed, then leaned
her body more firmly against Helen. Helen felt Alison relax.

"Jesus, you feel good," she whispered into Alison's neck. Her fingers traced the line of Alison's spine from the neck to the swell of her buttocks, then back up again. "Do you always feel this good?"

"I think so," Alison muttered, still half asleep. "What are you doing?"

"Physical therapy." Helen's hand slipped around Alison's side. She caressed Alison's breast, locating the nipple and squeezing gently until she felt an answering tremor in Alison's body and a hardening of the soft tissue. "It's a medical fact that making love is the most important method known to humanity of healing what ails you."

"And where did you learn that?"

Helen lifted her head from Alison's shoulder. "From long experience and practice."

"Oh, really?" Alison managed to shift in Helen's grasp enough to peer up at her. "You mean, prior to meeting me?"

"Well, of course! I have, however, made a very careful study, with a variety of test subjects."

"Oh, so now I'm an experiment. Not too flattering."

"No, no," Helen said, shaking her head and gently pushing Alison's hands aside. "This morning I'm making love to you."

"Are you sure?"

In answer, Helen slipped her hand between Alison's legs. "Well, let's see," she said, watching Alison's expression change. "I'm not too sure, but I know how to find out." Her hand went in deeper, then deeper still, seeking and then finding moisture and heat in the center.

Alison smiled. Her breath caught in her throat as Helen played with the warm, sensitive folds of skin. Helen gingerly raised herself up on her elbow and, watching Alison's face in the dim gray light of a foggy morning, felt with her thumb for the hard nub of flesh. Under steady, rapid movements of Helen's thumb, Alison's clitoris enlarged and grew harder.

Alison arched her back slightly, straining toward her hand. Helen kissed her briefly on the lips, then moved downward to her breasts. The nipples stood erect, firm pink against the paler skin. Alison moaned. Lifting her head again, Helen pushed in deeper with two, then three fingers, her thumb never leaving Alison's clitoris. Suddenly, without any warning, she withdrew her hand and began to play with the curls of hair below Alison's belly.

"Bitch," Alison whispered. She spread her legs farther apart, inviting her lover back.

"Well, you didn't seem too sure of the medical benefits of sex, so I thought I should give you a chance to reconsider."

"Oh yeah?" Alison grabbed Helen's hand and moved it down. Helen let her fingers trace the soft wet lips, teasing and tickling without going inside. "I'll show you medical benefits if you don't —" Suddenly Alison caught her breath as Helen thrust two fingers deep inside her and pressed with her thumb at the firmness just above. She began a slow circular motion that gradually grew faster, thrusting even deeper. Her thumb flicked back and forth,

Helen closed her eyes and smiled as Alison's body surged and closed around her fingers. Waves of heat followed the rush of moisture that flooded over Helen's hand. She moved her thumb away from the swollen nub of flesh and slowed her pace. Alison moaned softly as her thighs trembled, and Helen slowly withdrew her hand.

Even in the dim light of the bedroom, Helen could make out the heightened color of Alison's face. "I feel kind of selfish, Helen."

"Don't be silly." Helen gave her a quick kiss on the cheek and struggled with the rumpled sheets until she was sitting up. "I wanted to make love to you. Sometimes it's more fun to be on the giving end of things."

"But if you're feeling good enough to take care of me . . ." Her hands strayed to Helen's waist and she tried to pull Helen closer. "I'd love to return the favor." Alison put on a ridiculously somber face and intoned, "I'll be gentle, my dear. And it's already morning, and I already respect you, so what the hell?"

Helen struggled away. "Not this morning. Remember, we have to go to the doctor, and you . . ." Helen leaned down to kiss Alison on the cheek again. "You have to get back to work sometime today." Helen tried to ignore the panic that fought to overpower her as she looked down at her lover, warm and naked and flushed from sex in the early-morning light.

Alison sat up and watched Helen, all humor gone. "Right," she said in a flat tone. "God forbid that Helen Black, famous butch private eye, scourge of all women, actually let her girlfriend make love to her. She might enjoy it, and then what the fuck would she do?"

"Hey, it's just a raincheck." Helen gaped at Alison, stunned by her reaction.

"If you're sure." Alison watched as Helen moved away from the bed into the bathroom.

"Listen, as soon as the doctors tell me I'm going to live past lunchtime today, you can count on getting your hands on me." Helen saw Alison smile just before she got into the shower.

The hot water, creating a cloud of steam that misted the tiny bathroom, felt so good on her aching back and shoulders that Helen stayed in the shower much longer than usual. By the time they got into Alison's car and headed for Alta Mira Hospital, the warm glow of the shower had faded. Although she felt much better than the previous day, Helen's whole body still felt like a thin piece of fragile porcelain. The dull ache had dissipated, but she feared that the least pressure would send the pain knifing back in.

"I'm not too sure you ought to go to that protest thing

191

today." Alison shut her door and walked around the car to offer Helen a helping hand. "You're still not feeling too good."

"Nothing a couple of aspirin won't keep under control." Helen patted Alison's hand. "I'll be fine, I promise."

Alison checked her watch. "We'd better get moving. I told my office I'd be there by lunchtime."

But before they could get settled in the waiting area, Helen saw a familiar face standing at the nurses' station in the emergency room. With a promise to Alison that she wouldn't be long, Helen made her way through several clusters of people to the long counter.

"Kim? Is that you?"

The nurse from the free clinic turned, startled, at Helen's voice. She stared at Helen in amazement. "My God, what happened to you?"

Helen gave her as brief an account as she could manage. "I'm here for one more checkup this morning, actually."

Kim sighed and shook her head. She wasn't wearing her white lab coat, but there was a stethoscope slung around her neck, and her name badge revealed that she was on the staff of the hospital. "I was going to try to page you, Helen. I'm afraid I have some bad news."

The smile froze on Helen's face and with a sinking heart she knew what she was about to hear. "It's Amelia, isn't it?"

"Afraid so." Kim turned to confer with one of the nurses, then she picked up a chart from the counter and studied it as she continued, "I got a call last night. She showed up right when they were closing up for the day. Thanks, Cindy," Kim said to one of the nurses, "I'll take care of that from here." She slid the chart back into the rack and leaned against the counter. Weariness was etched into her face. "I'm not sure where Amelia had gotten to, but she was badly beaten. Lost a few teeth, almost lost an eye. And there's been quite a bit of internal bleeding as well. If we could have gotten her in here sooner, things would look a little better now."

"What are you saying, Kim? How bad is it?"

"I'm not going to lie to you — it doesn't look good. There's been internal bleeding, for several hours. We don't know for how long, because Amelia has been unconscious since before we got the ambulance to bring her here from the clinic. As it is, we'll have to transfer her to the county hospital if she gets off the critical list."

"But — can you tell?" Helen followed Kim as she walked hurriedly through the hall in what seemed to be a labyrinthine maze of rooms and patients and gurneys. "I mean, what happened?"

"Best we can tell, she got jumped and beaten up last night. The cops who brought her in think it was a couple of guys going around Berkeley and hitting street people. She's had X-rays and blood work done, and they're going to take her into surgery now, try to find where she's bleeding." Kim stopped outside a baize-covered door and ran a hand over her brow. "Look, I'll page you as soon as I know something. I've already told the clinic I'll be here all morning, keeping an eye on her. I have to go."

Helen watched her go through the doors, which continued swinging back and forth for several moments. After realizing that she was blocking the way she made her way slowly back to where Alison was waiting near the main entrance.

"But we just saw her yesterday afternoon! What could've happened?" Alison said as she sat down with Helen a couple of minutes later.

Helen shook her head and leaned back against the uncomfortable cushion of the chair in the waiting room. "Not all that unusual. People on the streets often get beaten like this. Who knows why? Someone might have thought she had some money, or some drugs. Maybe it was a rape. Or it could have been a hit-and-run. Whatever it was, it doesn't look good."

The image of Amelia on the operating table, hooked up to a variety of machines that monitored every function of her weakened body, stayed with Helen throughout her own brief examination. It was too much like all the times she'd gone to the hospital as a cop, when shootings and stabbings and beatings ended horribly, brutally, in blood and screams and tears. She kept waiting for her pager to beep while the doctor made his final remarks, but it hadn't gone off by the time she went out to join Alison.

"I'm fine," she told Alison as they left the waiting area. "Nothing serious. Just a few bruises to get in the way of winning that beauty pageant," she joked lamely.

"Do you want to see if we can find anything out about Amelia before we go?" Alison said, glancing over at the nurses' station under the sign marked EMERGENCY.

Helen paused, tempted to track Kim down for an update, but shook her head. "We shouldn't get in the way. I know Kim is making sure they do all they can."

As they were walking back outside, Helen heard footsteps behind them. "Just a moment! Just a moment!"

Helen turned around to see a woman trotting after them. She wasn't wearing anything that indicated she was part of the medical staff, but she did have a clipboard tucked under her arm. Her tight blond permanent curled over ears that sagged under the weight of heavy gold hoop earrings. "Are you related to — ah, what was her name? Oh, yes, are you next of kin to Amelia Wainright?"

"No, no, I'm not." Helen stared at the woman, confused. "Why?"

"I saw you talking with Kim, so I wondered if you were the one taking responsibility for payment."

"Excuse me?"

The woman tapped a pen on her clipboard and pursed her thin lips into a red wrinkle. "Well, we have no

194

insurance for this patient. She'll be sent to the county hospital as soon as possible. If she requires anything beyond emergency treatment, the money will have to come from somewhere. We're hoping to get hold of next of kin to assume financial costs of hospitalization, and —"

Helen spun on her heel, seething with rage. Was this going to be the epitaph on Amelia Wainright's life? That no one could pay the hospital for her deathbed?

It was a silent ride back to Helen's office. Helen caught a glimpse of her own car as they passed Helen's office building in search of a parking space.

Helen cleared her throat and said, "Guess Hitch dropped my car off before getting a ride over to the demonstration."

"That was nice of him." Alison parked the car on a side street off of Shattuck Avenue, and they sat quietly for a few minutes. Finally Alison reached over and took her hand.

"I'm so sorry, Helen. I wish there was some way we could do something, contact someone."

"That's just it. People like Amelia don't have anyone to contact. They don't have jobs, they don't contribute to our marvelous little capitalist society that demands you produce before you count for anything. They don't have insurance. They aren't deemed worthy. And let's not forget, she's queer as a three-dollar bill. Absolutely no reason to be alive at all. No one gives a fuck." Helen looked down at her silent pager again, then sighed.

"That's not true, Helen. That no one gives a fuck, I mean." Alison refused to let go of Helen's hand when she tried to pull away. "Look at me." Helen turned and saw Alison's bright green eyes swimming with tears. "Helen, I care. Kim, the woman from the clinic — she cares. And you care, too. Even if you do try to act like you don't."

Helen stared out at the street, not seeing the grimy asphalt and the peeling paint on the aging buildings. She swallowed hard and the urge to cry went away. "What makes you think I do care anymore? Jesus, I'm so sick and tired of fighting for air all the time." She squirmed around in her seat and stared at Alison, who was wiping tears from her cheeks. "After all those years as a cop, and now a few years lurking around in the shadows and digging up dirt on people's private lives and calling it investigative work — it's just really hard to care about much of anything anymore."

Alison looked up with a sad smile. "You cared enough about a woman who was being beaten by her husband to help her. Remember? You got me out of that hell, into a new life. I think that counts for something."

Alison released her hand and Helen shifted her gaze back to the street outside. "I'm sorry, Alison. I just — I just don't know if I have the energy for this anymore."

"I don't believe it." Alison spoke almost in a whisper, leaning closer until Helen could breathe in her scent. "No one who said what you just did is without emotion. Your feelings have just gotten buried, so deep that it feels like it's completely lost."

"Maybe they are lost, Alison. This is just — it's just too much for me right now."

Alison sat silent. "And by 'this' do you mean your work? Or dealing with people like Amelia?" She turned on Helen with a fierce look on her face. "Or do you mean me? Us?"

In the street, a trash hauler rumbled by, redolent with the gatherings of an early morning run. Helen realized with a start that it was already Friday morning. She hadn't visited her office for quite a while. Suddenly the dilapidated chamber where she conducted business seemed like a tantalizing sanctuary. "Alison, in the last three days I've trekked back and forth from home to the lair of a drunken idiot who happens to be paying me a great deal of money. I've been beaten up and checked over by doctors. And now I just need a little time to gather my wits about me while I get ready to go mingle with a throng of political fanatics."

Alison, her face stony with hurt and anger, switched the key in the ignition. "Fine. Take yourself and the planet you're carrying around with you on your shoulders back to your office." Helen opened the car door just as the trash hauler reeled by again with its fresh load. "I'll talk to you later."

Helen waited until Alison's car had gone back down Shattuck before heading slowly to her building. She realized as she entered through the garage that she'd not had a chance to put out her own garbage for the pickup that had just passed them by.

"Fuck," she muttered, staring at the oily concrete. "Just add a week's worth of garbage to my list."

"Helen! Oh, Helen!"

With a heavy sigh Helen recognized the voice of Tina Merrick. "Oh, Helen, I've left you so many messages on your office phone! Where were you yesterday?" The plaintive whine turned into a gasp of shock when Tina saw her face. "Lord, look at you! What happened to you?"

Helen took her by the arm and began to steer her toward the stairs to her office. "I ran into a little trouble the night before last —"

"Yes, the day before yesterday. I wanted to talk to you about that. About what you found in my poor dear's office."

Helen took a good look at Tina Merrick's face in the unforgiving light of day. For someone who'd been steadily drinking ever since Helen had met her, Tina looked remarkably well. She must have slept off the strain of Leslie's death. Tina looked positively rosy in her tasteful black suit and pink silk blouse that showed a dangerous amount of cleavage. Then Helen remembered the healthy influx of cash that Drake had injected into Tina's life.

"So, you see, Helen," Tina babbled as they toiled up the stairs, "I think we should wrap things up, don't you?"

"I beg your pardon?" Helen stopped on a landing and looked down at Tina, perched like a plump bird on the step below. "Are you telling me the investigation is off?"

Tina took a step up, standing next to Helen, and spoke

in a soft conspiratorial tone. "Well, the police wouldn't have said my poor baby —" She paused for a sniffle and a feigned wiping of tears — "my little girl died the way she did unless they had proof, would they? So I guess there's no real point in going on with your investigation."

Tina batted bright blue eyes at her, and realization sank into Helen's mind. "The insurance company came through, didn't it? You've got your money now."

Tina's mouth rounded into an astonished circle. "Helen, that has nothing to do with anything! My heart is still broken over Leslie, and it always will be." Her voice caught and broke, almost convincingly, Helen decided, watching Tina fumble in her purse for a tissue. Helen wondered briefly if the flask had been transferred from purse to purse. "So why don't you just send me a bill and we'll take care of the whole thing? Unless you'd like a check right now."

Helen stared. The switch from grieving mother to efficient businesswoman had happened before the tissue made it up from the purse to Tina's nose. "No, no, that's okay. I'll — I guess I'll mail you an invoice."

"That'll be fine." Tina reached over and patted Helen's hand. "Actually, I was just going to slip a note under your door, so it's a good thing I bumped into you."

"Well, I'm sorry you came all the way out here —"

"Oh, but Richard and I are having lunch today, so I'm in town anyway."

No wonder she looked so good — maybe there was more money to come. Richard, huh? "Since you're here, would you like to come up anyway?"

"No, I don't think so." She babbled her way back down the stairs, and Helen followed her to her car. As Tina sped off to luncheon with the kingpin of Centurion Sportswear, Helen went back to her office, debating whether or not she should call Alison or go on over to the protest site.

A moment's debate was all it took. Helen remembered

Manny, and Linda. With a sigh Helen turned on her heel and headed for her car still parked out on the street. Better to drive over to Oakland now, she reasoned, so she'd be there for the demonstration. The office could wait. Helen glanced at the note Father Hitchcock had tucked under the windshield wiper and folded it into her pocket. She'd be seeing him soon enough. She took her cell phone from her shoulder bag and locked it into the glove compartment before starting the car.

She didn't see the crack in the windshield, in the dim light of the garage, until she drove out into the street. Helen slammed on the brakes and her eyes took in the damage. Right in front of the driver's seat, positioned so that it would have centered right at the driver's head, was a neat round hole that could have come from a bullet.

Chapter Fifteen

Helen spotted Linda almost immediately. Standing near the intersection of Broadway and Fourteenth Street, the group of protesters was quickly increasing until they threatened to overflow into the lanes of traffic that sped back and forth from Jack London to the freeway on the other side of Oakland. Linda Hernandez stood with her back toward Helen, listening intently to something Father Hitch was telling the group. As she picked her way through gathering protesters, curious onlookers and people in business suits scurrying with faces determinedly aimed at the ground, Helen couldn't make out what he was saying.

Whatever it was, it seemed to galvanize the demonstrators, and they nodded and smiled at one another.

Linda carried a picket sign. At the moment it was perched rather casually on her shoulder, and it bobbed back and forth as she shifted her weight from foot to foot. The placard was turned away from Helen's line of sight. Helen reached the edge of the crowd and slowly worked her way up to the front, to where Linda stood at Hitch's side.

"Need a sign to carry?" Hitch said to her with a smile as she greeted him. He looked a lot better than the last time she'd seen him. Already that nasty bruise over his eye was fading, and the cuts on his chin could have come from shaving instead of a few well-landed punches. He leaned over and peered more closely at Helen. "How are you, anyway? Been back to the doctor?"

"Just got checked out this morning. They say I might live, after all. Besides, my head is way too hard. Oh, before I forget, thanks for getting my car back to me."

He grinned. "Had a little help from a parishioner who used to hot-wire cars before I got hold of him."

"Father Hitchcock! Father Hitchcock!" A reporter — it looked just like the one who'd accosted Helen and Tina at the memorial — yelled out over the crowd. Everyone turned around to look at him, and he shoved his microphone into the air over their heads. The bright lights of a video camera blazed into their eyes. "Any comment on the protest today?"

Hitch shook his head and held up his hands in a gesture of negation. "I'm not the story here, folks. Stick around and watch the activities today — what Centurion is doing in Mexico is the reason we're all here."

"Is there any connection between the death of Leslie Merrick and the assault on you two nights ago, Father Hitchcock?"

"Father Hitchcock, do you have any comment on Richard Drake's denouncement of PAN and its activities?"

Hitch shook his head and grimaced at Helen. Leaning

over to pick up his own picket sign, he murmured to her, "I hate reporters. They're a necessary evil, but I do hate them." He glanced over Helen's shoulder and smiled grimly. "Speaking of necessary evils, don't look now but we have a police presence in the mix."

Helen followed his gaze and saw a couple of black-and-whites situated over behind the Centurion building. At the moment, the four uniformed officers were just getting out of their vehicles with absolutely no sense of urgency. She could make out the steam rising from the Styrofoam cups of coffee as they grouped around the cars, speaking into shoulder mikes and eyeing the demonstrators.

"Doesn't look like they expect any excitement," she said. A third car joined them, and the total of six officers leisurely sauntered out from behind Centurion and positioned themselves unobtrusively around the group of protesters in a wide circumference.

Hitch shrugged. "We did all the necessary paperwork weeks ago." He waved grandly at the sawhorses that ringed the plaza in front of the building. "All above board, all by the book. I just want to be sure those cameras get this on the evening news."

Linda snorted and adjusted her picket sign on her shoulder. Helen saw that her face was flushed a deep pink. "I'm surprised Manny isn't running out here with them, yelling and screaming for me to get back into the kitchen and whip up some tortillas." She turned on Helen. "Or is that what you're here for?"

"I'm an independent observer today," Helen said. "Hi, Linda. Haven't seen you in quite a while."

Linda hugged Helen with her free arm and laughed. Her small delicate dark face glowed with happiness. "Oh, come on, Helen, I know exactly why you're here. My dear darling husband couldn't stand the thought of my doing this, and he hired a baby-sitter."

Helen shook her head. "The last thing you need, Linda,

is a baby-sitter." She craned her neck to get a good look at the sign Linda carried. "But you're right, he did tell me he was worried about you."

Hitch had wandered off to talk to a couple of people huddled at the edge of the crowd. Helen saw a microphone dart into the air, catching his words. Radio people, maybe — certainly the major local non-profit listener-supported station would be in attendance. And she could make out, over in the next block, a couple of television news vans parked alongside the crumbling office buildings. Apparently they blocked the way for construction workers, for Helen could see a couple of vociferous arguments developing between people in hard-hats and orange vests and men and women carrying microphones and heavy camera equipment.

The construction workers threaded their way through the crowd, muttering and sneering as if to suggest they'd prefer to see all these people buried in the rubble of the building across the alley. Helen watched them trailing across the pavement until they disappeared into the shadowy interior of the framework behind the Centurion building.

"Well, you're here making history, Helen! Let's go!" She felt Linda tugging at her sleeve, and Helen gently pulled away. Linda turned and looked back at her, an odd expression on her face.

"You really are baby-sitting, aren't you?"

Helen shook her head. "No, not really. I will tell Manny I saw you here, but that's all." She waved and took a couple of steps backward, letting the protesters surge around her. In spite of the crowd, which looked to be close to a hundred people, it seemed that at least half of the people who'd been listening to Hitch were merely well-wishers. The group split almost exactly in half, one set surging forward into a messy conga-line of people circling on the flagstones in front of the Centurion building, the other set bunched together with their backs toward Broadway, watching the pageant unfold before them.

203

Helen positioned herself at the front of the self-made audience, where she could see Linda and Hitch conferring as they took their places in the circle of people carrying signs. They moved slowly, holding the placards so that people driving or walking by could see the lettering clearly. A couple of photographers knelt down to get a good shot of the circling demonstrators, asking one or two to stand still for the camera. At the other end of the plaza, Helen saw three — no, it was four — setups of television reporters, positioned in front of cameras and talking into their microphones.

Helen let out a deep sigh and was surprised at the sense of relief washing over her. She didn't quite know what she'd been expecting, but certainly the protest seemed to be shaping up quite tamely. To her right and left, four people emerged from the small crowd, holding flyers that they offered to passersby. Most of the people trotting up and down Broadway ignored them completely, turning away with expressions of irritation or disgust on their faces. One or two slapped at the papers offered them, but a few actually accepted the flyers and either looked at them or tossed them into the street as they hurried on about their respective errands.

Caught on a cool breeze that gusted through the wind tunnel created by tall buildings lining the street, one of the flyers lifted up into the air in front of the Centurion building. The white sheet unfolded in the breeze and floated toward the top of the building. Following its course, Helen saw that quite a few people were lined up at the windows of the Centurion. Every floor sported its own audience to the quiet pacing of the protesters.

Helen tried to make out familiar faces among the pale visages lined up behind the faux marble walls. She succeeded only when she saw Vicky Young, all alone, leaning out of the open seventh-floor window. Perhaps she was still sitting isolated up there, Helen thought, away from everyone else.

Just then Vicky spotted Helen at the back of the crowd watching the picketers. Vicky waved hesitantly, as if hoping not to attract attention to herself. Helen lifted a hand in greeting, and they both went back to watching the demonstrators. She hoped there was a way to catch up with Vicky later, maybe chat for a few minutes, or to get a bite of lunch. It was almost noon, after all.

The sun, which had made only a weak showing up to this point, tucked back behind clouds that were gathering and spreading from the bay. The air took a cold turn, and wind continued to gust around sharp corners with sudden energy. More than one of the demonstrators, caught in an erratic burst of cold air, fought to control their picket signs as they wavered precariously from side to side. Wishing she'd brought a jacket with her, Helen hugged herself and watched as the circle shifted, reformed, and started its slow procession on the flagstones once again. The reporters had backed away from the scene. Some still held their microphones and kept their eyes intent on the groups clustered around the demonstrators, eagerly awaiting any sign of disruption. A couple of them were chatting, looking bored and cold, their mikes nowhere in sight. Camera crews still held their equipment ready, but Helen saw that one van, at least, had side doors slid open and cameras and lights loaded inside.

The police presence remained a backdrop to the scene. They stood around, a half-dozen officers forming a loose circle around the plaza, now and then murmuring into their shoulder mikes. Yet another black-and-white pulled up along the section of Broadway marked for buses. One officer, a woman, got out, chatted to the uniform standing there, then got back in the car with a wave.

Helen saw that Linda had broken from the circle of

people holding picket signs. She took a water bottle that someone in the crowd fished up out of an enormous cooler. Helen jammed her hands in her pockets. Should she hang around any longer? It was clear that this was a very peaceful, even dull, demonstration. Beyond the hope that Father Hitch's PAN group would get some much-deserved attention and support, Helen couldn't see that her presence was making a damn bit of difference to anyone. Certainly not to Linda Hernandez, who had rejoined the line and calmly continued to hold up her picket sign.

Before she'd made a definite decision to walk away and give Alison a call, was somewhat surprised to see Christine Santilli walking out of the building's entrance, putting a cigarette between her lips. Before Helen could disappear through the crowd back to her car, Christine spotted her and headed over to join her.

"So what the hell are you doing here today? Going to fall in with the bleeding-heart liberals, as our friend McFarland would call them?" Christine took a deep drag and blew smoke out over Helen's head, in the direction of the traffic.

Helen forced a smile. "You never know. Anything is possible." At the moment, Helen's escape route off Broadway was blocked by a surge forward of a large contingent of teenagers thrusting their way off a bus and running across a plaza — probably on their way to one of the dark and noisy game arcades in the mall on the lower level and completely unconcerned about being in school. A bus chuffed and honked a path away from the stop in front of them, and another took its place, puffing black exhaust into the air. This one unloaded two people in wheelchairs. A gang of riders stood knotted by the bus doors, waiting their turn to board. Helen's path out was effectively blocked.

"So what are you doing here, anyway?" Christine's eyes narrowed through the smoke as she peered at Helen.

Helen was thankfully prevented from answering by the

arrival of Bob Tyrell and Lily Mapa. "So you managed to get out, too," Bob said, jerking his head toward the demonstrators. "I didn't know what they might do to us, you know?" He was sweating and nervous, his gaze darting back and forth from Lily and Christine to the protest. "Oh hi, Helen. Are you here with the — uh — with them?" Bob asked, gesturing over to the circle of demonstrators.

"No." She smiled but refused to elaborate. Bob and Lily exchanged glances, then turned back to Christine.

"You know better than standing out here. Donna will have your ass on a silver platter if you don't get back inside. Remember the meeting yesterday? They told us specifically to stay inside." Lily frowned, elbowing Christine.

"So what the hell are you two doing out here, then? And what am I going to do when I need to smoke? Not to mention grabbing a sandwich or something for lunch."

"How about quitting?" Lily suggested.

Bob smiled again. He whispered conspiratorially, "The coffee here is awful. You can get a really good mocha over at that café in the mall." Then, with a somber expression, he said to Christine, "You'd better wait here until I get back. Then I can get both you and Lily inside safely."

Lily rolled her eyes at this display of machismo courtesy and smiled at Helen. "Would you like a mocha, too?" she asked her. "Or a sandwich?"

"That's very thoughtful. Thanks, but I'll pass."

They ambled off to the mall in search of coffee and lunch after one final glance at the front of the Centurion building. Christine pulled out another cigarette.

"Not afraid?" Helen asked.

Christine shrugged. "They won't do anything. They just want to get on the nightly news, not go to jail."

"Well, it looks pretty calm so far," Helen agreed.

"Not very exciting," Christine said. She took a few puffs, then dropped the cigarette butt to the flagstones and ground it under her shoe. "But it's better than sitting in yet another meeting about our sales goals this quarter." She scratched at the skin around her wrist braces absentmindedly.

"I should think after last week a little boredom would be more than welcome."

Christine shook her head. "Have you taken a look at their flyers? Apparently we represent all the cruelty and decadence of late twentieth-century evil."

Helen looked away, back toward the protesters. "Well, it's hard to ignore the information they've gathered. About the Korean women, I mean. Not once you see the photographs."

"Shit, I can ignore anything as long as it doesn't affect my morning commute."

Almost as if in response to her remark, someone cried out from within the group of demonstrators. Helen looked over quickly, her first thought for Linda. Manny's wife stood stock still, her picket sign frozen in mid-air, staring at the front of the Centurion building. Helen moved away from Christine, and as she walked across the plaza she got a glimpse of Brian Reilly, the security guard, waving his hands over his head. She couldn't make out his words as the noise increased. To her right, Helen saw the camera crews tumble back out of the vans, hoisting equipment over their shoulders and following in the wake of reporters who quickly adjusted suits and ties and skirts as they hustled to the source of the commotion.

It was almost impossible to tell what started the melee that ensued. Some people said that Reilly made an insulting remark to Father Hitchcock. Others believed it was the result of an angry exchange between one of the uniformed officers and the people in charge of keeping water handy for the marchers. It might even have been passersby who were trying to get through the crowds to go to their offices, or lunch dates, or an ATM machine.

"Shit," Helen muttered, moving forward through the

small throng that gathered at the crux of violence stirring up. Christine followed her, but she paid no attention, focusing on making sure that Hitch and Linda, at least, were going to be all right.

Helen managed to get a couple of steps in front of the reporters, and the uniforms dotted here and there on the plaza were right behind her as she scurried around the crowd. By the time she'd worked her way back up to where the two women guarded the cooler, she was struggling harder to push through the mass of bodies confronting her. She felt the shoves get harder and meaner as she got closer to the picket line.

Christine backed away from the plaza, then darted around the side of a bus bench as two men came running from around the corner of Fourteenth Street. Just before she slipped through a break in the mass of bodies, Helen caught a glimpse of Bob and Lily, *sans* mochas, joining Christine by the bus stop. Together the trio of Centurion employees worked their way around the crowd toward Twelfth Street — presumably to a back entrance of the building.

By the time Helen had squirmed and struggled toward the front of the crowd, someone pushed someone. Then another person did some pushing, followed by a couple of choice epithets. The uniforms hovering at the perimeter called terse requests for backup into their shoulder mikes and shoved forward to where Brian Reilly, red-faced and breathing hard, had just pulled a gun from his belt.

Shocked — why the hell was Reilly armed? — Helen watched the scene crumble slowly at first, then deteriorate into a brief but nasty free-for-all. The commands of the police were lost amid the shouts welling up from the demonstrators.

Helen got a quick look at Hitch, reaching over his cohorts and trying to make himself heard, before he sank into the midst of the confusion. The news cameras wedged their way into the group, which had now grown to include people just passing through, Centurion employees who'd come outside to watch, and protesters. Something sharp and heavy hit Helen in the back, and she found herself being barreled over by the same reporter she remembered from the memorial.

When she stood up again, things had gotten louder and more violent. Someone grabbed one of the picket signs and Helen watched it break. She heard the ugly crack and the dull rip of cardboard. Brian Reilly and his gun had melded into the crowd. Sirens blared in the distance. A couple of people were sprawled onto the flagstones, and then there was the flat smack of a fist hitting flesh.

"Fuck you, asshole!"

"Fuck yourself!"

Similar epithets followed, and Helen was nearly swept into a tight knot that included a couple of the people she'd seen get off the bus, Father Hitch, and a man wearing a very expensive-looking suit. Hitch's face reappeared momentarily, and he weaseled out of the cluster minus a part of his sleeve.

"Linda! Linda Hernandez!" Helen shouted out. "It's Helen! Where are you?"

"Over here!" Helen squirmed around and pushed herself up, using someone's shoulder as leverage. Cornered on the steps leading up to the entrance of Centurion, Linda held the ragged end of the post that had carried her picket sign. At her feet lay someone whose nose was bleeding profusely. Helen saw a fist swing up at her, but Linda darted backward, shrinking against the wall. Helen made a painful push forward, found herself lifted off the flagstones, then landed on solid ground again just in front of Linda. "Jesus, are you okay?"

"Yeah. Someone tried to slug me, but I'm all right." Linda gazed at the scenario playing itself out, blinking as a news team switched on lights to get a good shot of the scene. "What the hell happened?"

"Right now we just have to get you out of here."

"No, I'm staying. I mean it, Helen." Helen looked down at her. There was going to be a nasty bruise on Linda's cheek, and her shirt was done for, but Linda's eyes glittered with determination. "I'm going to see this through."

There was no point in arguing. Besides, the police, now increased in numbers, had formed a loose cordon that began to tighten around the center of the brawl. Helen saw more than one nightstick drawn, but so far she hadn't seen anyone using one. Her shoulders were undergoing a steady rain of sharp pains. Someone must have hit her harder than she realized.

"Did you see him? Did you see Hitch?" Linda asked.

"For just a second." Helen ducked down as something — a rock, maybe — slammed with a loud crack on the wall over her head. "He was right in the middle of it — no, there he is."

The two officers flanking Hitch tried to steer him off toward the edge of the plaza, but he kept turning around, calling out to the demonstrators. Helen heard the static of a bullhorn warming up.

The sight of Brian Reilly, unconscious on the flagstones, distracted Helen from the commands bellowed out over the bullhorn. His face, scratched and bruised, was pale. Moments ago it had been reddened with exertion. Most of the buttons on his blue uniform suit had been torn off, and he seemed to be gasping.

"Jesus," Helen whispered. Had he had a stroke? Helen looked up, hoping to see a uniform nearby, but the crowd was still weaving in a miasma of noise and confusion. Afraid that someone was going to trample him further, Helen looked over at Linda. "Help me drag him up the steps," she shouted. Linda moved nervously away from the wall and crept toward Helen. Together, sweating with the effort, they managed to pull him along the plaza the three or four yards to the building. Helen tried to open the glass entrance doors, but someone had locked them. She pounded on the thick glass and shouted hoarsely, "We need help out here! Goddamnit, let us in!"

There was a flurry of activity near Lily's reception area. Christine and Lily turned around — perhaps calling to someone out of sigh — and then Bob appeared, peering around a corner.

Helen pounded on the door again. "Jesus fucking Christ, open the door! He's hurt!"

Bob was suddenly at the door, fiddling with the locks. Christine and Lily held the doors open while Bob helped Helen and Linda to drag the unconscious security guard into the lobby.

Helen looked beseechingly at Linda, but she shook her head and ran out. With a sinking feeling that she'd somehow failed Manny, despite her own disagreement with his attitudes, Helen shut the doors. Lily, gasping and terrified, strained up for the lock with trembling fingers and switched it shut.

"Oh, my God, he's dead!"

"No, Lily, he's alive, but he doesn't look good." That was when the rock — or brick, or something — hit the doors. They didn't shatter, but from the circle left by the impact, the glass cracked in a web of bright shards. It reminded Helen of the crack in her car's windshield, and she shuddered.

Lily screamed, and Bob hugged her. He looked over Lily's shoulder at Helen. "We've got to get an ambulance."

Helen shook her head. Suddenly the events of the last couple of days caught up with her, and combined waves of nausea and pain swept over her. She'd pushed herself too hard, not allowing her body to heal from the beating she'd received the night before. Unable to move another muscle another inch, she leaned back against the wall and watched the others as they scrambled for telephones, to call for help and to run uselessly back and forth. The police would be there soon. Let someone else do it, she thought.

She slumped against the wall. It was probably only minutes, but it felt as though years had passed before she could bring herself to look over at Reilly.

It struck her at that moment that Brian Reilly's gun had disappeared.

Chapter Sixteen

"Well, ma'am, there was a lot of confusion around here — are you sure you saw a gun?" The kid couldn't have been more than twenty-one. His cheeks, round and pink and healthy, showed the scratchy evidence of that morning's razor scraped across flesh that bore little or no traces of a beard either before or after shaving. And his Oakland police officer's uniform was so new and freshly minted that it practically squeaked whenever his arm moved.

Behind him, on the plaza, Helen observed the cleanup in progress. A handful of uniformed officers, holding rifles, gathered the remaining protesters into a group next to a van that was probably headed for the jail downtown. The fire truck someone had called proved to be an unnecessary presence, and it rumbled back down the street to its station. She saw spectators queued across Broadway, in front of the drugstore on Fourteenth. A line of police officers kept a tentative guard against them, preventing them from surging forward onto the plaza. Traffic, slowed almost to a halt, plugged the intersection where two more officers attempted to keep cars moving in a relatively orderly fashion. The blaring of car horns, courtesy of frustrated commuters who'd hoped to reach the freeway before the Friday afternoon rush, provided a noisy yet somehow appropriate backdrop to the scene.

Helen propped herself against the wall of the Centurion lobby and held tight to her temper. That edge of control was becoming increasingly difficult, though, given the activities of the last hour and a half. The denouement of the protest, replete with fists and shouts and tussles, had taken only a few minutes. The aftermath, however — reporters and police and ambulances and tears and exhaustion — looked to be a much longer venue. And it wasn't over yet.

She briefly turned her attention away from the overgrown child standing before her and shifted so that she could see the plaza. The area still had the look of a battle zone. There were two ambulances parked on Broadway, blocking the path of buses, and a third was pulling away with lights flashing and siren wailing. News vans outnumbered paramedics. Helen counted no fewer than six reporters wrangling for good positions at the perimeter of the scene, facing their video cameras and contriving tense expressions that conveyed to their audience that they were true media heroes, risking life and limb to bring viewers live coverage. If they got the angle just right, the backdrop included shots of the police and the paramedics. And those were just the news teams.

At least Linda Hernandez had walked away on her own two feet. She'd looked scared and tired, but still defiant as she stood with two other women talking to a reporter. Once the reporter had determined that they weren't actually very interesting, the trio had ambled off toward Twelfth Street, unassailed by anyone else. Helen was sure Linda would get home safely — good thing she hadn't been bundled off to jail, like some of the others. Probably staying with Helen and Reilly at the steps leading to the building's entrance had kept Linda from having to make a very awkward call to her husband to bail her out. And, even though Helen disagreed with Manny's view on his wife's participation in PAN, she was grateful that neither he nor Linda would have to deal with that.

Hitch hadn't been so lucky. The last Helen had seen of her old friend was the way he called out, with a tired smile, to a knot of reporters as he climbed into the police van that would take him downtown. The other protesters who'd been arrested for civil disobedience cheerfully pulled him inside, for all the world as if they were off to a party. Helen remembered her own days on the beat, and the handful of times she'd been called on to break up gatherings that had grown "troublesome." She sighed and shook her head. Many of those demonstrators were too young to know what it was like to go through that. She'd seen a few old hands in the crowd, but for the most part getting arrested was going to be a new experience to the occupants of the van. Hitch, however, seemed to have achieved his purpose in his own arrest, which was faithfully recorded by several video cameras.

"Uh, ma'am?" The young officer rubbed his jaw with his pen, looking up at her curiously. "You all right?"

"Yeah. Just make sure you find that gun." Helen fought down the urge to grasp him by the scruff of the neck and shake him like the silly puppy he was. It wouldn't do much good to insist on talking to his superiors, she knew — she was already marked as another nutcase, ranting about some non-existent firearm. The harder she pushed, the more likely it became that her claims would evolve into a weirdo's insistence that she'd seen a laser rifle from outer space. Maybe she could call Macabee tonight, she thought, ask him if he'd do what he could to pursue the matter.

"Well, we got your statement now."

"Right." Helen gave him her name and address. His eyebrow lifted when she described herself as a private investigator, but he made no comment. Great, Helen thought, just one more item to laugh over with the guys, a crazy woman who played Samantha Spade.

While she'd been standing there making her statement, most of the staff of Centurion had ambled through the lobby to get a look at the excitement. Shielded as they were from any real danger, they had for the most part taken on a carnival air. Remote from the cacophony and confusion on the plaza, the staff wandered in and darted out, as if fearing contagion of some kind.

Kid Cop ambled off somewhere, and Helen made a quick check of her aches and pains. Except for the terrifying few minutes when she and Linda had pushed and shoved poor Reilly up the steps and into the lobby, Helen hadn't been in any danger. She was amazed that she felt no aftereffects from the event. A bit shaky, but that was all. The beating she'd taken two nights ago had left some bruises, but aside from vertigo not much more.

The same couldn't be said for Brian Reilly. His face, which Helen recalled as being usually quite flushed, shone like a pale moon over the collar of his bright blue shirt. Except for his collar, his uniform was covered with the thin white blanket the ambulance techs had wrapped around him. The two men in the team hovered over him, babbling to each other in jargon that Helen couldn't decipher. What the hell had made him collapse like that? Perhaps he had some kind of heart condition, and the stress of the demonstration had brought on an attack. Helen seriously doubted, though, that he'd be employed as a security guard if he had a history of heart trouble.

"All right, let's do it." On the count of three the two technicians heaved Reilly's body up onto the gurney. High over his head one of them carried a bag of clear fluid attached to an IV drip that snaked out of the guard's right arm. Helen realized she was standing in their way, and she moved quickly to help hold the doors open. She didn't see McFarland or Donna Stethins until the doors slammed open wide.

"What's wrong with this man? Did one of those idiots hurt him?" McFarland barked. Helen took in his mussed hair, the suspender that flapped, unattached to his waistband, and the rings of sweat darkening the pristine shirt at the armpits. Donna hovered behind him, her eyes avoiding Helen as they would a bug on a wall.

But the techs were too busy to pay much attention. "Don't know, sir," one of them shouted out as the gurney was slowly and cautiously bumped down the steps. "The hospital will have to do some tests."

"There's no obvious sign of injury," the other said as he carefully kept the bag of fluid positioned above Reilly's body. "It could be a stroke."

Cameras whirred and people shouted out questions as the men trundled toward the ambulance. "Where are you taking him?" Helen called to them from the doorway.

"Alta Mira," one of them shouted. Helen tried to wrench the doors shut while the crowd reluctantly made way for the gurney, which jostled gently back and forth on the plaza. Before she succeeded, one intrepid reporter, her hair flying wildly in her eyes and her neat beige suit askew on her skinny frame, wriggled an arm into the lobby. McFarland, his chiseled mouth twisted with rage, unceremoniously shoved her down. She landed at the point on the steps of the building where Helen and Linda had

218

recently crouched over Reilly. The reporter, whose face Helen immediately recognized from the nightly news broadcasts, slammed straight back into her cameraman, whose equipment dislodged from his shoulder and landed with a resounding crash on the plaza. The reporter's response to this sequence of events wasn't audible through the thick glass of the building's doors, but if Helen's lip-reading was up to snuff those remarks were going to be edited out. A couple of other reporters, sensing a story, hurried up to watch.

At least she'd seen Reilly and Linda and Hitch get out in one piece. A wave of relief swept over her, and she turned back to the lobby, where further drama was unfolding.

McFarland, his suspenders still swinging free, put both hands flat on the reception desk and glared down at Lily, who cowered in her chair. "Drake's called a meeting, in the fifth-floor conference room. Everybody up there, now." He turned a haggard face to Helen. "What are you doing here?"

"Got caught in the shuffle," Helen started to say. "We had to get an ambulance in here for Reilly, and —"

Donna Stethins broke in with a shriek of fury. "Get that woman out of here! She doesn't belong here! Get her out of here now!"

"Donna, please." McFarland tried to interject with a calm deep voice, but Stethins was pointing a red-tipped, trembling claw at Helen.

"She's a sick pervert. She's as sick as that bitch Leslie Merrick."

Bob and Lily stared in fascinated shock as McFarland pinned Donna's arms behind her and looked down in disgust at her twisted face. "Please! Calm down, Donna! You're humiliating yourself with this!"

She seemed to melt into his arms, clinging to him, whimpering, her eyelids fluttering. McFarland managed to hold her away from his body while still supporting her arms. He blushed when he saw that the two people at the receptionist's desk were avidly drinking in the scene, then he turned to Helen.

"You'll have to leave now," McFarland said to her, his face grim with exasperation. Donna Stethins cowered behind him, now and then fearfully peeking out around his side at Helen. "We're going to lock the building, and without a security guard here there will be no one to let you out."

Bob Tyrell appeared in time to see McFarland hustle Donna off to the elevators, bending over her protectively. "Well, that ought to make Stethins' day," he muttered as he went over to Lily.

"Well, Drake and McFarland and that old hag Stethins can just go right to hell! I'm not going!" Lily spat out. Her words echoed in the sudden, sepulchral stillness of the lobby. "As far as I'm concerned I earned double pay just for showing up today!"

Bob had turned a waste can upside down and was perched on it next to Lily's chair. The remains of the sleeve that had been sacrificed to the struggle outside dangled precariously from a couple of slender threads as he reached out to stroke Lily's trembling arm.

"Now, come on, we can't just walk out. Drake will kill us."

"Screw Drake. I'm going home."

"Hey, I know — I'll take you for a drink after the meeting, okay?" His brow furrowed and he pushed his glasses further up the bridge of his nose. For the first time Helen saw that one of his lenses had cracked in a neat diagonal seam. "We can go over to Jack London Square, to Kincaid's, over by the water." He gently wiped tears from Lily's cheek. "How about it?"

Lily sniffled. "Margaritas?"

"Doubles." Bob and Lily got up and headed to the elevators. Helen saw a huge pile of keys lumped in Bob's

220

hand. They glinted in the light as he vaguely gestured at the door. "Sorry, Helen, I'm going to have to —"

"Look, I really could use a bathroom right now. Isn't there some back exit, or something I could use?" Helen put as much anxiety into her expression as she could muster.

Bob and Lily glanced at each other as the elevator doors slid open and a soft bell chimed from within. "Well — Drake will kill me —" he began.

"Bob, you're such a wuss! Helen practically saved Reilly's life out there. The least we can do is let her use a bathroom!" Lily nudged Bob with her elbow, then turned her tear-stained face to Helen. "There's a staircase at the other end of this hallway, and an exit door there. It locks from the inside as soon as you shut it, so once you go out you can't come back in."

"And a bathroom?"

"Right — there's a ladies' room two doors before the stairs. Just follow this hall around, you can't miss it." Lily managed a final wave as the doors closed.

Helen hurried back around Lily's enormous desk. The hallway was formed like a wide spiral, circling around an inner core that housed elevators and stairwells. The bathroom was right where Lily said it would be. The EXIT sign glowing in green and red over a door facing the carpeted steps. Taking a deep breath, Helen began her climb up the flight that would lead her to Vicky. Even if she'd been dragged into a meeting with Drake et al., Helen wanted a chance to make sure she was all right, that she hadn't somehow been caught in the fray.

By the time she hit the fifth floor her chest was heaving as if she'd been climbing in the Himalayas. A moment's pause was all she allowed herself, and she trudged upward again, moving slower and slower. Upon reaching the seventh floor, Helen rested against the door, gasping, leaning over so her face came close to her knees. She didn't think more than a couple of minutes passed before her breathing slowed and the ache in her side eased a bit. Finding a waste can tucked behind her against the wall, Helen pulled the heavy door open and propped the waste can there — she didn't want to take any chances with getting locked inside of the Centurion building once everyone had gone home for the night.

The staircase opened out into the hallway on the seventh floor just past the bank of elevators near Vicky's desk. "Vicky?" Helen took in the empty room, its cubicles still unoccupied, the long windows bright with late afternoon sun. Once she saw that she was alone, Helen entered Vicky's work station. The fax machine bleeped softly, its lights flashing, and a sheet of paper hummed into the plastic tray protruding from its side. Behind that, Helen saw a messy pile of confetti-like strips heaped beside the shredder. On the desk a litter of papers and pens splayed across the calendar blotter, which was smudged with blobs of ink and dirt. Candy bar wrappers lay next to a half-eaten Twinkie. The creamy filling oozed out onto a blank piece of paper marked with the Roman columns of Centurion's letterhead. The computer screen before it displayed a screen saver of stars shimmering by in rapid flight. There were a handful of disks next to the monitor and a thin stack of manila folders next to those.

A flyer from the demonstration lay beneath a coffee mug close to the disks. It was only half the flyer, though. Helen could see the ragged edge curling around the porcelain mug, the paper stained with stale coffee that had slopped onto it.

Vicky's purse was open on the chair. Her wallet, flaccid and open, spewed out a couple of twenties for all and sundry to see. A cold feeling spread up from Helen's stomach into her chest. She couldn't imagine anyone leaving personal items out like that, meeting with Drake or no meeting with Drake. Something was very wrong.

222

Seeing the desk littered with papers, wrappers and the odds and ends of Vicky's working day reminded Helen of their conversation over at the Youngs' house. Had that really been only two days ago? Helen suddenly realized what it was she'd been trying so hard to remember, what kept creeping into the surface of her thoughts. And it was Vicky who had pointed it out, two days ago. It was Vicky who'd told her what she'd needed to know in order to discover what had happened to Leslie Merrick. That meant it was Vicky who might be in serious danger.

Helen made a quick check of the cubicles lined up behind Vicky's desk, but the room was empty. There weren't even any chairs in the cubicles yet — just rows of blank beige squares, each displaying an unused phone jack and a Formica work area that was gathering dust.

She took a moment to glance down at the street far below. The window near the center of the room, where Vicky had waved to her earlier, was still open. A few people still lingered on the plaza. There were no news types in sight, and the ambulances were long gone. Men and women dressed as office workers stopped in their progress down Broadway, pausing to take a look at the location of so much activity during the past week. A cold gust of air blew up into Helen's face, and she shivered, pulling the window shut as she backed away.

The fax machine hummed again as Helen walked by. As it buzzed another sheet of paper into the tray, she gazed blankly at the neat array of office equipment surrounding the desk. Where the hell was Vicky, if she wasn't in Drake's meeting?

She went back to the stairs and hurried up to the eighth floor and into Leslie's office. Nothing. With a sigh, Helen went back to the desk and looked it over again. The picture was very wrong, and it meant something, but she had no idea what. A sense of urgency swept over her, though Helen didn't quite know what to do with it. Slowly she made her way back to Vicky's desk on the floor below. She grabbed the phone.

"Alison? It's me. Yes, I'm okay. Well, you might see me on the evening news, but — yes, Hitch is okay for now. What? Oh, well, if Manny calls back tell him Linda is fine. No, I'm sure of it. I saw her walk away."

Then came the hard part. "Listen, have you heard from your mom? Oh. No, it's nothing. They're having this meeting, and I was hoping to say hello to her. Would you mind paging me if she calls you, though? Well, no reason, really — just checking up. Okay. Alison — look, can I stop by tonight? Really? Thanks, sweetheart. Yes, I know we need to talk. All right. 'Bye."

Damn. Helen wasn't sure what to do now. She really shouldn't hang around anymore. The meeting was likely to break up at any moment, and the last thing she wanted was to be found lurking in the building. Behind her, Helen heard the elevator shaft echoing with motion. People were on the move, and it was past time for her to go.

As she headed back to the staircase, Helen's pager buzzed at her waist. She stopped cold. It was the hospital. In all the commotion of the day Amelia had disappeared from her thoughts. But she didn't want to risk taking the time to call the hospital from this building. Although she could hear voices beyond each door she passed, no one else entered the stairwell, and she emerged at last into a parking lot.

It took her a couple of minutes to thread a path between the parked cars to the entrance gate. No one sat in the booth at the moment, and Helen was able to squeeze her way past the wooden barrier guarding the lot from trespassers. With a sigh of relief she took her bearings and came out on Broadway again.

The spiked pattern of glass in her windshield was no worse than when she'd left it this morning. At least, looking like that, she reasoned, no one would try to break into her car. She slid into the driver's seat and sat still for a moment as the pent-up emotion of the day threatened to overwhelm her. With shaking hands she reached for her pager, and then for her cell phone.

Kim came on the line almost immediately. "I'm sorry, Helen," she said in a tired voice. "Amelia didn't regain consciousness before she died. And no one knows if she has any family around here."

Helen, exhausted and worried though she was, felt a stab of grief for the woman in brown. Helen had thought herself worn beyond the point of feeling any deep emotion for the stranger. "Kim, what can I do?"

"I'm sorry," Kim said again. "It's out of my hands."

"What do you mean?" Helen asked as yet again that day, she felt the sensation of control slipping through her fingers into nonexistence. "What's going to happen?"

"Nothing. There'll be an autopsy since she died as a result of being injured, whether it was a beating or a car. We — we don't have a next of kin, Helen. Leslie was the only person in her life, as far as we can tell."

Helen shuddered, remembering how as a cop she'd observed more than one autopsy in cold morgues stinking of chemicals with the underlying scent of death beneath the procedures. She had a brief, sharp memory of her as she'd clutched her pitiful garbage bag in the back seat of the car. Whoever Amelia Wainright had been, whatever she'd been, she deserved better than this. Helen made a quick decision.

"Helen? You still there?"

"Yes, Kim. Sorry. I just had to think a moment. Look, as soon as the body can be released, I'll take care of it." She shook her head at her own impulsiveness, hoping she wasn't making a big mistake by getting involved.

Kim sighed. "Thank you, Helen. I really appreciate this."

"And now, I need a favor. Not regarding Amelia, though. If you have a minute, that is." She described Brian Reilly and related the circumstances of his admission to the hospital. "I'd like to find out his condition, if that's possible."

"Well, I'll see what I can do. What's this about, Helen?"

She explained briefly then hit the disconnect button. The interior of the car darkened suddenly, and Helen looked up. The sun had slipped below the top of the Centurion building. Helen glanced down at her watch. It was five o'clock. She doubted if Vicky would have joined the rest of the Centurion staff for the drinks Bob had mentioned earlier, but at least she could find out if Vicky had attended the meeting with the others.

Tired to her bones, worried sick and knowing her day was far from over, Helen strained to see through the distortion wrought by her broken windshield and headed over to Kincaid's.

Chapter Seventeen

Kim's promise to call her again haunted her on her way to Kincaid's. For once that day she was in luck — a handful of the Centurion staff were gathered around a table on the restaurant's patio, and Bob hailed her as she came in. Helen hadn't been at Kincaid's in quite a long time. Situated near the water in Jack London Square, at the end of Broadway, the restaurant provided its patrons with the deep cushioned seating and rich leather Helen always associated with steak-and-baked-potato venues. She refused the offer of beer and ordered the most expensive bourbon on the list.

"Oh, you mean the temp agency person? The one they put up on the seventh floor?" Bob said in response to her query.

"Right. Was she at the meeting with you?"

Bob shook his head and glanced at Lily, who shrugged and looked quizzically at Helen. "No, I didn't see her there. Did you, Lily?"

"No. I guess none of us see much of her, you know? The way she's up there all alone, typing letters or whatever for people. Unless you have to go shred something."

"Yeah, that's the only working shredder in the building right now. Except for McFarland's." Bob tossed back the last of his beer and reached for the pitcher with a grin. "And heaven help you if you ever even ask him if you can go into his damned office." He grinned and drew a cigarette out of the pack on the table. "God, I need this tonight."

It was difficult for Helen to fight down the rising panic that made her want to take these two people, calmly sitting at the bar and relaxing with drinks in hand, and bang their heads together. Of course, they had no idea of Helen's fears, and it was entirely possible that her fears were completely unfounded. Still, it was maddening to hear them speak in such careless tones about a woman whose life might — if Helen was right — be measured in hours, or even minutes.

Helen sipped at her bourbon and let its warmth slide down her throat. She rarely drank in bars these days — another sign of her domestication — but after talking to Kim the drink was more than welcome.

She jumped as she felt the buzz of the pager at her waist. Slipping aside her jacket she glanced down at the digital readout. It was Alison. "Listen, I have to make a phone call," Helen said as she got up from the chair. "Would you mind waiting for me for just a couple of minutes?"

As soon as she got their confused nods, Helen wove a path through the smoke-filled bar, squeezing past clusters of patrons celebrating the beginning of the weekend. She had to wait several minutes for a phone, and she kept straining to look back into the bar to make sure Bob and Lily were still there.

It was difficult to hear Alison over the guffaws of a couple of men emerging from the restroom at her back. "I'm sorry, what did you say?"

"Helen, it sounds like you're in a bar, or something. Where the hell are you?"

"Long story," she shouted into the receiver.

"Well, I just got a call from Dad. Mom hasn't come home yet."

Fear froze Helen, standing at the phone booth, and all the boisterous sound receded into the background. "Not home? When does she usually get there?"

"It's about, what, six o'clock now? Usually not later than five, but with all the stuff that went on in Oakland today I think he's a little worried. You should see the evening news, Helen, it really —"

"Has he called anyone else? The police, I mean."

Silence rang at the other end, and Helen waited tensely. Then Alison said, "I doubt it. Look, what's going on? Do you think he should?"

Helen briefly closed her eyes and felt a surge of frustration. Damnit, there was something she'd seen and heard, something involving Vicky in all this — something important that she just couldn't piece together. What the hell was it? "I hope I'm going overboard with this, but yes, honey, I think he should."

"All right, Helen." Fear strained Alison's voice, and she spoke so quietly Helen had a difficult time making out the words. "I guess there's not time to get into this now, is there?"

"No. Honey, I'm sorry, I have to go back to the Centurion office. She — your mother might still be there."

"Then I'll call Dad, tell him to get on the phone.

229

Helen —" Her voice grew louder and more confident. "I'm coming out there."

"Alison, please —"

"I'll wait outside the building for you. I'll be at the café across the street, where we had lunch. Don't try to talk me out of it."

Before Helen could object the dial tone sounded in her ear. She nearly slammed the telephone down but resisted the urge. Resolutely biting down on rage she wheeled around, parted the sea of male bodies gathered near the restroom and went back into the bar.

"What happened?" Bob turned a blank face up to her as she tossed a couple of bills onto the table, and Lily kept looking back and forth between them.

"I'm sorry, I have to get going," Helen called out over her shoulder. A few minutes later, waiting to get out of the parking lot, she seethed with anger. Who the hell did Alison think she was, butting in where she'd only get in the way? Helen ignored the tiny protest her mind reeled out, reminding her that Vicky was Alison's mother. Besides, there was no time to waste. The way everything had been strewn all over the desk, spilling out onto the blotter —

That was the moment, while Helen was sitting at a traffic light waiting to speed on up Broadway, that the puzzle locked into place. She was too caught up with her own epiphany to get angry at the idiot in front of her who tried to invent his own lane down the middle of the street. Helen veered around the offending car, ignoring the blares and beeps of horns sounding all around her, and flew through a light turning from yellow into red. A couple of pedestrians hopped back up onto a curb as she sped by, and then she saw the bright lights that edged the awning over the café.

True to her word, Alison was waiting for her outside the café's entrance. A dark silhouette on the clear white brilliance of the café's windows, she stood stiff and

230

immobile with tension. "Dad called the cops," she said in greeting. "I don't think there's a whole lot they can do yet."

Helen tried to put concern into her voice as she took Alison by the elbow and steered her inside the café. "I'd like you to do me a favor," she said, nodding to the waitress who led them to a table near the door. She handed Alison the cell phone she'd tucked inside her jacket. "Would you call this number and ask Lieutenant Macabee to meet me here?" Helen dug into her pockets for the card she was sure she still had — yes, there it was stuffed into the inside pocket of her jacket, wedged in with lint and some string and a theater ticket stub.

"Helen, tell me what's going on. Where's my mother?" Helen was relieved that Alison kept her voice soft, but she could hear the steel beneath the words. "No, don't give me that look," Alison went on. "Not now."

Helen leaned over the table, gripping it with both hands and straining to keep her voice calm. "I believe that the same person who killed Leslie Merrick —"

"Then you think she was murdered?"

"The same person now has your mother — and the security guard's gun."

Alison picked up the cell phone with trembling fingers. "What should I tell him?" she asked.

"Exactly what I just told you. I'm going out to see if I can find your mother's car in the parking lot, find anything out there." Helen stroked Alison's cheek with her fingers. "Alison, this person isn't used to killing — I think your mother will be all right, but we have to get to her. Please, do this for me? Okay?"

Alison turned her pale face up to Helen and nodded. Helen turned away quickly before she could change her mind, and she walked out of the bright lights into the darkness of downtown Oakland with a chill at the pit of her stomach.

She paused by her car long enough to get her own gun

out from under the dashboard. Helen slipped the weapon into her waistband and it snuggled down against her back, its cool metal a comforting shape on her skin. Her jacket fell loose over the gun and she hurried back up to Broadway and the Centurion building.

Helen spotted Vicky's car right away. It was the same boat the Youngs had parked outside Alison's apartment building earlier that week. It stood in isolated, gas-guzzling splendor in the center of the otherwise vacant parking lot. Before she even got to the car Helen knew that there wouldn't be a trace of Vicky there, but it was all she had at that moment. She slapped a hand on the hood in frustration.

The construction site was just across the alley. Helen stood still in total darkness, looking around. It was as if some giant had put together a doll-house for its monstrous offspring — the façade was completely gone, exposing the interior to the elements. Semi-transparent thick plastic, tucked around the skeletal frame, puffed silently in the eddies of air that flowed in odd currents through the city streets. To her right, Helen made out a concrete staircase that snaked up the side of the ten-story site all the way to the roof. Slipping her gun out from her back, she eased off the safety and moved quickly across the street. The soft snick of the metal was muffled against her palm and helped quell the fear that rose like bile in her throat.

Knowing that each moment counted, Helen took the time to consider. What would she herself do, faced with dragging an unwilling hostage around and keeping a gun aimed at her? Certainly she wouldn't try to force an unwilling Vicky Young up those stairs. It made a lot more sense to get her out of sight on the bottom story, as quickly and quietly as possible.

Helen took a couple of deep breaths and moved forward, trying to focus. There was no telling what lay inside the gutted structure. There was some dim, reflected light that seeped in from street lamps overhead in the alley, but the sickly yellowish beams only outlined some indeterminate lumps without revealing their nature.

A few rats, perhaps a family of them, scuttled across her path, and some angry birds shrieked and fluttered at her face as they flew by. Except for that, nothing stirred inside the cavernous maw of the construction site. Helen made out evenly stacked rows of concrete blocks under clear plastic tarps. Fortunately for her, the construction crew had cleared away a great deal of rubble. Unnameable piles of gray stone and dust were heaped all through the first floor. Helen found herself glancing at the huge concrete pillars that held up the roof — no way to tell how safe it actually was in here. She had almost persuaded herself to go back outside and wait for Macabee — where was that fool? — when she heard a muffled cry.

Helen gripped her gun tightly and cautiously made her way across the floor. She couldn't imagine that Vicky's abductor would not hear her stumbling around, but the darkness could work for Helen as much as against her. She had made her way deep into the building, perhaps halfway, she judged, when she felt the shove at her back.

"Stupid bitch. You sound like a fucking elephant, clumping around in here. What the hell did you hope to get out of this?"

Very slowly, Helen started to turn around.

"Drop the gun." She did so, clicking the safety back on and tossing the gun down onto the heap of rags at her feet.

Christine Santilli bent over and picked it up. Even in the weak light from outside, Helen could see that the wrist braces were off, revealing what must have been a nasty set of bruises, marking where Helen was sure Leslie Merrick had clung for her life as Christine pushed her out the window. As Helen gauged her chances of kicking her on her ass and getting the gun away from her, Christine stood up and grinned at her. "I'm amazed, Helen. Never would have thought you'd have the brains to put it all together." She poked her in the chest with Reilly's .45.

Helen shrugged and did her best to still the pounding of her heart. "Never would have thought you'd be so stupid as to think you'd get away with this. But then, people are always full of surprises, aren't they?"

"That they are." Christine gestured with a jerk of her head toward the back of the building. "Including that stupid old woman they had working up on the seventh floor that day. In fact, why don't we go back there and say hello to her?"

Not bothering to answer, Helen preceded Christine across the hollowed-out site. Her eyes had finally grown accustomed to the dim gloom broken intermittently by moonlight, and she could make out a narrow path cleared by the construction crew. Passing rows of huge concrete supports, Helen finally got a glimpse of Vicky, half-hidden in the shadows. Duct tape gleamed dully in the weak light as she moved aside to let Helen get by. Her eyes glittered like hard agate, shining with terror and confusion.

"Get down there next to her. Come on, now!"

Helen crouched down, her eyes fixed on Christine, her hands feeling the dusty floor around her for some kind of weapon. Christine set Helen's gun down just out of reach and picked up a huge roll of silver duct tape from the floor.

"I'm curious, Helen," Christine said conversationally as she tore a strip of tape off. Frozen with fear, Helen watched the hand holding the gun — it had to be very awkward, wielding the tape and a weapon. That gun might go off at any time. "What tipped you off? Couldn't have been this idiot over here." She paused long enough to kick Vicky in the side, getting a moan out of the woman for her efforts. "So what was it?"

"Those wrist braces, for one. Perfect for covering up the bruises Leslie must have put on you when she tried to keep you from pushing her to the window ledge." Helen tried to keep the fear out of her voice as she watched Christine's hands. "It's not like you ever seemed to do a lot of typing or computer work — Lily said as much. And then there was the way Leslie's room was set up. There was no way she could have jumped without Reilly's stopping her — if he'd even been in the room."

Christine shook her head in mock sadness, positioning a strip of tape so it dangled from one of the concrete supports, and then began to tear off another strip. "Too bad about poor old Reilly. Old fat fart should never have lied about his health to the security company. Wonder if he'll live long enough for me to thank him for the gun?" She smirked.

"I figured he had to be in the bathroom down on the seventh floor, nowhere near Leslie's office — maybe having another attack. That's when you showed up."

Christine sighed and shook her head. "If only Leslie hadn't decided to save the world! I didn't really mean to do it, you know." She stopped and faced Helen. "She was going to take me down with her, so there was nothing else I could do. All that shit about the Koreans and the Mexicans. This fucking job was all I had!"

"What do you mean, take you down?"

Christine knelt down beside her. Helen could smell her sweaty clothes. "Do you have any idea, you fucking queer, what it's like to be one paycheck away from oblivion? To have a bitch like Donna Stethins reminding you every day that at any moment the assholes that run Centurion could throw me out on the street without so much as a fuck you?" She stood up again. "No. I didn't think so."

"But they gave you another position —"

"Oh, right! Like that would have lasted longer than a

month!" Christine went back to the concrete pillar. "All they needed was an excuse to get rid of me once Leslie was out of the way. Anything would have done. My house, my car, my whole fucking life was about to be shitcanned. And it was all Leslie Merrick's fault. Little Miss Goody-goody — who the fuck was she, to screw up my life for me?"

"So you had an argument," Helen went on, hoping that her words would cover the sound of Vicky's terrified weeping. "You got into a fight that morning, up in her office on the eighth floor."

"Look, I was just going to make sure she didn't take my stuff when she left! How was I to know that Reilly was passing out in the bathroom? It's Leslie's fault, anyway. She started it, calling me stupid and useless, threatening to go to the papers with the stuff she learned down in Mexico."

The sound of the tape being torn off in neat, methodical strips nearly drove Helen mad. And of course there was nothing — no bricks or stones or pieces of wood — near to hand. Vicky sat very still, hardly breathing, although her eyes still gleamed bright in the gloom. Helen knew that Macabee would never get there in time to help them. And it wouldn't be all that difficult to dispose of two corpses, not in all this rubble and mess. No doubt there were convenient holes in the flooring, or under the remains of the building, for Christine to dump their dead bodies when she was finished.

Christine kicked Vicky again. This time Vicky made no sound. "You go first, bitch," Christine said in a soft voice. "If you hadn't started working by the shredder that day, no one would have known I wasn't at that fucking shredder all morning when Leslie died. Everything would have been perfect, especially with this construction work going on. No one heard a thing, what with all the machines running here." Then she looked back at Helen. With her free hand,

Christine lifted the first piece of duct tape. "Your turn now, Helen. You get to watch her get it before you get it."

Helen's hands closed on a thick pile of dust behind her. This was the only chance she and Vicky were going to get. She looked up at Christine, forcing calm into her face and voice. "Well, come on then. Quit fucking around and go ahead with it."

Christine frowned, then pointed the gun at Helen's head. "Maybe I ought to kill you first, after all," she muttered. "Just to get you to shut the fuck up."

Helen waited until she could smell the stench of stale cigarettes on Christine's breath. Then she brought both hands up, fists as full of dust as she could manage, and thrust the chalky concrete dust into her eyes. Christine shrieked and jumped back. Helen jerked her right leg up into a kick that landed squarely in Christine's crotch. She howled with pain and doubled over. Helen followed the kick with a fist shoved into her stomach, then watched Christine crumple to the floor.

Still, however, Christine held on to the gun. Helen glanced quickly behind her — Vicky had managed to shove herself down behind a pile of concrete blocks, and Helen could see her huddled behind them. Helen grabbed her own gun from the heap of tarps behind Christine, then bent over Christine, prepared to wrench Reilly's gun away from her.

She never got the chance. The shot, which Christine fired blindly, hit Helen in the abdomen. Strange, all those years as a cop, followed by several years as a private investigator, she had never once been seriously injured. The oddity of it all was the first thought in her mind as her body registered a sharp burst of warmth in her stomach, followed by a stab of fiery pain that spread out from her torso to her whole body. She barely felt the concrete floor slamming up into her back as she tumbled flat.

And she wasn't sure, at first, when the police cars began swirling their strobes of light onto the building, if she was hallucinating or having one of those near-death visions. It wasn't until Macabee's broad white face loomed over her that she believed help had arrived at last.

What the hell was he saying, though? Helen couldn't make out the words, and a weird drowsiness stole over her, mingling with the pain. Vicky's face swam in and out of her line of sight.

There was too much commotion to try to take in with the last shreds of consciousness that Helen could muster. There were the lights and strange, disconnected noises all around her. Damnit, she just wanted to go to sleep. Couldn't they understand that and leave her alone? She swallowed at the odd coppery fluid that suddenly surged into her mouth. Blood, but it didn't seem to matter.

"Helen." That was Alison — where did she come from? Helen tried to smile, but it was too much work. She tried to look down, and saw that Alison's hand gripped her own. So why couldn't she feel it? Actually, she couldn't seem to feel anything. Not even the floor beneath her.

There were other hands on her, too. Someone kept fussing with her clothes and putting things on her. Helen gave up trying to understand it. She could tell they were lifting her up when the scenery changed. She was placed on something that was moving forward, taking her out of this strange dark place. She was going to where there were lights and people and sounds, but as she approached, everything kept creeping away.

Someone placed something over her mouth, and at that moment she saw vague figures on the concrete flight of stairs exposed at the side of the building. There was someone — someone she should know, someone who'd tried to hurt her — standing at the top of the stairs. Christine. Helen tried to motion toward her, but her arm refused to obey any commands from her weakening mind. As she was

238

being lifted into the ambulance, Helen watched the pageant displayed near the building's roof. Christine, poised there, spun around once, then twice, while others scrambled up the stairs. Just then, Christine pitched forward and fell, sailing bright against the moon, into the blank well of nothing far below.

Chapter Eighteen

It was so dark that she couldn't be certain she really was awake. And she couldn't feel anything. Nothing. It was all so weird, so strange, that she was much more curious and amazed than afraid. Nothing to see, to hear, to feel — everything was blank and still, beyond quiet.

Somewhere there was pain. A lot of it. A vague awareness of the pain made itself felt to Helen. Where the hell was it coming from?

And there were voices. She knew them, although the pain seemed to make the voices softer, farther away.

"They still aren't sure," someone said. "She's not out of the woods yet. But she got through the night, and her condition is stable. They told me that much, at least."

Then the voice and the pain were the same thing, or was it that the soft, gentle voice sounded so hurt? So tired?

"Little Alley Cat, you have to get some rest now."

"But who's going to stay here?" The voice cracked. Feeling welled up from it, feeling that washed over Helen as if it were a wave of cool fresh water splashed on fiery sand. "No, I can't leave. I have to be here, right here, when she wakes up. I won't leave her alone."

"Honey, she's being watched around the clock. She's getting the best of care."

"It doesn't matter, Dad. I have to be here. I know she knows when I'm sitting here, talking to her."

Talk. Yes, that made sense. People in the room talking. Yesterday — was it yesterday? Hard to tell now — it had been Manny, telling her how Howard Mitchum was going to stay locked up for a long time, despite Drake's attempts to buy his way out of that predicament. She remembered Manny as a warm, vital presence, someone she was very close to for a long time.

"Alison." This voice was deeper and stronger but still overflowing with that strange mix of emotion and hurt. "Why don't you try to get some sleep? Your parents can take you home. I'll stay here until you get back."

"But, Father Hitchcock —"

"Hitch. Helen always calls me Hitch."

"I have to be here for her!" There was anger in the voice. With her growing awareness of the emotions swirling around her in the blank darkness Helen felt a faint twinge in her own body. It was as if the thoughts and feelings of the others were making her more solid, more real. More alive.

"Alison, sweetie, let's go. You can get some sleep, and Hitch here will call us if anything changes."

"Of course I will. Mrs. Young, are you sure you're all right?"

There was a heavy sigh. "Yes. I was only scratched a little. She — she saved my life, she really did, you know."

This voice, too, broke and swelled over Helen. Again, she sensed her own fragile presence and her own broken body. She didn't quite know how it had happened, but the vague blankness was beginning to take on recognizable shape. Yes, this was her body. And there really were other people nearby, other bodies with substance and voices and powerful emotions that seemed to swim in and out of the soft, blurred boundaries of their physicality.

There was another brief flurry of sounds and motions, then Helen was alone. No, not quite alone. The utter blankness had gone, replaced by a dim murk of consciousness broken here and there by eddies of noise. And someone else remained.

"Helen, it's Hitch."

Her hand. There was pressure on her hand. The voice came nearer.

"Look, I don't know if you can hear me right now. I'll just talk to you for a while, in case you can. I thought you'd like to know that Amelia was buried at St. Joseph's yesterday. It was a beautiful day, Helen. It felt like summer. Alison was there, and Kim from the hospital. Oh, and your friends from that coffee shop, Mother Hubbard's. They came, too. I wanted you to know that Amelia wasn't alone."

The words went back and forth over her, making a pattern that she couldn't decipher. Still, the warmth and gentle pressure on her hand kept her tethered to the feel of the sheets over her body.

"And you should see the flowers Drake sent! It's like a whole garden over here on the table. That security guard,

Reilly, stopped by yesterday to see how you were. I know he feels terrible about his gun, but his physical condition seems to be improving."

Helen struggled to make some kind of response to him, to move a finger or an eyelid or make a sound. Her efforts were all in vain. She gave up and focused her will on remaining attentive to the words that floated around her.

Hitch fell silent. He stayed next to Helen. And while Helen slowly and painfully came up out of the well of nothingness, the blurred shapes began to solidify. She couldn't recognize the things around her, not yet — that would come later. For now, though, she could know that she was someplace, that the other people were in fact real, that the blank darkness wasn't so blank after all.

But with each moment of awareness she gained, Helen felt the maw of piercing pain closing over her as she lay in the hospital bed. She clung to the pain, knowing somehow that her grip on it was a link to whatever pulled her up out of the nothing.

Then the shapes and sounds that whirled around her began to slow, becoming objects that she could understand. The bed. The lights. A carafe of water beside her gleamed as the sun rose and glowed orange-yellow through that square called a window. Cool white sheets swathed her body, their touch both pleasant and uncomfortable as they reminded her of how much she hurt.

Hitch — that must be Hitch sitting on the thing she remembered was a chair. Yes, yes, she could hold onto that, hold onto how she could make the connection with chair and person and window and water. That ability to link *thing* with *nothing* would be enough.

And it was enough. Hitch leaned over the bed, elbows on knees, his head hung down. For the moment his attention wavered from her face. She watched him, unable to move or speak or acknowledge his presence. But it didn't matter. In a few moments, when Hitch looked up, he'd see that she was awake. For now, Helen thought, it was enough to be alive.

A few of the publications of
THE NAIAD PRESS, INC.
P.O. Box 10543   Tallahassee, Florida 32302
Phone (850) 539-5965
Toll-Free Order Number: 1-800-533-1973
Web Site: WWW.NAIADPRESS.COM
Mail orders welcome. Please include 15% postage.
Write or call for our free catalog which also features an
incredible selection of lesbian videos.

FALLEN FROM GRACE by Pat Welch. 256 pp. 6th Helen Black
mystery.   ISBN 1-56280-209-7 $11.95

THE NAKED EYE by Catherine Ennis. 208 pp. Her lover in the
camera's eye . . .   ISBN 1-56280-210-0   11.95

OVER THE LINE by Tracey Richardson. 176 pp. 2nd Stevie
Houston mystery.   ISBN 1-56280-202-X   11.95

JULIA'S SONG by Ann O'Leary. 208 pp. Strangely
disturbing . . . strangely exciting.   ISBN 1-56280-197-X   11.95

LOVE IN THE BALANCE by Marianne K. Martin. 256 pp.
Weighing the costs of love . . .   ISBN 1-56280-199-6   11.95

PIECE OF MY HEART by Julia Watts. 208 pp. All the
stuff that dreams are made of —   ISBN 1-56280-206-2   11.95

MAKING UP FOR LOST TIME by Karin Kallmaker. 240 pp.
Nobody does it better . . .   ISBN 1-56280-196-1   11.95

GOLD FEVER by Lyn Denison. 224 pp. By author of *Dream
Lover.*   ISBN 1-56280-201-1   11.95

WHEN THE DEAD SPEAK by Therese Szymanski. 224 pp. 2nd
Brett Higgins mystery.   ISBN 1-56280-198-8   11.95

FOURTH DOWN by Kate Calloway. 240 pp. 4th Cassidy James
mystery.   ISBN 1-56280-205-4   11.95

A MOMENT'S INDISCRETION by Peggy J. Herring. 176 pp.
There's a fine line between love and lust . . .   ISBN 1-56280-194-5   11.95

CITY LIGHTS/COUNTRY CANDLES by Penny Hayes. 208 pp.
About the women she has known . . .   ISBN 1-56280-195-3   11.95

POSSESSIONS by Kaye Davis. 240 pp. 2nd Maris Middleton
mystery.   ISBN 1-56280-192-9   11.95

A QUESTION OF LOVE by Saxon Bennett. 208 pp. Every
woman is granted one great love.   ISBN 1-56280-205-4   11.95

RHYTHM TIDE by Frankie J. Jones. 160 pp. . . . to desire
passionately and be passionately desired.　　ISBN 1-56280-189-9　　11.95

PENN VALLEY PHOENIX by Janet McClellan. 208 pp. 2nd
Tru North Mystery.　　ISBN 1-56280-200-3　　11.95

BY RESERVATION ONLY by Jackie Calhoun. 240 pp. A
chance for true happiness.　　ISBN 1-56280-191-0　　11.95

OLD BLACK MAGIC by Jaye Maiman. 272 pp. 9th Robin
Miller mystery.　　ISBN 1-56280-175-9　　11.95

LEGACY OF LOVE by Marianne K. Martin. 240 pp. Women
will do anything for her . . .　　ISBN 1-56280-184-8　　11.95

LETTING GO by Ann O'Leary. 160 pp. Laura, at 39, in love
with 23-year-old Kate.　　ISBN 1-56280-183-X　　11.95

LADY BE GOOD edited by Barbara Grier and Christine Cassidy.
288 pp. Erotic stories by Naiad Press authors.　ISBN 1-56280-180-5　　14.95

CHAIN LETTER by Claire McNab. 288 pp. 9th Carol Ashton
mystery.　　ISBN 1-56280-181-3　　11.95

NIGHT VISION by Laura Adams. 256 pp. Erotic fantasy romance
by "famous" author.　　ISBN 1-56280-182-1　　11.95

SEA TO SHINING SEA by Lisa Shapiro. 256 pp. Unable to resist
the raging passion . . .　　ISBN 1-56280-177-5　　11.95

THIRD DEGREE by Kate Calloway. 224 pp. 3rd Cassidy James
mystery.　　ISBN 1-56280-185-6　　11.95

WHEN THE DANCING STOPS by Therese Szymanski. 272 pp.
1st Brett Higgins mystery.　　ISBN 1-56280-186-4　　11.95

PHASES OF THE MOON by Julia Watts. 192 pp. . . . . . hungry
for everything life has to offer.　　ISBN 1-56280-176-7　　11.95

BABY IT'S COLD by Jaye Maiman. 256 pp. 5th Robin Miller
mystery.　　ISBN 1-56280-156-2　　10.95

CLASS REUNION by Linda Hill. 176 pp. The girl from her
past . . .

　　ISBN 1-56280-178-3　　11.95

DREAM LOVER by Lyn Denison. 224 pp. A soft, sensuous,
romantic fantasy.　　ISBN 1-56280-173-1　　11.95

FORTY LOVE by Diana Simmonds. 288 pp. Joyous, heart-
warming romance.　　ISBN 1-56280-171-6　　11.95

IN THE MOOD by Robbi Sommers. 160 pp. The queen of
erotic tension!　　ISBN 1-56280-172-4　　11.95

SWIMMING CAT COVE by Lauren Douglas. 192 pp. 2nd
Allison O'Neil Mystery.　　ISBN 1-56280-168-6　　11.95

THE LOVING LESBIAN by Claire McNab and Sharon Gedan.
240 pp. Explore the experiences that make lesbian love unique.

　　ISBN 1-56280-169-4　　14.95

COURTED by Celia Cohen. 160 pp. Sparkling romantic
encounter.   ISBN 1-56280-166-X   11.95

SEASONS OF THE HEART by Jackie Calhoun. 240 pp. Romance
through the years.   ISBN 1-56280-167-8   11.95

K. C. BOMBER by Janet McClellan. 208 pp. 1st Tru North
mystery.   ISBN 1-56280-157-0   11.95

LAST RITES by Tracey Richardson. 192 pp. 1st Stevie Houston
mystery.   ISBN 1-56280-164-3   11.95

EMBRACE IN MOTION by Karin Kallmaker. 256 pp. A whirlwind
love affair.   ISBN 1-56280-165-1   11.95

HOT CHECK by Peggy J. Herring. 192 pp. Will workaholic Alice
fall for guitarist Ricky?   ISBN 1-56280-163-5   11.95

OLD TIES by Saxon Bennett. 176 pp. Can Cleo surrender to a
passionate new love?   ISBN 1-56280-159-7   11.95

LOVE ON THE LINE by Laura DeHart Young. 176 pp. Will Stef
win Kay's heart?   ISBN 1-56280-162-7   11.95

DEVIL'S LEG CROSSING by Kaye Davis. 192 pp. 1st Maris
Middleton mystery.   ISBN 1-56280-158-9   11.95

COSTA BRAVA by Marta Balletbo Coll. 144 pp. Read the book,
see the movie!   ISBN 1-56280-153-8   11.95

MEETING MAGDALENE & OTHER STORIES by
Marilyn Freeman. 144 pp. Read the book, see the movie!
                                              ISBN 1-56280-170-8   11.95

SECOND FIDDLE by Kate 208 pp. 2nd P.I. Cassidy James
mystery.   ISBN 1-56280-169-6   11.95

LAUREL by Isabel Miller. 128 pp. By the author of the beloved
Patience and Sarah.   ISBN 1-56280-146-5   10.95

LOVE OR MONEY by Jackie Calhoun. 240 pp. The romance of
real life.   ISBN 1-56280-147-3   10.95

SMOKE AND MIRRORS by Pat Welch. 224 pp. 5th Helen Black
Mystery.   ISBN 1-56280-143-0   10.95

DANCING IN THE DARK edited by Barbara Grier & Christine
Cassidy. 272 pp. Erotic love stories by Naiad Press authors.
                                              ISBN 1-56280-144-9   14.95

TIME AND TIME AGAIN by Catherine Ennis. 176 pp. Passionate
love affair.   ISBN 1-56280-145-7   10.95

PAXTON COURT by Diane Salvatore. 256 pp. Erotic and wickedly
funny contemporary tale about the business of learning to live
together.   ISBN 1-56280-114-7   10.95

INNER CIRCLE by Claire McNab. 208 pp. 8th Carol Ashton
Mystery.   ISBN 1-56280-135-X   11.95

LESBIAN SEX: AN ORAL HISTORY by Susan Johnson.
240 pp. Need we say more? ISBN 1-56280-142-2 14.95

WILD THINGS by Karin Kallmaker. 240 pp. By the undisputed
mistress of lesbian romance. ISBN 1-56280-139-2 11.95

THE GIRL NEXT DOOR by Mindy Kaplan. 208 pp. Just what
you d expect. ISBN 1-56280-140-6 11.95

NOW AND THEN by Penny Hayes. 240 pp. Romance on the
westward journey. ISBN 1-56280-121-X 11.95

HEART ON FIRE by Diana Simmonds. 176 pp. The romantic and
erotic rival of *Curious Wine*. ISBN 1-56280-152-X 11.95

DEATH AT LAVENDER BAY by Lauren Wright Douglas. 208 pp.
1st Allison O'Neil Mystery. ISBN 1-56280-085-X 11.95

YES I SAID YES I WILL by Judith McDaniel. 272 pp. Hot
romance by famous author. ISBN 1-56280-138-4 11.95

FORBIDDEN FIRES by Margaret C. Anderson. Edited by Mathilda
Hills. 176 pp. Famous author's "unpublished" Lesbian romance.
ISBN 1-56280-123-6 21.95

SIDE TRACKS by Teresa Stores. 160 pp. Gender-bending
Lesbians on the road. ISBN 1-56280-122-8 10.95

HOODED MURDER by Annette Van Dyke. 176 pp. 1st Jessie
Batelle Mystery. ISBN 1-56280-134-1 10.95

WILDWOOD FLOWERS by Julia Watts. 208 pp. Hilarious and
heart-warming tale of true love. ISBN 1-56280-127-9 10.95

NEVER SAY NEVER by Linda Hill. 224 pp. Rule #1: Never get
involved with . . . ISBN 1-56280-126-0 11.95

THE SEARCH by Melanie McAllester. 240 pp. Exciting top cop
Tenny Mendoza case. ISBN 1-56280-150-3 10.95

THE WISH LIST by Saxon Bennett. 192 pp. Romance through
the years. ISBN 1-56280-125-2 10.95

FIRST IMPRESSIONS by Kate 208 pp. 1st P.I. Cassidy
James mystery. ISBN 1-56280-133-3 10.95

OUT OF THE NIGHT by Kris Bruyer. 192 pp. Spine-tingling
thriller. ISBN 1-56280-120-1 10.95

NORTHERN BLUE by Tracey Richardson. 224 pp. Police recruits
Miki & Miranda — passion in the line of fire. ISBN 1-56280-118-X 10.95

These are just a few of the many Naiad Press titles — we are the oldest and
largest lesbian/feminist publishing company in the world. We also offer an
enormous selection of lesbian video products. Please request a complete
catalog. We offer personal service; we encourage and welcome direct mail
orders from individuals who have limited access to bookstores carrying our
publications.